ANCIENT GUARDIAN

ANCIENTS RISING
BOOK NINE

KATIE REUS

D1452404

Cover Art by Sweet 'N Spicy Designs

Editor: Julia Ganis

Proofreader: Tammy Payne

Author Website: https://katiereus.com

Publisher's Note: This is a work of fiction. Names, characters, places, and incidents are either the products of the author's imagination or used fictitiously, and any resemblance to actual persons, living or dead, or business establishments, organizations or locales is completely coincidental.

Ancient Guardian/Katie Reus—1st ed.

ISBN: 9781635562187

PRAISE FOR THE NOVELS OF KATIE REUS®

"…a wild hot ride for readers. The story grabs you and doesn't let go."
—*New York Times* bestselling author, Cynthia Eden

"Has all the right ingredients: a hot couple, evil villains, and a killer action-filled plot. . . . [The] Moon Shifter series is what I call Grade-A entertainment!" —Joyfully Reviewed

"I could not put this book down. . . . Let me be clear that I am not saying that this was a good book *for* a paranormal genre; it was an excellent romance read, *period.*" —All About Romance

"Reus strikes just the right balance of steamy sexual tension and nail-biting action….This romantic thriller reliably hits every note that fans of the genre will expect." —*Publishers Weekly*

"Prepare yourself for the start of a great new series! . . . I'm excited about reading more about this great group of characters."
—Fresh Fiction

"Wow! This powerful, passionate hero sizzles with sheer deliciousness. I loved every sexy twist of this fun & exhilarating tale. Katie Reus delivers!" —Carolyn Crane, RITA award winning author

"A sexy, well-crafted paranormal romance that succeeds with smart characters and creative world building."—Kirkus Reviews

"You'll fall in love with Katie's heroes."
—*New York Times* bestselling author, Kaylea Cross

"Both romantic and suspenseful, a fast-paced sexy book full of high stakes action." —Heroes and Heartbreakers

"Katie Reus pulls the reader into a story line of second chances, betrayal, and the truth about forgotten lives and hidden pasts."
—The Reading Café

"Nonstop action, a solid plot, good pacing, and riveting suspense."
—RT Book Reviews

"Exciting in more ways than one, well-paced and smoothly written, I'd recommend *A Covert Affair* to any romantic suspense reader."
—Harlequin Junkie

"Sexy military romantic suspense." —USA Today

"Enough sexual tension to set the pages on fire."
—*New York Times* bestselling author, Alexandra Ivy

"*Avenger's Heat* hits the ground running...This is a story of strength, of partnership and healing, and it does it brilliantly."
—Vampire Book Club

"*Mating Instinct* was a great read with complex characters, serious political issues and a world I am looking forward to coming back to."
—All Things Urban Fantasy

For all the dog lovers. You're my people.

PROLOGUE

Violet slid off her backpack and set it on a small boulder next to her before stripping off the rest of her clothes.

A cool breeze kicked up, making her shiver as the stream bubbled past her. The sound of the small waterfall thirty or so yards away was consistent, soothing. All this land had once been part of a national preserve but that didn't matter anymore. The federal government, as she and her small community knew it, was gone, destroyed.

For months after The Fall they'd kept waiting for someone to show up and help. The National Guard or...someone. When it had become clear that they were on their own, their small farming community had banded together and taken stock of the situation. Things had been running smoothly enough but today had been long and she needed to be alone.

Didn't matter how cold the water was at this point, she needed the shock to her system anyway. Biting back a gasp, she waded up to her waist, then shoved out a shaky breath. She had an actual shower back home, but something about being in the stream always cleared her head and— She froze as she saw a man at the top of the small cliff's edge.

He was covered in red clay and *naked*. He blinked down at her, his eyes a little wild. There were red streaks across his chest that looked darker than the natural clay around here. Oh God, had he been hurt? She held up her hands to show him that she meant no harm.

"Are you okay?" she called out, already hurrying from the water as she called up to him. "I'm a doctor, I can help!" She grabbed a towel and glanced down at herself as she started to quickly dry off, but when she looked up again, the huge man was gone.

They hadn't had many strangers traveling through the Robichaux parish in the last year, but the ones who had, had stayed for the most part. A couple had simply left in the middle of the night with no good-byes, but that was just the way it went. Some people wanted to explore, see what was left of the world.

"Sir?" she called out again as she rapidly dressed, shoved her feet back into her hiking boots. As a precaution, she tucked one of her younger sister's knives in the back of her pants as she made her way over the rocky terrain toward the edge of the waterfall.

They were only a couple hours from what had once been Baton Rouge, Louisiana and most people didn't realize that there were water-falls in the state—what had once been the state. She wasn't even sure what they were anymore. A state, a country? A territory? They didn't have a government anymore. Not that she knew of anyway. Not that it mattered now, she thought as she hiked up the small rocky incline that looped around the cliff's edge to where the waterfall started.

Where the man had been.

But when she got there, she saw muddy, reddish footprints on one of the boulders, and…nothing else.

No footprints on the surrounding boulders, and it was too far for the man to have jumped to the grass and rocky area a good thirty feet behind the pooling water and boulders.

Frowning, she glanced around the underbrush, looked into the clear water, then even up in the trees. She contemplated trying to find the man, but what was the point?

If he'd wanted to make contact, he could have. Clearly he didn't want her help. But it was the doctor in her—she wanted to help when she could.

Sighing, her private bath ruined now, she started the climb back down and continued hiking until she reached her family's farm. She shouldn't have left anyway, but she'd gotten in an argument with one of her younger sisters over…something stupid.

Rolling her shoulders, Violet slid her backpack off as she stepped inside the farmhouse she and her sisters had inherited from their parents.

"Hey, you're back." Mari hurried out of the kitchen, her expression a mix of excitement and worry as she carried Violet's medical bag. "Ava's in labor. Contractions are ten minutes apart, so everything is still good, but she's ready for you."

"Where's Luke?" Ava's husband.

"Still hunting, but I sent someone to grab him."

Violet nodded, taking the bag from her, already going into doctor mode. Thankfully Ava's pregnancy had been fairly easy, but she was weeks early and anything could happen.

She shelved thoughts of the stranger she'd seen in the woods, but made a note to tell her sisters and the others later.

Right now it was time to deliver her neighbor's baby.

CHAPTER ONE

One year later

Orion slowed his descent, cupping his wings slightly as he watched the darts of movement through the trees below.

Too fast to be human. And the scents wafting up from the forest and hiking trails weren't ones he recognized.

His dragon silently snarled.

Vampires. Predators.

And they were making their way toward the humans he lived with, the ones he protected. Soft, kind beings who'd opened up their home to him without knowing what he was.

They were far too trusting.

That was okay, he kept them safe.

On a burst of speed, he flew ahead of the vampires—six, he counted —then silently dove into a thicket of trees, hooking his backpack onto a branch high up in one of the pine trees before he landed and shifted to his human form.

Though they were quick and fast, Orion could hear the vampires moving in his direction.

Using a bit of ancient magic, he created a ball of light in his hands, then threw it up into the air, illuminating the nearby trees. It was as if he'd turned on what the humans he lived with called a lamp.

The movement in the trees stopped, the forest going eerily still.

"I know you're there. Show yourselves." Orion stood where he was, naked as the day he was hatched.

A moment later, a male vampire with long, blond hair and ice-cold eyes the color of rich amber stepped into the spotlight. He wore dark navy pants and a matching T-shirt, no visible weapons on him. Other than his fangs.

Orion could sense the others moving around him, likely thinking to trap him, then attack. His dragon smiled darkly, ready for a fight, though deep down he knew this would be over quickly. He'd had no real fights since rising from his long Hibernation. Because these vampires weren't a true match for his strength.

But he would give these vampires a chance to leave if they meant no harm. "You're in my territory. I suggest you turn around and return whence you came."

"Whence?" The male snorted, swaggering forward, flashing his fangs. "I suggest you shut the hell up and listen to what's going to happen. We take what we want, when we want. And we're going to drain and probably fuck everyone in this territory, starting with you." The male's eyes flashed bright and Orion sensed the vampires in the trees jumping down on him.

He mentally extinguished the light even as his beast took over, the wildness of his magic pushing out in a rush of sparks and power.

He kept his wings pulled in tight as he chomped his jaws down on the obnoxious mouthpiece, ripped the vampire in half.

"Hell," one breathed out as he landed on Orion's back.

"Shit," another muttered as the sound of feet racing away greeted Orion's ears.

He turned, whipping his tail out behind him, striking the fleeing vampire as he bit down on another that raced at him, fangs out. What did this tiny vampire think he was going to do? Chomp through his scales? Fools. All of them. Bloody fools.

6

As he bit yet another vamp in half, ash coating his mouth, he shook wildly, throwing off the vampire who kept trying to stab him.

The male landed on a tree trunk, clutching onto it like a cat.

Orion leaned down in front of him, exhaled smoke over the cowering male.

He wasn't going to breathe fire only because he didn't want to risk starting a forest fire. It was too cold and there hadn't been much rain the last few months.

"Please, we didn't know you were a dragon." Raw fear rolled off the male, the stench cloying as the sound of more footsteps racing away filled the otherwise quiet forest.

As if their ignorance made their actions acceptable?

He batted the male off the tree hard with his claws, the predator in him smiling as the male started to run, slipped in a cluster of fallen leaves, scrambled up and tried again.

Orion pounced, bit down hard, sneezed as more ash filled his mouth.

It didn't take long to hunt down the other vampires—it was pathetically short, in fact—and turn them to ash. Once he was certain they were all dead he retrieved his pack, then made his way to the small waterfall where he'd first seen and scented Violet.

He hadn't understood her language then, had just seen the most beautiful naked female wading into icy waters—icy by human standards.

He'd gone into Hibernation here long ago, long before Violet had been born, before anyone in this territory had taken their first breath.

He'd left after seeing her, not wanting to deal with a human as he figured out the world he'd woken into, but something had compelled him to return months later.

That same *something* had compelled him to stay.

It was her scent. She called to him on the most primal level.

As he rinsed off the grime of the evening, he paused at the faintest change in the air. Then ignored it because he recognized the scents. Hayes, Tyler and Bentley.

"How many were there this time?" Bentley asked as he stood on the stream's edge, dressed much the same as the vampires Orion had just killed. In dark clothing with no discernible weapons.

"Six." Shaking off, he strode out of the water, grabbed a towel as he looked at the three males. Wolf shifters who were hiding their nature from the humans they lived among as well.

He wasn't sure why, but didn't care. He had secrets too. And these were good males, protecting a cub and the territory they all lived in.

Between the four of them, they'd managed to keep out all predators in the last year who would have hurt his humans if given the chance. And yes, he realized he thought of the humans as his. He'd tried to keep his distance, but they were too trusting and naïve. Someone had to keep them alive.

"The attacks are getting more frequent," Bentley said again. As the oldest, he was usually the speaker of the three.

His two brothers stood behind him, their expressions dark.

"I know," he said as he tugged on a pair of pants, not bothering with a shirt. "It's not just here," he continued. "In the north and to the west, I've found former human encampments ravaged. All killed by vampires." Beyond that were established territories, run by different Alphas.

"They've got to be coming from somewhere," Bentley said again, running a hand over his closely shorn hair. "They're too well fed and they're not setting up camp that we can find. And they're not bringing any supplies with them."

"It's crossed my mind that someone might be sending them." Because Bentley was right. They had to be making a base camp somewhere. They'd been coming in waves, usually in groups of six, sometimes eight. Unfortunately vampires moved with supernatural speed, which meant they could cover a lot of ground in one night. So pinpointing where they'd come from was almost impossible.

The territory he lived in now was in good shape, untouched by the destruction much of the globe had suffered because of unstable dragons who'd sought to enslave humans and supernaturals alike. *Fools.* Dead fools now. The attack—or The Fall as humans called it—had happened before he'd woken from his Hibernation, but he'd picked up enough information since then to know what had occurred.

"Why?" Hayes, the youngest, stepped forward slightly. "There aren't many humans in this territory and it's small. It can't be for the food source."

Orion looked at Bentley, saw that he already knew why. "That's exactly why they've targeted it. They want the territory, the land, the humans in it. They think it's ripe for the picking. And there are plenty of people here for a food source—young humans they can keep for a long time." And there were two big territories on either side of their home. New Orleans was to the east, and as far as Orion knew, no one there was even aware of this small, human-run territory. He'd kept a wide berth when he went out flying, not venturing into that territory.

Then there was Opelousas territory to the west. A small area, just like his own, and he'd seen vampires there during some of his night flights so his money was on them sending out scouts. The area south of that, Lafayette, had been severely damaged during The Fall, according to what he'd seen, so he didn't think the vampires were from there.

One thing he knew, regardless of who was sending the vampires: whoever was in charge would get tired of their people disappearing, never to return again. Because he hadn't left any survivors from any of the attacks. "Where's Kayla?" he asked, referring to the young cub who lived with the wolves. They'd told the humans that she was Bentley's daughter, but Orion didn't think so. The scents were too different. She might be a cousin, but the wolves had never offered up the information and he'd never asked. It was clear they'd give their lives for the girl, and she was a happy, healthy cub.

"With friends, having a sleepover," Bentley said.

"Good. Fan out, tighten the perimeter tonight. Check on all the homes in the outer ring." He didn't have to specify where or who anymore. He'd created a grid map nearly a year ago and they'd been diligent in keeping all the people who lived here safe, even if the humans had no idea about the supernatural threats lurking in the night. They *knew* about supernaturals, of course, but not that their parish was being infiltrated.

He would protect this place until the day he died—though he didn't plan on that happening. He was here for Violet and would keep her safe. It was the reason he'd returned to this small territory. The compulsion to watch out for her was too great for his beast to ignore.

CHAPTER TWO

Exhausted, Violet hitched her bag on her shoulder as she walked through the dormant orchard, the harvesting season a few months past.

As she stepped out of the small orchard, she saw something near one of their spherical growing pods... A shadow that moved. Then another, smaller shadow, and she inwardly smiled.

She was pretty sure she knew who that was.

Glancing around, she looked for any other signs of life, wasn't surprised it was quiet at three in the morning. A haze of clouds had drifted over the half-moon, and though they had plenty of solar lights set up around their farm and the surrounding ones, they weren't overly bright.

As she approached the pod that was as big as her first studio apartment had been in a lost city destroyed years ago, relief punched through her when Orion and his pup Bowie stepped out from the interior of it. "Hey, what are you doing out so late?"

"I could ask you the same thing."

The frown tugging at that harsh mouth did nothing to negate the raw hotness of the man. And she hated that term, *hot*. But it was appropriate for Orion in every way—six foot seven, midnight dark hair, emerald green eyes, and the barest hint of an accent she couldn't begin to guess the origin of. And he might as well have been carved from granite. Men like him didn't exist. Well, apparently they did because he was standing in front of her, but some days he didn't seem real. As if he should be on a movie screen. With that jaw and the "come hither" eyes, yep. Movies.

Bowie, on the other hand was about thirty-five pounds, a mutt of indiscriminate origin, with three white paws, pointy ears and dark, chocolate eyes that might as well be human. She swore that dog could read her mind, or at least her emotions.

"Oh, I had a callout." She lifted her medical bag, gave a tired laugh as she petted Bowie, who'd already nudged up against her calf insistently.

Orion's frown deepened and he immediately took the bag from her as if it weighed nothing. To him, it probably didn't, considering he had arms like The Rock. "You're supposed to take someone with you when you leave the farm. That's the rule."

One of his many rules. They'd only known each other a year, but he had this habit of bossing her and her sisters around. She wanted to be annoyed by it, but the only things he was ever truly bossy about revolved around her or her sisters' safety so getting mad seemed stupid.

"I didn't actually leave, I was at the bunkhouse—and I *did* go to your room to tell you, but you weren't there." She wanted to ask him where he'd gone in the middle of the night but bit her tongue.

They were just friends.

Friends, friends, friends. Bah. He simply happened to live with her and her sisters. A year ago he'd been passing through, and had saved a bunch of their chickens from being devoured by a coyote. She'd recognized him as the man she'd seen covered in clay with the wild eyes from before and he'd apologized for running off—though he'd never offered an explanation for why he'd been naked or anything.

And she hadn't pushed. He'd ended up staying so they'd offered him a room in their home since the bunkhouse had two different families living there now. He'd fit right in with her and her sisters, his presence comforting—even if it made her wildly aware of how long she'd been without a man. And no one on his scale of hotness, ever. But he'd put her firmly in the friend zone. So she lived in the same house as a man she fantasized about on the regular and he had all sorts of rules she didn't mind following. She hated that she wondered if he had "rules" in the bedroom. Maybe dirty ones?

Gah, she was such a freaking pervert.

"Oh." His frown didn't lessen and somehow that made him even more attractive, which was just plain annoying. "Hayes radioed me, thought he saw something at the windmill farm, so I headed out there."

"With Bowie?"

"Ah, no, he must have snuck out." He looked down at Bowie, his expression softening as he scooped the dog up.

Bowie acted like an actual human baby sometimes, but only with Orion. It was so ridiculous and adorable her ovaries couldn't stand it. Orion held him like one might a baby and rubbed his belly as they started back for the house.

"Is everything good?" The windmill farm in their parish had been an experiment—they'd been given a grant from the federal government before The Fall thanks to her parents' hard work.

The windmill farm had been a success and she was beyond grateful they had it since it was the only reason their small territory had relatively consistent power when much of the world didn't. Or she assumed it didn't. The info they received about the outside world was scant and scattered.

"Everything's fine. What about your call?"

"Oh, yeah, everything's good. Ava's little one had a fever but nothing to worry about." Still, Violet worried all the time. She tried not to, but it was difficult when they had such limited medical supplies now. People were careful, but a simple injury could have longer-lasting effects, sometimes fatal. Not to mention they'd lost a few people in the beginning who'd depended on various medicines and hadn't been able to get them. That had been so hard, accepting that she knew how to help them, but was unable to because of a lack of supplies.

She knew it was out of her control, but it didn't stop her from feeling the weight of responsibility to the people of the parish she'd grown up in and loved. It didn't matter that she'd moved away after high school; this had been her home for her formative years and she loved it and the people in it.

Orion opened the front door of the farmhouse, looked around as if expecting to be attacked, then nodded that she could enter even as he set Bowie on all fours.

Violet had a feeling he'd been a soldier of sorts, though he'd never specifically stated. He'd once told her that he'd "fought for my people" but it had been a vague statement and then he'd clammed up on her so she hadn't pushed.

Her parents had been scientists, but one of her uncles had served in the Marines and he hadn't liked talking about his time in Vietnam so she figured it was the same deal. Though Orion was far too young to have been in Vietnam. She guessed he was in his early thirties like her but again, she'd never pushed.

Because deep down she had this fear that one day he'd just leave. Just up and leave and she'd never see him again. That shouldn't fill her with such terror, but the thought of never seeing him again carved a hole in her chest.

"Come on," he murmured in that same commanding tone as he shut the door behind them.

She didn't even think to question him because she recognized that tone—he was going to make her tea. Which seemed at odds with the giant man with callus-roughened fingers and scars all over his body.

"You don't have to make me tea," she murmured even as she sat at the round kitchen table that had been her mother's.

He snickered slightly. "I can see you're fighting me quite hard on that."

She groaned as she slumped in her chair. "I was saying it to be polite. You don't have to call me out on it."

His mouth curved up ever so slightly and heat punched through her, just curled tight in her belly. God, this man could bring her to her knees —and at that thought, she had to shut down the thought of her on her knees in front of him. Or him on his in front of her, and oh my God, she needed sleep.

And tea.

She realized Orion was watching her, his emerald eyes seeming almost darker than normal. "What?" she asked.

He cleared his throat, shook his head even as he turned toward the stove, giving her his very broad back. "Nothing," he murmured, his voice low, gravelly. *Delicious.*

Jesus, maybe she should just close her eyes so she would stop ogling him like she was the queen of the perverts.

"Rough night?" he asked.

Nope, closing her eyes didn't help either. His delicious voice wrapped around her and she realized that it didn't matter if her eyes were open or closed, she was hot for this man. Which was stupid because she was pretty sure he was sneaking off to meet with someone. Why else did he sneak out at all hours of the night? "Not too bad," she murmured. "Just long."

"I found a couple treasures earlier," he said when she didn't expand.

She opened her eyes as he spoke again, the darkness of his voice wrapping around her, soothing all the frayed edges of the last day. "Yeah?"

As the kettle started to rumble on the stove, he unzipped his backpack and pulled out a bag of coffee from a brand she'd once been in love with.

"Oh my God," she breathed. "Where did you find this?" She saw that it had expired over a year ago, but so what if it was stale? It was ground coffee. She clutched it to her chest, and the intense look he gave her she felt allllll the way to her core.

But then he blinked and pulled out more treasures, setting each one on the table.

"You always find the best stuff," she murmured, looking at the little display he'd spread out. She picked up a handheld multi-tool. "Mari's going to fight you for this so you might want to hide it." Because Mari was always taking things apart and putting them back together. Or just fixing things in general.

He pulled out a similar looking one from his pocket, grinned as he held it up. In that moment he looked youthful, the harshness of his life fading to the background as he full-on smiled at her.

15

She forgot to breathe for a moment, her heart kicking against her chest. He rarely smiled and it felt like a gift that he was now.

"Thank you for all this stuff. I hope you know how much we appreciate you living with us, helping out not only us but everyone else." Their parish was only about seven hundred people, give or take, and the community was fairly spread out, but he went out of his way to come on house calls with her and help out wherever anyone needed it. Whether it was patching up chicken coops, or providing a large portion of the meat for the town. He was really good at hunting too, apparently, though she'd never seen him leave with a weapon. He probably provided eighty percent of the meat for everyone, which was unreal.

He blinked, looking surprised by her compliment, and it wasn't the first time she'd noticed that. For some reason he always seemed surprised when she or anyone else thanked him.

"In case I don't say it enough," she continued, reaching out slowly, barely skimming her fingers over the top of his hand. He'd been skittish of touch when they'd first met so she tried to be respectful of that, but then she'd realized that he seemed almost touch starved. And she so wanted to touch him. All over. All the time. "I hope you consider this your home." She felt vulnerable as she put it out there, but she was sleep deprived and punchy, and hell, she *wanted* him to know.

In the almost year he'd lived with them, he hadn't made any changes to the room they'd put him in. Absolutely none. He slept there and that was it. She and her sisters had given him little gifts that he seemed to like, but he hadn't changed anything in the room at all. She wanted him to put his stamp on his space, to give some indication that he felt comfortable here and considered this his home too.

That he wasn't planning on leaving in the middle of the night and never coming back.

He opened his mouth to respond, then the teakettle whistled and he stood abruptly, shoving the chair back with a clatter against the hardwood as he did.

"So what do you have planned today?" she asked, hoping a change in subject would dispel the awkwardness she'd decided to bring down on them. It might be three in the morning, but she knew him well enough that he'd grab only a few hours of sleep, then be back out again.

"The Bouchet ranch needs a few extra hands in the morning, then I'm taking some of the youth tracking. They want to learn to hunt better and that starts with tracking. I'm going to teach them what tracks to look for, how to be silent."

She inhaled the scent of the chamomile tea, smiled at him from behind the mug that had been her mother's favorite. It had a chip in the handle, but she didn't care. "I wish I could go with you."

"Come, then. Your presence is always welcome."

Oh. "I need to do a check on some of the older residents today." After she got a few hours of sleep. "It's been over a week since I've seen some of them."

He paused and she swore she could read his mind.

"You're not canceling your plans to come with me."

"Fine, but Hayes is going with you. You will take an escort."

"Don't you need to ask him first?"

"Nope." There was a slight challenge in his eyes and she wasn't sure exactly what it meant.

But she wasn't surprised by his confidence that Hayes would do what he asked—almost every man in the area and surrounding farms seemed to listen to every single thing he said. If he'd been in the military, she was betting he'd been an officer.

She took a sip of the hot tea, sighed in appreciation. "You'll have to teach me how you get everyone to listen to you so easily."

"Everyone but you and your sisters listen," he murmured, almost grumbling. "Because Mari isn't home, and I'm fairly certain that Rose is about to walk through that door alone." He chin nodded at the side door and to her surprise, Rose stepped in, looking as exhausted as Violet felt. "Despite the fact that I've asked *all* of you to take escorts with you on late jobs," he added, giving Rose a hard look.

"Hey guys," Rose murmured, slipping her work boots off with a sigh. Her dark curls were pulled up in a bun on top of her head. "Are you really giving me grief at three in the morning?" she asked Orion even as she made her way to the teakettle, grabbed a mug of her own.

"There are dangers everywhere. I need you to be careful, especially when traveling at night." He kept his gaze on Violet as he spoke. "You need to travel in twos."

She narrowed her gaze right back at him. "What about you?"

"The world is cruel to soft h—females."

Rose smacked him gently on the back of the head before she sat at the table. "We aren't soft."

He just snorted and stood. "Get some rest," he murmured, the words very much like an order.

"You too. You work just as hard as all of us," Violet said.

"I need less sleep than you."

He gave her a long look she couldn't decipher, then he was gone, disappearing upstairs, Bowie racing after him, and Violet could breathe normally again. That band of constriction around her chest eased, but only when he wasn't in her direct vicinity. Because if he was near, even the act of breathing became something she had to think about.

"Is he in bossypants mode tonight?" Rose murmured.

Violet snickered slightly. "Always. So where were you?"

"Delivering a foal. And I'm grabbing a quick shower after this, so please tell me there's hot water."

"As far as I know there is. Laurel went to bed hours ago and she took a short shower." She wanted to ask Rose if she knew where Mari was, but held her tongue. Even though she hadn't checked her sister's room yet, she had no doubt that Orion was right that Mari was gone.

Mari had been sneaking out in the middle of the night, and since she was a grown woman Violet hadn't asked her about it. She was curious what her sister had been getting up to though.

Because Violet didn't think she'd been sneaking off to meet up with someone. If she was, good for her—Violet wished she was sneaking up to Orion's room right now.

But that was just a fantasy and one she wouldn't act on. Orion hadn't ever hinted that he wanted anything more than friendship from her so she'd kept her feelings to herself. She might be the queen of the perverts in her head, but that was it.

Besides, he lived with them now. And if things changed between them, then went south, it would screw up the dynamics of everything.

Okay, who was she kidding? She didn't care. If he ever showed any interest in her romantically, she would jump at it. For a chance with him, she'd risk it.

She'd risk everything.

CHAPTER THREE

"I agree, it would be easier if we moved closer to the farms," Lili said quietly, glancing over her shoulder at the little house she lived in with her grandmother. "But you know how my nana is."

Violet nodded, suppressing a sigh of frustration. Aurélie was ninety-two and didn't want to move from her home, which Violet understood. But she and Lili were too far out from the center of things.

They didn't have a real downtown or central area in the Robichaux Parish. Before The Fall, their town had two main streets and a historic downtown that had brought in a lot of the wealthier people from Baton Rouge on weekends for different festivals. But the majority of people here had been lower middle class or living below the poverty line.

Violet had left when she'd graduated high school because she'd wanted to see the world and to have more job opportunities, but she was forever grateful that her little hometown hadn't been scathed by dragon fire or supernaturals fighting.

Now the majority of people lived on the connecting acreage of her and other families' farms. There were a few outliers, like Aurélie, who simply didn't want to leave—had never even ventured out of Louisiana at all.

"I know I've said this but there are plenty of abandoned homes you two could move into. They're a little bigger and we can get everyone together to bring all her stuff. It won't take but a day or so to do it. We've been keeping up with all the homes so that everything is clean and livable."

Lili's full mouth pulled into a line. "She doesn't want to live in some 'fancy house' with no soul. Meanwhile, I'm terrified that if something happens to me, she'll have no way to contact anyone and..." She swallowed hard, shook her head.

"Have you told her how you feel? Truly feel?"

Lili started to answer, then snapped her mouth shut. "No, not really. I've been pretty vague, I guess, just saying how nice it would be, to be closer to everyone."

"Tell her the truth. Be blunt. She needs to live closer for more than just medical reasons. We do a lot in the evenings with all the families and it'll be good for both of you to be there. I worry about you too, not just her. She needs to be around her community and so do you. And... there are security issues too. If something happens out here, there's no one close to help."

Lili nodded, her expression determined. "I'll talk to her now, tell her that we're moving and explain why it's important. You just tell us when you can get people to help and I'll make sure we're ready."

As Lili headed back inside the small, one-story ranch-style house that had been built in the sixties, Violet strode back over to where Hayes was waiting with their horses. Because Orion hadn't been wrong; Hayes had shown up exactly at nine to help her do her rounds.

"That's the last stop of the day," she said as she stuck her foot in the stirrups.

"Sounds good. You think they'll move?" he asked as they headed down the quiet street of mostly abandoned homes. This had been a quiet street even before The Fall, with mostly retired people—who had either moved in with family or passed. The only two left were Lili and Aurélie.

"I do. Lili had that determined look in her eye."

"So why'd you become a doctor?" Hayes asked as they reached the end of the street, made a left onto what was now an unused four-lane highway.

She was surprised by the question; Hayes was the youngest of his brothers and usually quiet around her. "Well, before all this, I was a pediatrician. And someone in my life was being hurt as a kid, and their doctor realized what was happening and got them the help they needed." A very condensed version of the real story. "And once the world went mad, it made sense that I step into the role of doctor for the parish since we don't have anyone else right now." She hadn't been living here when The Fall had happened, but after her own city had been destroyed —which she'd only seen on the news because she'd been on vacation— she'd slowly made her way home. Thankfully her sisters had been of the same mind, all of them making their way back here to a place that had always given them love and shelter.

"You're good with people," Hayes said, squinting as they rode right into the sun.

She slid her sunglasses on, glad that had been the last house. "Thanks. So how'd you and your brothers end up here?"

He lifted a shoulder.

"So I answer questions, but you give me nothing?" she asked teasingly.

He seemed a little startled, by her teasing tone or what, she wasn't sure, but it pulled a smile out of him. "Ah…we'd already left home when everything happened and this seemed like a good place to settle so we did."

Something told her it wasn't as simple as that, but he and his brothers, and Kayla, had been a welcome addition to their little community. He and his brothers worked as hard as everyone else to keep things running smoothly, and Kayla had immediately made friends her own age. From what Violet could see, she was a sweet kid, with a big heart. She liked to follow Rose around and ask questions about helping animals so maybe she'd get training from Rose and become a vet.

She started to respond when he stilled his horse, going immobile in the same way that Orion sometimes did. It was a little unsettling. She figured it was a former soldier thing, since his brothers did it too.

"What?" She stilled her own horse, though not as gracefully as him, or as quiet. Pickles was still shifting slightly, her body energy nervous. Probably because Violet had never been completely secure on a horse, but it was the best, easiest way to travel now.

"Someone's coming."

She frowned slightly, looking down the open, curving highway, not seeing anything or anyone other than what had always been there. A couple restaurants that had been boarded up long ago and the local high school that they used now as a meeting place more than anything.

"Wh—" She stopped when she heard the soft whine of an engine, recognized it immediately. Her sister Mari's restored motorcycle. It ran on some kind of vegetable oil or potatoes or something, Violet wasn't totally sure, but Mari loved the thing and treated it like her baby. "It's Mari."

Moments later, her sister crested around the curve in the wide-open highway, heading straight for them. Violet patted Pickles gently, waited until Mari pulled to a stop.

"We have newcomers. A lot of them. They came in from the east. New Orleans." Each word was clipped, hard. "A lot of supernaturals. Some humans."

Her heart rate kicked up a fraction. "What do they want?"

"To talk to who's in charge. You and Orion. Come on."

Violet started to argue that she wasn't in charge, but her sister had already shoved her helmet back on after a brief nod at Hayes and turned around, expecting them to follow.

Well, hell.

ORION KEPT his expression neutral as he stood with the wolf shifter, Darius, and his mate, Hazel. The female was a shifter of some kind, but he wasn't sure what. Something peaceful, and likely vegetarian, he sensed. Which was a big reason why he was reining in his natural aggression. His instinct was to battle natural predators, not peaceful beings.

But interlopers were in his territory. Didn't matter that he hadn't officially claimed it. Didn't matter that his humans didn't know that he was a shifter and that they were under his protection. They were his to keep safe all the same.

Two truckloads of supernaturals had shown up an hour ago from the territory of New Orleans. Wolves, mostly, along with some other types of shifters, a couple witches, and though he hadn't seen them, he knew there was a dragon or two nearby.

He could sense it, even if he couldn't scent it.

His beast half flat-out knew there were more like him nearby. And he wanted to challenge them out of raw instinct, to force them to submit.

"I saw the windmill farms on our way in. They're impressive," Hazel said into the quiet.

There were a few other families nearby, standing behind Orion, with his wolves in between him and the families. Creating a barrier between them and the humans. And whether the humans realized it or not, they'd fallen right in behind them.

"What are you?" he asked boldly, eyeing the slender female with dark curls and ocean blue eyes. "Because you're not a wolf." And he didn't like not knowing things, especially now. This could be one big trap, even though his instinct wasn't flaring to life, telling him they were in danger. No, that part of his brain was quiet.

But there were strangers invading his territory, and he didn't trust them.

Orion's blunt question made Darius bare his canines and step forward. "It's rude to ask that."

"Why is it rude?" It was standard practice to ask other supernaturals.

Hazel laid a gentle hand on her mate's forearm and gave Orion a soft smile. "It's fine. I'm guessing you're...a bit older than we are."

He lifted a shoulder, glanced in the direction Violet should be coming back from. He should have gone with her today, but he'd had to stop being so obsessive about her. *Never*, his dragon purred, deciding to chime in now. As he often did when it came to anything involving Violet. *She is ours.*

Hazel continued. "Well, if you are older, and it used to be common to ask about someone's identity or perhaps to smell them to identify, it's not anymore—"

Orion cleared his throat, not wanting to discuss any of this in front of the few humans behind him and the wolves. He knew his time had come to tell his humans he was a dragon, that he would have to tell Violet what he was. But he wanted to do it on his terms. Luckily the humans were back too far to hear their conversation.

"Look…" He paused at the sound of hoofbeats in the distance and the very faint scent of Violet on the air. She smelled like jasmine, lavender and something sweet that was all her, and he would recognize it anywhere, among any number of people. His beast calmed a fraction, knowing she was nearby. He wanted her close to him, where he could protect her.

"I grow corn, beans, and broccoli on my farm," Hazel said, as if they'd been having a conversation about it. She tucked one arm through her mate's. "And we've also got chickens and a pet dragon. Well, I don't, but my neighbor and best friend does."

He went very, very still at her words. "Pet dragon?"

"A dragonling. A baby, really, or more like a toddler. And not a shifter, if that's what you're thinking. Her name is Willow and she's pretty bossy but she's the sweetest thing. Also, to answer your other question, I'm a deer shifter."

"Why are you telling me all this?" He glanced between her and Darius, still wondering if this was some sort of trap. It wasn't a very good one, if so. Or…maybe she was just trying to disarm him with her guilelessness. Then it was actually a good idea and it was sort of working.

"Because you look as if you want to crawl out of your skin and I was hoping to distract you a bit while you wait for your Violet to return."

My Violet. That was what he'd called her when they'd approached and asked who was in charge. It had just slipped out and now he couldn't take it back.

Though Darius hadn't asked who was in charge, he'd simply walked right up to Orion as if he'd known who he was.

He just grunted and stared at Darius until the male was forced to break eye contact. The male was clearly a leader among his pack, but he wasn't an Alpha like Orion. No one that he could sense in the vicinity was.

Though it felt as if the eternity of his existence stretched out, a few minutes later Violet was there, her expression tense as she slid off her horse, strode toward them. She raised her eyebrows at Orion, her gray eyes flashing with curiosity, but he just lifted a shoulder as she came to stand right next to him. He could breathe again now that she was close. It was clear she'd had a long day; her dark curls were falling out of their braid and her clothes were rumpled and all he wanted to do was kiss her senseless and take care of her. She was small compared to him, though most people were, and she was fairly lean given how often she rode horses, hiked or biked to different homes around the territory. Not that it took away from the curves he was desperate to explore. And she had a presence that made her seem larger than life, approachable. It was why so many people in the community trusted her. Why she was such a good doctor.

"Hi, I'm Hazel." The deer shifter stepped forward before her mate could stop her, Orion thought, moving quickly, her hand out, a big smile on her face. Oh no, she was another one of those trusting shifters.

"I'm Violet." She took the female's hand, her smile a little unsure but kind.

"We're here from New Orleans, reaching out because it's come to our attention that you have a great setup here, a lot of farms, and are mostly humans." Hazel flicked a quick glance at Orion that he didn't think Violet even noticed.

"Ah…yes, we have a lot of farms. Why are you here though?"

"We'd like to set up an allyship of sorts. And I know this is a lot to dump on you, to just show up at the end of the day and drop this, but there was really no other way to contact you. Most of our pack is waiting a few miles back behind your territory lines, but my mate, Darius, and I," she said, motioning to him, "thought it would be best if we and a few humans arrived first. From what we understand, you're in charge?"

Violet let out a tired snort as she brushed back a few curls that didn't want to stay in the tie she'd secured them with. "Ah, no one is really in charge. I mean, we all look after each other, take care of each other."

"You're in charge, darlin'," said one of the older human males from the back—a farmer who Orion liked, but was now reconsidering since he'd called Violet darlin'. "She and her three sisters organized everything after The Fall and kept us all going. Because of their continued organization, everyone here's been fed and taken care of. And because of their parents' forethought to the changing climate, we still have power."

Darius had moved up closer now so that he was next to Hazel, motioned for the human male to step forward. As the male did, he glanced at Orion subtly, for permission.

Orion nodded, but held up a hand for him to stay behind Orion a fraction—he didn't think these two would hurt anyone, but he wasn't taking the chance they'd attack this human. And a fraction of a second could matter when it came to a fragile human life.

"How long have you lived here?" the wolf asked Hank.

"My whole life. Moved to Baton Rouge for a few years for work, but that was decades ago. Didn't like it, so I moved back and helped out on my dad's farm. My farm now."

"Would you say that your opinion is shared widely that Violet is the one in charge?"

"Violet and Orion." He gave Orion a half smile. "Even if he won't say it outright. These two, along with a handful of others, keep things running in an orderly fashion. This place is named after one of her great, great, great, whatever grandmothers. Their family has always been a strong presence here."

"Anyone here disagree?" Darius called out. He looked pointedly between Orion and Violet when no one said anything. "All right then, I think it's established for now that you're the two people we want to talk to. Look, I know we're dropping a lot on you, and we'll leave if that's what you want. But I think our territories can be of help to each other. You have a lot of food, but you're eventually going to need more things like textiles and medical supplies. So I hope you'll at least listen to what we have to say. Because…" He rubbed a hand over the back of his head, looked uncomfortable for a moment.

Hazel nudged him. "Just say it."

"You're a small territory." He spoke to Orion, his expression hard. "And we're not trying to annex you. But eventually, predators are going to come for a territory this rich in supplies. And no matter how strong you are, you need allies. Everyone does in this new world."

"We haven't had any issues with predators," Violet murmured. "Not the kind I think you're talking about anyway."

"He means vampires, mostly," Hazel said. "We've had a recent uptick in rogue vampires roaming on the edges of our territory. We live in a small farming community outside what you would have known as New Orleans proper. And we've seen a definite rise in attempted attacks."

Violet frowned slightly. "We haven't seen anything like that."

Orion cleared his throat, glanced back at his wolves. Bentley lifted a shoulder. Yep, it was time to come clean.

"We actually have had some issues with vampires," Orion said, giving Violet a sideways glance, gauging her reaction.

She blinked. "Why didn't you say anything?"

"Because we took care of them." He hadn't wanted her to worry, which in hindsight might not have been the best thing. But he liked taking care of her.

If she wanted to ask what he meant by "we" she bit her tongue and turned back to the others. "Okay, so what exactly are you proposing?"

"To have dinner, talk, get to know one another and see if an allyship is a viable option."

Before Violet could respond, Orion said, "Traditionally, an Alpha makes that offer."

If Darius was surprised by his statement, he didn't show it. And Orion didn't think he was surprised. "You're correct. But King, my Alpha, is currently dealing with diplomats from a neighboring realm. And he didn't think it was wise to stroll in here to this territory without touching base first. I'm following all the proper protocols."

Orion simply nodded because the male was correct. He looked at Violet, who was now staring at him as if she'd never seen him before.

Hell. "I think it would be wise to host a dinner and hear what they have to say," he said to her.

She blinked, then glanced back at the others, including two of her sisters—Mari was missing—then looked back at him before she nodded. "Okay. We'd planned to do a big roast tonight anyway. How many…ah, people would you like to bring?"

Darius looked at Orion. "Is ten acceptable?"

"How many supernaturals and how many humans?" Orion asked even as he deeply inhaled, though subtly. Because there was a scent he recognized on the air as the wind shifted. That of a friend. One he hadn't seen in millennia. One he missed, as she was one of the few beings he cared about who still lived.

"For tonight, one supernatural other than us. The rest will be humans."

Orion looked at Violet and nodded.

"Okay, then. I guess, meet us back here in about two hours?" she said.

Darius nodded and Hazel smiled broadly. "I'm looking forward to it. I'll bring some treats."

"Thank you," Violet said, almost dazedly.

Orion knew she was trying to process everything and thought she was doing a damn good job. He wanted them gone now, however, so they could talk.

Because he knew she had a lot of questions—and he wasn't sure if he'd just made a mistake in allowing these people into the territory.

He kept guard, watching as the strangers left, but the moment they were alone Violet turned toward him, her eyes narrowed. And he knew his time was up. "Okay, what the hell?"

CHAPTER FOUR

"There were vampires in our territory and you're just now telling me?" Violet had her hands on her hips, her mouth pulled into a tight line as she looked up at him. Even in this colder month, her skin was a glowing olive tone. She'd once told him she had a French and Portuguese heritage. He hadn't understood the reference then, but he did now.

He looked down at her, resisted the urge to run his fingers through her dark hair, free her curls from their braid. And to wipe away the slight smudge of dust along her jaw. He wanted to touch her all over. But he didn't have that right. *You could,* his dragon snarled.

"I took care of the problem."

"What does that mean?" she demanded.

"I killed them." No need to hide the fact. They would never be together; Orion knew he never had a chance with a female like Violet, even if his dragon couldn't get that through his thick skull. So it was better she knew this about him, even if it would make her look at him differently. He would simply live with her disappointment.

Bentley stepped up then, his brothers behind him. "We did too. You've all welcomed us into your community and we've been keeping the border free of danger."

"While you guys figure this out," Laurel, Violet's youngest sister, said, "I'm going to talk to the rest of the families and set up a big cookout. If we're going to meet these newcomers, we'll just make it into a party."

Violet looked a little dazed as she nodded at her sister, and when she turned back to Orion she grabbed his hand and tugged him away from everyone, stalking toward the dormant orchard fifty yards away. There were growing pods next to the orchard where they grew mini crops and she was using one of them as a way to block them from everyone else.

Eventually she dropped his hand and stalked away in front of him, and he enjoyed the view of her angry walk because her ass was absolute perfection. *Goddess.* He shook himself, knew that was not the most important thing right now—though her ass was a close second.

"So, vampires have been threatening our parish and you and apparently the 'broody brothers' didn't tell anyone that you'd been killing them. Not even me," she hissed. "Are you kidding me with this?"

He blinked. "Broody brothers?"

Violet shook her head, made an exasperated sound. One of her curls bounced free, framing her face. "Why didn't you tell me?" Her jaw was tight and her expression angrier than he'd ever seen. Even her gray eyes seemed shades darker as she glared up at him.

He stemmed the urge to push her curl back out of her way, but didn't think she would welcome the touch. "I didn't think you needed to know. They never ventured into our inner territory. They've always been on the outer rings, and you never go that far at night without me." He frowned. "Well, last night is the exception," he growled, his protective urge swelling up again. Though technically she hadn't gone far, she'd just gone out *alone.* Which was unacceptable.

"Oh no, you don't get to be mad. Oh my God, you know all these supernatural rules too? I'm going to put a pin in this whole *vampires in our territory* thing for now but I'm still mad about it." She glared at him, but that quickly faded as she continued. "So what do you think of the newcomers? I liked Hazel. She seems pretty nice."

"The way they've approached us is the correct protocol and they don't..." He couldn't tell her that their scents were fine, that if they'd been here with malicious intent, he'd have scented it. Hell, their group would have simply infiltrated in the middle of the night and attacked if they'd wanted to claim this area. He also couldn't tell her that he'd scented a friend from long ago on the air, which further made him think this situation was exactly what it seemed to be: another territory hoping to set up a line of communication with a future ally.

But he had to tell her something. "In my former life, I was a soldier—"

"I knew it!" Her eyes widened slightly, then she grinned. "Sorry, I thought so."

He watched her carefully, drinking in all of her, the way her pale gray eyes flashed as she watched him right back with no fear, no looking away at all. Goddess, he should just tell her that he was a dragon. But… dragons had destroyed most of the world, gotten her parents killed. And she'd already been given a lot of information to process for one day.

Lie to yourself, his dragon growled. *Our human will understand, but she won't understand if you keep the truth from her. You will hurt her even more by waiting.*

Sometimes he hated his other half. The smug bastard. Orion cleared his throat. "As I was saying, in my former life I was good at reading people. Still am. For now, I trust them. Because if they'd wanted something from us, they could have invaded at night using violent means." He decided to add that last part because it mattered and he needed her to understand.

She shoved out a breath, looked around, but he didn't think she was really seeing anything as she digested his words. "They said they would trade medical stuff. It would be incredible to get my hands on medical supplies. I've been running on fumes the last few months…" She trailed off, met his gaze again. "Okay, if you trust them, then I do too. Let's get this party together, then."

Her trust in him shook him right down to his marrow. Sometimes he didn't understand this female, her open nature and kindness. She should be more wary, distrusting. The world was a dark, violent place; he knew firsthand. The thought of it snuffing out her light was the only thing that gave him nightmares. "That's it?"

She batted at the stray curl now, made an annoyed sound. "What do you mean?"

"You just…trust me?" he asked.

She lifted a dark eyebrow. "Should I not?"

I would die for you, kill for you, set the world on fire for you. And you can always trust me to keep you safe. He kept all those words to himself and simply turned, headed in the direction of Violet's home, the one he slept in. "Come on."

"That's not really an answer, but whatever. I need to shower," she said more to herself than him. "And oh my God, we'll get to learn more about the outside world too. You know, if these people aren't serial killers hoping to wear our skins."

He paused, nearly stumbled.

She stopped next to him. "What?"

"Why would someone want to wear our skins?" Long ago he'd battled ancient clans who'd liked to behead their enemies and put their corpses and heads on spikes, but no one had ever worn skin. That was disgusting. "Or kill…cereal?" That could not be right.

She blinked, then let out a startled laugh. "So that was a reference to a movie I'm guessing you haven't seen."

Damn it. She often made references he did not understand. "I did not have much time to watch movies in my previous life." A sort of lie. He'd seen a handful of movies since waking up because Violet had showed them to him. He hadn't understood the purpose of them at first, but they were entertaining. Like plays, but better. And they often made her laugh, which was purpose enough.

"And serial killers are murderers who kill random people with, like, patterns and, ah, it doesn't matter," she said on another laugh. "Okay, so am I good to take a shower? Do you need help with anything right now?"

The thought of her upstairs in the shower, naked, rubbing soap all over her body…*nope.* He had to lock that thought down tight and bury it forever. "Take care of yourself. I have things under control here."

She narrowed her gaze slightly, then hurried inside. And he didn't stop himself from staring at her ass as she opened and shut the door behind her.

"Where have you been?" he asked before turning around, scenting her younger sister Mari.

This female was different than her sisters—harder, though her heart was no less big than theirs. She just had an edge of wariness to her the other three did not. She was a human who understood the darkness of the world, that much his dragon sensed.

As he turned, she was sliding her backpack off and rolling her shoulders slightly. Her hair was short, her curls tighter and springier than her sisters', though she had the same pale gray eyes. "Spying on the newcomers. There are two truckloads of people ten miles away. But you must already know that."

"I do." And he was about to do another aerial recon, see if there was any new movement.

"So what's the deal? You invited them to dinner tonight?" she asked.

"Ten of them have been invited to dine with anyone in the community who wants to be here. The others will remain on the outskirts of the territory."

"How do we know they're not psychopaths who want to murder us all?"

"We don't. But I don't think they are."

"Yeah, I didn't think you'd invite them here if you thought that. So… put me to work. I want to help out with security. You and the brothers are always sneaking off to kill vampires and—"

"What?"

She gave him a dry look. "Yeah, I know about that."

He eyed her carefully, glanced around, though he knew exactly where everyone was. Laurel was ordering people around near the barn as they set up tables and strung up new lights. A handful of kids were playing hide and seek in the orchard—and doing a terrible job at hiding —and a couple humans were chopping extra wood. Likely for a bonfire. And Violet had just started the shower inside the house. She was likely naked right now, something he absolutely could not think about if he wanted to focus. "What else do you know?"

"That you're not human."

Hmm. Okay.

"I figured if you wanted to hurt us, you could have done it long ago. Same with the broody brothers."

"Does everyone call them that?"

"Yeah. You want to know what they call you?"

He blinked at her teasing tone. "Not really."

She snickered. "Probably a good thing."

Now he kind of wanted to know. "Who else knows about me?"

"You and the brothers, you mean? I don't know. I certainly haven't told anyone."

"Not even your sisters?" That truly surprised him.

"Figured you were keeping it a secret for a reason."

"Do you know what I am?"

She sighed. "No, but I know the brothers are wolves. I thought you might be like a bear or something but…" She shrugged. "You're too sneaky and too fast. I've only ever seen you running around the woods naked—and I did not look at your junk, for the record."

"You are quite stealthy," he murmured, ignoring the junk comment. He didn't care about anyone seeing his "junk." Other than Violet. He definitely had feelings about her looking at him naked. Many, many feelings. "I didn't even scent you following me."

"Well, I wasn't actually following you. One night I saw a couple vampires and killed them when they threatened me. Then later I saw you and the brothers having a secret meeting in the woods, talking about killing vampires. It wasn't too hard to put it together after that."

"You've been killing vampires too?" He hid his shock, but he should not be surprised. Humans could kill vampires. Perhaps not as easily as supernaturals, but there had been human vampire hunters for ages.

"Yep." And the way she said it made him think it wasn't her first time.

"Were you a soldier before everything?"

"No. But…I dealt in secrets." She glanced around, then eyed him again. "You're gonna need to tell Violet what you are sooner or later— I'm guessing you're a dragon because of the lack of tracks you *don't* leave behind. That's your business though. Until then, I want to start working with you and the brothers on security. I've started setting up traps for vamps and I want to make sure we're not overlapping each other."

"Okay. Tell Bentley to loop you in on everything."

"That's it? You're not going to tell me that I'm just a human?"

"Why would I do that? You're clearly capable and we need to make sure this territory is as secure as possible." Because though he and the brothers had been working hard to keep everyone safe, there were just four of them. It wasn't a long-term solution and he knew it.

"Huh. Okay, then." She plucked up her backpack, slid it on with a grin that was slightly terrifying. She reminded him of a deadly dragon female in that moment. "I'm going to try and catch up with them."

As she hurried off, Orion knew he needed to tell Violet not only what he was, but that her sister was apparently out there killing vampires. Because if she found out he'd kept that from her, he wasn't sure she would ever forgive him.

CHAPTER FIVE

Violet felt as if she was going to crawl out of her skin as she stood next to Orion and her sisters while they waited for the small group of outsiders to arrive at their farm.

Her sister Laurel and some others had set up a big party atmosphere at the last minute outside their barn, with about twenty tables, and everything looked amazing. Country chic, as her sister called it. A few of the younger teens had even set up an area right off the gazebo for their band. They hadn't started anything yet, were currently talking and laughing as if they didn't have a care in the world.

She wished she could be like that, but too much was at stake. A breeze rolled over her and she shivered, even under her thick puffy coat, knit cap and mittens. Orion had gotten it for her, from who knew where. He'd found it on one of his explorations and she treasured the gift. The temperature had dropped a solid twenty degrees since the sun had gone down and it only added to the panic punching through her.

This shouldn't be that big of a deal. In her before life, she'd interacted with so many different people from different cultures, had traveled all over the world. But since everything had changed and they'd created a quiet, thriving community in her hometown, she felt incredibly protective of it and all the people in it.

Especially her sisters and Orion.

Who'd been giving her strange looks tonight that she couldn't quite define, including right now.

"What?" she murmured.

Orion looked away. "Nothing."

"That look is *not* nothing."

"You look beautiful tonight," he said calmly, not looking at her again as he scanned the road that led up to their property.

His words took her off guard, made her brain go on the fritz for a moment. Did he just call her beautiful?

Then he continued all casual. "They're almost here."

She was going to put a pin in that too, and revel in it later when she was alone in her room. She listened, frowned, then heard the subtle rumble of an engine. Which wasn't completely foreign anymore, not when Mari and a few others rode motorcycles or four-wheelers around here that ran on whatever kind of fuel her sister had cooked up.

Their farm was fairly far off the beaten path, surrounded by a thousand acres and other farms, and the sound cut through the talking, laughing and other noise, making everyone quiet down.

There was a buzz in the air, and she couldn't tell if it was good or bad. "I can't believe Mari's not back," she said low enough for only Orion, who was standing at the edge of the group with her, in front of everyone, to greet the others.

"She's on security detail right now. Probably won't be back until after they leave."

"Security?" She could see the pickups rounding the long, winding bend, kicking up dust as the two vehicles headed down the drive toward them.

"Yeah, she's working with the brothers. They're heading up security now, keeping an eye on the perimeter. Which is something you and I need to talk about later."

Her tongue stuck to the roof of her mouth at his casually spoken words. So much was happening so fast. She couldn't be surprised that Mari was on security detail, however. Not when she knew her sister had secrets that she kept from all of them—and that she was very comfortable holding a random array of weapons. "Why'd she tell you and not me?"

Orion was silent, but she knew he wasn't ignoring her. "I don't know and I don't pretend to understand her mind."

"That's a fairly diplomatic answer."

He snorted softly. "No one has ever called me diplomatic before."

As the trucks came to a stop, she couldn't quell the tension coiling inside her, but when Orion took her hand gently in his, squeezed even more gently with his giant, callused hand, she managed to breathe.

Forget gentle; she linked her fingers through his and held on tight. Something about his hold was grounding, and it was like he'd thrown her a lifeline when she was drowning. So she wasn't going to be letting go anytime soon.

Thankfully he didn't seem to mind that she was clutching onto him like he was a security blanket.

After the vehicles parked, five people got out of the first truck and five out of the other. And...everyone looked normal. None of them were brandishing weapons.

She internally berated herself as she drew in another steadying breath. She was getting worked up for nothing.

Hazel smiled and waved as three men and four women grabbed coolers from the back and hefted them off. "Hey, everything looks great!" She approached with her mate a few steps behind and a pretty woman with red hair who somehow looked vaguely familiar.

"Violet, Orion, this is Luna O'Connor, one of our scientists. Since you're a doctor," she said to Violet, "I thought you guys might have a lot to talk about. Or at least speak the same language."

"Wait, *Doctor* Luna O'Connor? I read one of your papers on cell regeneration. It was a feature on Louisianan doctors. Your thoughts were revolutionary years ago and..." She held out a hand to the smiling redhead, couldn't contain her own smile. "It's a pleasure to meet you."

"You too, but just call me Luna, please. I'm so excited to be on this 'exploration.' As a human—which for the record is still weird to say—I haven't been out of our territory much, and honestly, it was terrifying to leave."

Violet let out a laugh as she admitted, "We, or at least me, have been kind of nervous about having so many new visitors, so I can imagine."

Orion placed his big palm at the back of her neck, squeezed in a comforting way she felt all the way to her core, before he stalked toward Darius. Then he just fell into helping, grabbing one of the coolers as if it weighed nothing, even though she'd seen two people struggling to carry it.

The man was ridiculously strong, and she hated that she noticed so much, that she wanted him so much. That she wondered far too often what it would be like to be pinned down by that giant man and... She sighed. They were just friends—even if he'd just told her that she was beautiful. But she wasn't going to read into it at all. Clearly he'd just been trying to calm her down when she'd needed it. It had worked too, because she wasn't freaking out as much.

And she needed to focus on the woman in front of her and the rest of their guests. Hopefully tonight was going to be a lot better than she'd thought.

～

"So tell me more about New Orleans, about life there. We've been so cut off from everything for the most part." Violet glanced over at Orion, who was talking quietly with Darius near where the band was playing. The others who'd arrived had started mixing with her community, but she and Luna had been more or less attached at the hip all night. And now they'd found a small table and were both drinking wine—which Violet hadn't had in years—underneath a bunch of paper lanterns someone had strung up.

"The city, or *territory*, really rebounded incredibly well and that's because of King, our Alpha. And now he's mated so we actually have an Alpha couple, and they've really got the territory running like a well-oiled machine."

"And supernaturals don't...look down on you because you're human?"

Luna snorted softly. "Not in my experience, no. I mean, there are some vampires who just seem to be dicks all-around, which is weird since the majority of them used to be human. But other than them, I've never personally dealt with any sort of bigotry. I work with witches mainly, and some bears. But the witches and I have been combining science and magic to do some incredible things with cell regeneration and prosthetic limbs, mainly. It's a whole new world and I'm embracing it."

"Fascinating," Violet murmured, taking a sip of her drink, enjoying the burst of fruity flavor.

"What about you guys? From what I've heard and the little I've seen, your community seemed to walk away relatively unscathed, and it looks as if everyone here is flourishing."

"I can't take credit for that. I mean, my sisters and I got everyone organized but it's been a real community effort. Everyone looks out for everyone and I think the fact that we're so small has made a big difference."

"Yeah, that makes sense. I heard you guys have a windmill farm too."

"Yes, and I'm so grateful for that. I have a limited amount of medical equipment and it's been lifesaving to have power for those."

Luna took a small sip of her drink, gave Violet a thoughtful look.

"What?"

"I'm probably not supposed to say anything..." She looked around, glanced in Darius and Hazel's direction. "But screw it. We've got a lot of extra X-ray machines, incubators, blood and urine analyzers, and oh, stethoscopes that we've built or retrieved from abandoned cities and hospitals. They'll definitely give you guys whatever you need, especially if you link up with healers. Whether or not you actually form an ally-ship with our territory, I know the healers will help you out. Just FYI. Doctors and healers help each other just because, so I'll put you in contact with one of my healer friends. Oh, and something you should know in case you don't already, healers—doctors—are considered off-limits during wartime. Or anytime. No one from a decent pack or clan or whatever will ever hurt a healer or doctor. It's part of supernatural rules."

"This all seems too easy," she murmured, hoping she made sense.

The other woman was offering her knowledge and a way to get medical supplies.

"Easy?" Luna snorted softly again. "Supernaturals are just different, or at least the ones running New Orleans are. And I'm going to exclude the vamps in this statement. Don't get me wrong, we've had our fair share of badness happen..." She trailed off, slightly shuddering. "Things I'll tell you about later because it's a little scary. But I know that King wants to form an allyship with this area because to the west of us and here is a growing...ah, territory. Run by vampires who aren't controlling their people. I don't know much, but I do know that there's a lot you could ask for and get," she whispered. "So don't be afraid to bargain."

"What do they want in return though?" That was the thing Violet didn't really understand.

"Trading rights. You guys have a lot of food, and while we do too, it just doesn't hurt to have allies. Especially when there are other territories who aren't like ours—ones who think they can take."

"And?" Because there was more she wasn't saying.

Luna took another sip, her green eyes sparking. "Okay," she said quietly. "I've heard talk that there are some supernaturals who want to move from New Orleans, move somewhere 'less settled.' I don't really get it, but they think our territory is too civilized, with little challenges for them, and they want to help a new territory grow. And King doesn't want to lose a lot of people. So if he forms an allyship with a trustworthy ally, then it only strengthens our territory."

Huh. She bit back any response as she saw Orion break away from Darius and Hazel and head toward her. "Where are you guys sleeping tonight?" she blurted instead.

Luna rolled her eyes. "In tents. I mean, they're like military-style, so nothing like when I was in the Girl Scouts, so I can't really complain."

Violet laughed lightly. "Maybe...well, we have some extra room here on our farm so maybe some of you could come by tomorrow and bunk here instead of sleeping in tents. Just a thought."

"I will happily take a bed over a sleeping bag but I'll let Darius and the others figure that out. I'm just along for the ride."

Orion nodded at Luna as they approached, then his gaze landed on Violet. And she thought it might be the alcohol, but his look seemed a little heated. Maybe. She squinted up at him, which, in hindsight, probably made her look like a weirdo. Or maybe constipated.

He paused. "Are you okay?"

"Yep, never better," she said, standing, smoothing out her ridiculous expression. "Is everything good with you?"

He stared at her for a long moment but nodded. "I think things are about to start winding down," he murmured, even as Darius made a sort of hand motion to his people. "I've told them that they can just leave everything here and retrieve it tomorrow. I wanted to invite them deeper into the territory, to see more of our farms and the windmills, but only if you're okay with it."

She wanted to ask if he trusted them—because she did. Or she at least trusted Luna O'Connor. The woman was brilliant and kind, and if she was part of some plot to...steal their land or something, then Violet would lose all faith in people. Since Luna was so close, she didn't ask Orion what he thought.

Because he wouldn't be asking her at all if he thought they were untrustworthy—he'd simply tell them to leave. She understood that much about this mysterious man. "I'm fine with it but we need to talk to the other families."

There were a handful of families that more or less made decisions in the area, but they almost always agreed with one another. When you'd lived in a rural community and were used to having to figure things out on your own because of lack of funding, it was easier to look at the greater good for the community.

"Okay." Orion looked as if he wanted to say more, but eventually nodded, then stalked off, all broody.

Because forget the broody brothers, they had nothing on him.

CHAPTER SIX

Orion crossed his arms over his chest and waited as Darius worked up to whatever he clearly wanted to say. He liked this wolf as much as he liked any stranger, but that didn't mean he totally trusted him.

"I'm giving you unsolicited advice," Darius said bluntly, glancing over his shoulder at the waiting trucks. Hazel was driving one of them, and with the exception of one witch Orion had scented, everyone else was human. "Claim this territory and do it officially. The humans here might not understand, but other supernaturals will. And this area needs an Alpha. You're already acting as one, so make it official."

"I don't make the decisions here," he said dryly.

Darius snorted. "Look, I've dealt with enough...of your kind, that I know how stubborn you can be. Claim it or don't, but this territory won't be safe forever. You simply don't have the supernatural presence, no matter how strong you are as an Alpha. So if you don't claim it, be prepared for the consequences."

"Bold words." His tone was mild.

Darius lifted a shoulder. "I think you care about these humans far too much to let those consequences happen."

Orion didn't have to look behind him to know the humans from his community were too far away to hear anything, but he still kept his voice down. "What do you know of my kind?"

"I know you're the most stubborn, arrogant beings I've ever met." But there was no rancor in his tone, more exasperation than anything.

He wasn't wrong about the arrogance, but the wolf could just be fishing for information. "When you come tomorrow, bring one of 'my kind' with you."

Darius eyed him once before breaking eye contact—because Orion's dragon was in his gaze. "You sure about that? I'd planned to leave them behind at our encampment."

So there was more than one dragon, as he'd suspected. "Bring the ancient female with you." Because he knew for a fact he scented Prima, an old friend. Or he hoped she was still a friend; there had been many years gone between them. And when she'd disappeared into Hibernation, her mind had started to fracture. He hoped the Prima he'd known long ago had resurfaced, that Hibernation had healed all those splinters. Because she was one of the few beings on the planet he'd trusted with his life. She'd saved him a long, long time ago.

Darius blinked, looked as if he wanted to ask something, but simply nodded. "You might regret that."

"Only one way to find out."

Orion waited as the two trucks drove off, then turned to find Bentley headed his way. The wolf had been running security with his brothers and Mari—whom he didn't see or scent anywhere.

"There was no movement from their encampment, and Mari managed to get close and eavesdrop—she's incredible, by the way." Bentley just jumped right into it and there was a hint of awe in his voice as he spoke about Mari. "And I know it sounds condescending, but I'm gonna say it, especially for a human. She moves like a ghost and managed to cover her scent so she could get far closer than we could."

Very interesting. "And?"

"Everything she reported back was benign. The people there were mostly talking about normal life stuff, though she heard a few conversations about the trip here. The topic of rogue vampires came up a few times though and there seemed to be a consensus that they were worried about this territory." Bentley had an expression of almost... surprise on his normally hard face. "They're worried about complete strangers being attacked by vamps, so I dunno, I'm leaning heavily toward trusting them. What happened here?" He motioned back toward where people were starting to clean up after the party.

"Just a party." Orion lifted a shoulder. "The supernaturals and humans who came tonight are what they seem." He didn't have any doubts now, not that he'd had many to begin with. "And I've invited more of them to visit tomorrow, including another dragon."

Bentley's eyes widened slightly. "How does that work with, well, you? I don't know much about your kind."

"More or less the same as with yours. This one is Alpha to her marrow but she doesn't want a territory." Or she hadn't thousands of years ago. That could have changed. He hoped he wasn't making a mistake by inviting Prima, but it was one he was willing to risk to see an old friend. He hadn't realized she was awake or he'd have searched for her and her twin.

"Oh, so you know her?"

"I did a long time ago."

"Can you define a long time ago?"

Orion blinked in surprise. Normally Bentley and his brothers just helped with security, but they weren't big talkers, something he preferred. Tonight apparently the wolf was breaking his normal routine and talking as much as Laurel did at the house.

"What?" The big wolf grinned at Orion's expression. "Look, my brothers and I respect you, and when you finally claim this territory, we hope things stay the same with us. Because unless you kick us out, we're not going anywhere."

"You don't want to challenge me for it?" Because Bentley had a lot of raw power. Not as much as Orion, but sometimes shifters got it into their heads that they could take him on.

"Hell no. I left one bad Alpha in the middle of the night with my family. And we've been here long enough that we trust you, even though you're pretty tight-lipped about your past and everything else."

"Your words are ironic, I believe."

"Fair enough." Bentley lifted a shoulder, smiling. He hadn't told Orion much about his past either. "I'm just saying, unless you end up being the opposite of everything you've shown us you are so far, we want to help you build this territory, strengthen it. Hell, expand it. I feel like we're in on the ground floor of something good."

Goddess, Orion felt it too. He had once been Alpha to a band of warriors. Males and females he missed to this day. He'd never had a family—not a good one anyway. Dragons were known for valuing their children, but he'd gotten the short end of that stick. Then been beaten with it within an inch of his life, over and over.

"We'll see what happens tomorrow," was all he could commit to. Because the thought of officially being in charge of everyone in this territory was... It reminded him of another life.

One he wasn't sure he wanted to revisit. He'd lost all the people he loved before. He didn't think he could do that again.

"Fine." Bentley's expression was good-natured. "For the record, you're my Alpha. In case that's not clear. My wolf recognizes you as my Alpha so it's a done deal. Same with my brothers. I know I've never explicitly said it, and I honestly don't know if it's different for dragons than wolves. My old Alpha simply knew, so in case you didn't, now you do."

Orion blinked, something warm expanding in his chest. He hadn't realized, perhaps because they were wolves. Long, long ago, he'd been linked to the clan of warriors he'd formed. A found family of mostly dragons who hadn't fit in anywhere else. They might not have been blood related, but they'd been linked all the same and he'd sensed their bond to him. And now that he concentrated...he could feel the slight tether to Bentley.

"You still didn't tell me what a long time ago means," Bentley continued.

"If that's your way of asking my age, I'm... I don't know for certain how old I am. Millennia upon millennia." It didn't matter.

Bentley blinked, then grinned. "Damn it. Now I owe Hayes. I hate when that little shit is right," he said in the way of a loving older brother. Then he straightened slightly. "We'll keep track of the perimeter for the rest of the night—Mari too, unless you want her home."

He did, but it was clear that Mari could handle herself—and had secrets. He could respect that. "As long as you team up with her. Violet can't lose her sister."

"Understood." Then he stalked off, heading away from the party, back to the edge of the woods.

Orion saw Violet watching him curiously as she secured some of the leftover food into a container, but then she quickly looked away. Not before he saw a spark of heat in her eyes.

He shoved down the punch of longing that swelled up inside him, demanded he go to her. Claim her. Possess her.

Then he turned away from her as well, reminded himself that she was simply his friend. They were from two different worlds and he didn't deserve a female like her anyway.

Never would.

ORION LOOKED over at his bedroom door as Violet stepped inside, wrapped in a faded blue fluffy robe, her long curls pulled back in a braid and had tattered slippers with pandas on the end peeking out from the matching panda-covered pants.

She should have dragons on her.

Or one dragon in particular inside her, his beast snarled sulkily. *Stupid pandas.*

"Hey, you busy?" she whispered.

He'd been about to sneak out and meet the wolves but shook his head. He was used to her stopping by his room to simply talk in the evenings. They'd fallen into a sort of routine.

One he cherished more than the treasure he had secreted away.

She'd let him see what a loving family looked like. And he would do anything to protect her and her sisters. No matter what happened, deep down he knew that she would always be his priority, even if he officially became Alpha.

"I saw Mari sneaking back in the house not too long ago. So...?"

She flopped on the end of his bed as he leaned against one of the dressers she'd told him had belonged to her grandmother. He could scent the lotion she often wore, twining through the air, permeating his space. He'd found the lotion for her on one of his flying trips. He'd taken a handful of the kind he knew she favored, and now one of their own humans made soaps and lotions for the community.

"So...?"

"What was she doing running security? Because don't believe I've let that drop."

"I haven't spoken to her yet, but according to Bentley she's skilled."

Violet bit her bottom lip as she crossed her legs under her.

"What?" he asked, loving that she was so comfortable with him.

"Years ago some random people from the government came to interview me, ask questions. And not just me, but everyone in the family, including our parents. Mari said it was because of some HR job for some random federal position she'd applied for but I never believed it. The questions were too invasive, and Mari hates being stuck inside with a passion. And I've seen her clean an animal with a knife. It's surgical in precision."

He had some idea where she was going with this, but he didn't fully understand all the nuances of the English language. And he didn't understand some words or colloquial phrases. Or even some very basic knowledge, so he tended to keep silent and let others speak.

Sighing, she flopped back on his bed and he knew it would smell like her later, wanted to bury his face in the covers right now.

Okay, he wanted to bury his face between her legs.

"It's not so crazy to think she was a spy, right?" He could tell by her tone that she wasn't looking for an answer.

Carefully, he lay down on the bed next to her, stared up at the ceiling.

Her sweet scent of lavender and jasmine wrapped around him, infused him as he just breathed her in. Around her he felt calm in a way he'd never experienced in his life before. He wanted to tell her what he was, knew it was inevitable. But he also wanted this quiet time with her where nothing else in the world mattered or existed.

"It's not crazy," he murmured. Because he understood the word *spy*. He'd had a small group of them in his arsenal high up on the mountain he'd once called home. It was on the tip of his tongue to tell her that he was a dragon, to lob the explosive news like a bomb, but years of self-preservation made him hold back. He would keep his secret for one more night.

For one more night it could just be Orion and Violet, two human friends.

Friends, his dragon sneered.

"I like Luna," she said, surprising him by the change of subject. "And I feel like a big jerk for admitting this, but I thought supernaturals would be...scarier, I guess. But the three here tonight were so nice. Stupid, huh?"

"Not stupid."

"So how do you know so much about supernatural rules and stuff?" She rolled over, propped her head up on her hand as she stared at him. "Because I told you we were going to circle back to this. Also, are there panda shifters? If so, are they almost extinct like their regular animal counterpart? And if we do create this allyship, then how does all that work? We'll be trading with another territory and..." Trailing off, she looked nauseous for a moment. Then she flopped back down, stared at the ceiling again. "Never mind. Just...never mind. Unless you know about pandas."

"I have never met a panda shifter. But they exist."

"Then I'm going to end this night on a high. I got to meet Doctor Luna O'Connor, panda shifters exist and..." She yawned loudly. "My sister was definitely once a spy."

He snickered slightly. "Pandas aren't that impressive."

She let out a sound of indignation and smacked him in the side, her touch ridiculously gentle.

He let out a grunt of pain.

"Oh my God, did I hurt you?" Clearly worried, she started to sit up, but stopped when he simply grinned at her.

"Your hits are like that of a butterfly," he said around a laugh, his entire body shaking. Goddess, she was the only person who'd ever made him truly laugh, feel free.

"Jerk," she grumbled, then elbowed him, but scooted a little closer, resting her head right at his shoulder.

And he froze in pure pleasure at the feel of her lying so casually in his bed like this. Touching him. He wanted to stay this way forever. Just freeze this moment in time.

"How are you so calm about everything?" she finally asked, curling into him, her voice sleepy.

"I'm analyzing everything. And I trust these newcomers." It was the only reason they were all still breathing. Because if they'd been a threat to Violet, this would have been their last day on earth.

She murmured slightly, but her breathing soon evened out in a way that told him she was sleeping.

He froze again, then risked a glance at her, and sure enough her eyes were closed, her face calm, relaxed in sleep. And he realized he could stare all he wanted. Goddess, she'd fallen asleep so quickly. And he knew it was because she was beyond exhausted from the day, but she also trusted him enough to be vulnerable.

Looking away, he stopped staring because that was an addiction he couldn't indulge in. Still, he remained where he was, curled his body toward hers, as if they were something other than friends who happened to live in the same house.

But when her breathing grew heavier, deeper, he adjusted her slightly so that her head was on a pillow and then he pulled a quilt over her—one her grandmother had made and she'd given to him. He still wasn't sure why she'd given him the gift, but he treasured it and everything she and her sisters had given him.

Though he wanted to stay and watch her, to guard her as a male should guard his female, he had important things to do—namely, keeping the perimeter secure.

Keeping her and her sisters safe.

Moving quietly, he eased out of his room and made his way out of the house like a ghost—and was actually surprised when Mari managed to sneak up on him outside.

"How do you not smell like anything?" he asked as she fell in step with him.

"I'm not going to tell you all my secrets. And speaking of secrets, have you told my sister what you are yet?" Her tone was tart.

"Which one?"

She cackled and shot him a dark look. "Oh, okay, we're playing that game?"

"Not yet," he murmured, his dragon amused by her cheeky tone.

Goddess, the Robichaux human sisters were so unafraid of him.

"Just tell her, dumbass."

"Violet thinks you were a spy," he lobbed out, wanting to move the topic off him.

Mari stumbled slightly, then cursed under her breath. "Do the others know?"

He shrugged as they reached the end of the orchard and neared the forest. Bright amber eyes glinted in the darkness—Hayes in his wolf form already.

Which meant vampires had been spotted. "You need—"

Mari had a long silver blade out before he could finish. "If you tell me to get back to the house, I might stab you with this."

"You could try," he murmured.

"I'm going."

"Fine. But you stick with Hayes and don't get killed. Violet will never forgive me if you die."

"Your concern is heartwarming." Her tone was dry.

He looked down at her, gently touched her shoulder. "I would never forgive myself."

She looked almost startled, then shrugged his hand off. "Jesus, Orion. Don't get all mushy. It ruins the tall, dark and feral thing you've got going on."

"Noted." His tone was as dry as hers.

And when she stepped into the woods with Hayes, he let his camouflage fall into place, stripped, then changed into his beast, welcoming the shift as he embraced the feral part of him, as she'd called him.

Then he took to the skies in a quiet leap, his flapping wings the only sound for a long moment as he ascended—and caught the faintest hint of vampire on the air.

It was time to go hunting.

Aware of the two in the forest, Mari riding on Hayes' back as the wolf raced through the forest, Orion put on a burst of speed.

He didn't care that they were capable. This was going to be his kill tonight.

HOURS LATER, after killing eight vampires—he got four and the others killed one each—he was still keyed up and desperate to see Violet as he entered the large farmhouse he shared with the sisters.

He needed to see with his own eyes that she was safe.

Because that bold wolf Darius was right: he could not protect the entire territory without more help. It was simply impossible. Eventually there would be a greater force of vampires or some other threat and they would breach the territory, hurt someone. He might come out on top after killing them all, but there would be many human casualties.

Unacceptable.

He had to make a decision—though he already knew what it would be. He wasn't leaving unless Violet told him to.

Even then, he wasn't sure he would. He wouldn't go far anyway, wouldn't leave her unprotected.

When he eased open his bedroom door, disappointment punched into him sharp and fast.

She was gone.

Of course she was. *And it is better this way,* he told himself.

Perhaps you are a dumbass like the human said, his dragon growled.

It is *better*, he told himself again, screamed the words in his head even as his dragon railed against him, told him he was the greatest fool who had ever lived.

But if he said it enough, maybe he would believe it.

CHAPTER SEVEN

"Thank you," Prima murmured to the delicate deer shifter who brought her a basket of food. "But this is not necessary." She could hunt if she chose. And right now she didn't want to do anything but sit here and feel sorry for herself.

"I know." Hazel sat next to her where she was propped up against the oak tree and crossed her legs. "I just thought you might like company. And I know the way to your heart is through food." The female was lean with long legs, light brown skin and pale blue eyes. Her curls were tamed into two braids and she had on a headband covered in ladybug print, making her look young and innocent. Well, probably more innocent than the self-professed hippie already was. There was a softness about her that was endearing.

Prima let out a startled laugh. This slender shifter might as well be human for the power difference between the two of them. Which just made Prima even more protective of her. She peeked in the basket, pulled out some dried fruit, sniffed. *Hmm.* Maybe she could eat. "So how was the dinner?"

"Fun. And the Alpha—who is still refusing to admit he is the Alpha, or a dragon, as far as I can tell—has asked you to come tomorrow. Well, he told Darius, who told me. And now I'm here letting you know."

Hmmm, indeed. She took a bite of the dried apple pieces, then finished the rest of the little bag. "That's good. And I'll go tomorrow." She sat back against the tree, ignoring the rest of the food even though she hadn't eaten all day. She was too...*in her feelings* as the humans liked to say.

An appropriate phrase right now.

"What do you think of Orion?"

Ah, it seemed she would have to have a conversation tonight. "He's a good male and I'm glad he lives." He was as old as her, had been hatched the same as she had, which was rare in itself. But his parents had been brutal and cruel. It was a miracle he'd turned out the way he had, especially since he'd lost so much in his long life. She'd met him when he'd been at his worst, vulnerable, recently escaped from those monsters. And she'd gotten to see him become the strong male he was supposed to. All before her mind had started to fracture and she'd been forced into Hibernation. But that was a time she didn't like to think about.

"Darius seems to like him too. This is all so exciting. I hope we form an allyship with them—I really like the humans we've met so far."

"Hmm." She couldn't muster more than that tonight.

Sighing, Hazel stood and then kissed Prima on top of her head, a bold move, her dragon thought. But welcome even if she would never admit it aloud. "If you need anything, let me know. Especially if...you'd like to *talk* about anything."

She just grunted. There was nothing anyone could do for her. She'd ended things with Arthur before coming on this trip, and while it was for the best, her heart ached in a way she hadn't thought possible. No, ached was too weak of a word. Her heart had shattered.

As she stretched her long legs out, Cale, another dragon she'd known a long time, strode up, his expression jovial as he sat, then lay down next to her. Why would these beings not leave her be? She simply wanted to rest under this tree in silence while she wallowed in self-pity. Goddess, save her.

"Beautiful night," he murmured, propping his head up under his hands. The male was pretty, with bronze skin kissed by the sun, dark hair and vivid green eyes. He often had an easy smile, his outer package an excellent distraction that had fooled many into thinking he was harmless.

She grunted again. "What do you want?"

"Nothing much. I heard you were formally requested to meet with the Alpha tomorrow."

Only because she knew Orion and he likely wanted to talk to her about what she thought of this allyship. She didn't respond to Cale. Maybe he would simply go away if she was silent.

"So do you think you'll stay here or go back to New Orleans? Or go see your sister in Montana?" he asked, undeterred that she hadn't responded to his first comment. "It's been a couple months since you visited."

Her sister was actually in another realm, but she didn't correct him. "Not sure what I'll do. The Alpha might not want me here at all after we meet up."

"Anyone who doesn't want you is a fool."

She shot him a sideways glance, narrowed her gaze. "What do you want?" Because flattery did not work on her, something he should know.

He let out a short sigh as he looked up at the blanket of stars. "Just to know more about this Alpha, what kind of male he is. I respect King, but...I need something different. My dragon needs more space, more stars, more...of a challenge. And I believe that enough time has passed that I've paid my blood debt to Greer."

"She never expected anything from you." Prima knew that much about the kind healer. Cale could have left New Orleans long ago if he'd wanted to.

"All the same. A debt is a debt."

"I'll know more about him tomorrow," Prima said, because if she didn't respond, she realized he'd never let this drop. "It has been millennia since I've seen Orion, but if he is the same as before, and if he makes an official claim on this territory, I'll tell him about you. Then you can meet and decide for yourself if he is the type of Alpha you would follow."

"Would you follow him? If you weren't...you?"

She gave him a ghost of a smile. She officially belonged to her clan up in Montana, was an Alpha right down to her DNA. But right now she lived in New Orleans and had pledged allegiance to King while she was there, but he wasn't truly her Alpha. No one was. "I would. He is a loyal male, would die for his people." And that was the standard which she measured by. Though it was more than that.

Orion had suffered greatly, but when she'd known him, he hadn't let it shape him into something ugly and twisted. If anything, he had always gone out of his way to look out for those weaker. He was a male she respected.

"Leave now, Cale. I need to be alone." Her dragon was right at the surface, ready to snap. And she didn't want to say something ugly to someone she cared about. Or worse, to injure someone because she couldn't control her dragon.

The last time she'd gone into Hibernation—been forced into it by her twin—she'd been losing her grasp on reality. Now she worried... She shook the thought off, not wanting to let her mind travel down that path.

She was fine, just dealing with the aftermath of a choice she'd made. One she'd had to, but it didn't make it any easier. Or less painful.

Nothing could do that.

Thankfully Cale left wordlessly, giving her a gentle touch on her arm —which made her wonder just how pathetic she looked right now.

After he was gone, she stripped and shifted to her dragon form. At least she could be useful here and keep their band of travelers safe. No matter what was going on, she would always remain vigilant. Would always protect those she cared about.

CHAPTER EIGHT

Orion had faced down actual armies of dragons and other supernaturals, and had all his bones broken by his father and mother when he'd been a child. More than once. He'd never felt fear in battle and he'd only felt hatred for his parents.

Today he was pretty sure that something akin to fear was pulsing through him as he strode toward the waiting humans outside Violet's barn. He'd requested this meeting with Violet, her sisters and the families who oversaw this territory with him. He'd planned to tell Violet that he was a dragon before the meeting but she'd been called out to attend to someone.

Now...*fuck*. He'd wanted to do all this at once. To talk about Darius and the offer from King, and tell the people he lived with that he was a dragon. The dragon was the only thing that worried him. Everyone had been accepting, but he knew how fickle humans could be.

Bentley stood as he approached, crossed the short distance to him. "We've got your back," the wolf murmured. "Lay it out there. They accept us or they don't."

He glanced behind him when he scented Violet, saw her racing his way, a smile on her face. Her curls were down, bouncing around her face, and she wore a flannel shirt and jeans that hugged her thighs perfectly. He'd had too many fantasies where she had those thighs wrapped around his head as he brought her all the pleasure. Finally tasted her.

If she rejected him after this...

He nodded once at Bentley, then waited for Violet as she stopped in front of him. "Did I miss anything?" she asked, slightly out of breath.

"I haven't talked with anyone yet. Listen, I need to tell you something before I tell the others." His pulse accelerated as he tried to force the words out.

He'd grown up keeping his emotions locked down tight, had been a goddamn expert at hiding anything and everything of importance to him. Because anything he'd cared about had been taken away or destroyed. But she was the most important thing to him and he wasn't certain he'd withstand her rejection. A small, kind human with big gray eyes and a wide smile could destroy him if she wanted.

Her face shuttered and he immediately missed the warmth of her smile, the light in her eyes. "Is this about where you're sneaking off to at night?"

"Yes." *Hell.* Did she know? Goddess, she must have seen him. Maybe Mari had told her? But no, he didn't think so.

"It's fine. We don't need to talk about it."

They didn't? She was being so calm about all this, if difficult to read. "Are you certain?"

"Yes." Her expression might as well be carved from rock now. And he couldn't get a read on her scent. There was a sort of chaos and pain rolling off her.

Oh, she knew, then. *Hell.*

"Ah...okay. I will be telling everyone today. As will Bentley and his brothers."

She blinked and her scent shifted but was no less chaotic. "Ooookay."

He wasn't sure what to say now. She didn't want to discuss the fact that he was a dragon. He...wasn't sure what to make of that. Couldn't tell how she truly felt about it. But he could sense the restlessness of the others behind him. "Let's talk to the families," he murmured, turning and waiting for her to join him.

They might not be mated, but he and Violet were who everyone in this territory turned to for guidance and protection. Now, he had to let all those people know who they'd been living with all this time. At least Violet didn't seem *upset* exactly. Or...maybe she was. He was still learning so much about humans and social cues.

As they reached the semicircle of people, he glanced at all the familiar faces. "Thank you all for meeting us. We've had the night to sleep on it and think about the offer of allyship. I think their offer is a good one. The New Orleans territory is run properly by a powerful and just Alpha. His people are happy and safe." Relatively safe anyway.

"How do we know they won't try to take over our land? And all of our...well, everything?" Cora, a blonde human female who ran the neighboring farm asked, her tone neutral. She was a widow in her forties with grown twins who lived on the family farm.

"That's a fair question. There are some treacherous Alphas who might try something like that, but his territory is large and they have many numbers. If they'd wanted this territory, they'd have simply started a war. They'd have come in the middle of the night and attacked. And with respect for all we've done to keep this place running, they don't need us. Their territory is considered prime." He thought that would be the right word to describe it.

"Well what about the vampires we've been hearing about?"

"There have been a growing number of vampire attacks in the area. I've been helping to kill them along with Bentley, Hayes and Tyler. And Mari," he added, which caused a couple gasps of surprise. "And we need to tell you something so you have the full details before you make a decision." He glanced at Violet, couldn't make out her expression at all.

She glanced away from him, her cheeks flushing pink.

Okay, then. Just rip the bandage off, as little Kayla liked to say. "I'm a dragon shifter, and Bentley and his brothers are wolves. I should have told you what I was sooner, but when I woke from my Hibernation it was into a strange world, one destroyed by my kind. I did not know who I could trust." And everyone he'd known before had been dead. Or he'd been unable to find them. He'd been all alone yet drawn back to this little parish, to a human female and her family.

Almost everyone was staring at him and the brothers in surprise, but he made note of the ones who didn't seem surprised. A few older humans who never seemed surprised by anything, so perhaps it was not a big deal to them.

"If I'd wanted to hurt anyone or do whatever some of you are likely thinking right now, I could have." *Easily*, his dragon scoffed. "I am no threat to you. Only to those who would harm us or try to take our territory. I want to stay and defend this territory. So now you have all the knowledge you need to make a decision."

No one said anything, just stared, but he could feel Violet's gaze on him.

As he turned to look at her, he was surprised by the shock in her wide eyes. "You're a dragon?" she breathed out, her words barely audible.

Wait... "You said you didn't want to talk about it," he murmured.

"I thought you were sneaking off to meet with someone in a romantic way and wanted to tell me about it for some insane reason. Then when you said something about Bentley, I thought you meant that you and he or his brothers were like... Oh my God," she breathed, staring at him as if she didn't know him at all.

"I'm still me." He kept his voice low, though his heart was pounding and he was aware of the others starting to talk amongst themselves in low tones. He took a small step toward her, but she jerked back.

He froze as if she'd slammed a spike into his chest. Was she afraid of him?_He didn't know what to say—and he didn't want to have this conversation in front of everyone else.

Wordlessly, she turned away from him and stalked back toward the house.

Shit. Go after her now, his dragon ordered.

"You waited to tell her until now?" Mari was in front of him then, her eyes wide.

"She said..." He scrubbed a hand over his face as some of the humans he considered friends approached, tentative smiles on their faces. That had to be a good sign.

Unless they were going to attack when they got close?

Ugh.

He really didn't want to hurt anyone today. Anyone other than vampires. All he wanted to do was chase down Violet, but he'd known her long enough to understand that she would want space.

Or maybe he was just being a coward.

～

"WHERE ARE YOU GOING?" Laurel jogged after her, slightly out of breath as she tried to keep up with Violet.

But Violet had built up a full body of steam and nothing could stop her—plus Laurel was a couple inches shorter. She'd gone straight home, packed a backpack and she was getting away from everyone. "For a hike." She didn't care what the hell was going on or who might need her —okay that was a lie, she cared about that. But she needed space right now.

And distance from that lying jackass.

"I know he should have told us before, but he looked kinda lost back there." Laurel's voice was soft, pleading.

It was the only thing that could calm Violet right now.

Sighing, she stopped at the beginning of the trail that would lead to what had once been a nature reserve with waterfalls and plenty of damn privacy. "He could have told me long before now. He's had an entire year." Why had he hidden something so important from her? Why hadn't he trusted her? Hell, all of them?

"Maybe he was scared of your reaction?"

She snorted, looked away from her blonde sister, the only one who'd taken after their mother in that department. Laurel looked just like her, and right now, she sounded like her. All calm and rational. *Ugh.* "Yeah, a dragon scared of me." She just...what the hell! Clearly she didn't know him and he didn't trust her at all. She felt like such an idiot. She would happily give him her freaking heart on a platter and he thought of her as...well, whatever. *Nothing.* "I'm such a stupid fool. Oh my God, I'm embarrassed too," she growled, more to herself than her sister. "He lives in our house and none of us knew."

"Mari knew," Laurel murmured.

Violet shot her a glare. "Oh, I'll talk to her later. Maybe." Right about now, she didn't want to deal with anyone or anything. The supernaturals from New Orleans were arriving in a couple hours, which gave her an hour to hike, clear her head and enough time to get back and shower.

And lay into Orion. Or maybe she'd do the super mature thing and just ignore him. No, that was impossible, considering the situation. *Gah!* "How's everyone else dealing with the news?" she asked, shifting her backpack slightly. Because despite everything, despite his damn lies, she still cared about him. Was still attracted to him.

Way, way too much. Which was probably feeding this feeling of betrayal and exacerbating it. It wasn't like she'd ever asked him if he was human, and now she felt so damn stupid that she hadn't realized. He was so huge!

"Okay." Laurel lifted a shoulder.

"Really?"

"Yeah. Everyone had some questions, but…no one really seems to care. He's part of our community, the brothers too. I feel stupid that I didn't realize he was a dragon," Laurel said on a laugh, mirroring Violet's own thoughts. "He's so big. I just thought he used to play football or something."

"I thought he was in the military." He'd told her he was a soldier, and now she wondered if that was true. "Listen…I've got my radio. I won't be gone long. Maybe half an hour," she said, cutting her time short. Because she did need to talk to Orion. But first she needed to get her own thoughts and feelings straight before she lost it on him and said something she'd regret.

"Okay." Laurel shoved her hands in her pockets and watched her with those "mom" eyes, even though she was the youngest. She was always taking care of all of them in little ways.

Violet softened. "In case I don't say it enough, thank you for all you do around the house. You take care of the three of us and make sure we have a nice place to come back to every day after long-ass work sessions, and you organize all the community gatherings. You do a lot and I think maybe we don't recognize that enough. At least not out loud."

Her sister stared in surprise. "Is this like a going-away speech? Are you…leaving over this?"

"What? No! I just don't think I tell you enough how much I appreciate you. And it's a lot." She pulled her sister into a tight hug, feeling overly emotional about everything. "I'm a mess right now and I love you. And I want to punch Orion's dumb, handsome face."

Laurel snort-laughed as she pulled back. "His face is handsome."

"Something you shouldn't be noticing," she grumbled. Because she didn't want anyone noticing him. Ever. Which was bonkers. But whatever.

Which made her sister cackle. "I'm not trying to stick up for him, but…I believe him, that he wasn't sure who he could trust when he woke up from his Hibernation."

Violet wasn't one hundred percent sure what Hibernation meant but could pretty much guess. She wondered how long he'd been asleep. Now she also wondered if that first time she'd seen him, covered in clay and naked…had he just woken up then? She was putting a pin in that and planned to ask that too. She'd been holding back questions for him but not anymore.

She was going to ask him every little thing she wanted to know. And he was damn well going to answer her questions!

"I'll be back soon." She patted her pocket where she'd stuck her radio. "And I'm not going far. I just need to clear my head."

Laurel nodded, her expression still tense and worried.

But Violet couldn't focus on that. Instead she headed into the forest.

The more minutes that passed, the deeper she got into the trees, the more she felt centered. Half an hour later, she realized that she was going to take a full hour. Because this had been the right choice after the bombshell Orion had dropped on her.

Violet breathed in the crisp morning air and tried to process that the man she was obsessed with could turn into a fire-breathing beast. She also wondered what he looked like as a dragon even as she fought the overwhelming sadness that he hadn't trusted her enough to tell her.

Maybe her feelings were misplaced, but even so, they were real and just plain sucked. She'd told him so much about her life and past and… She paused as she reached the top of a hill and realized she didn't hear anything.

No birds chirping, no squirrels climbing trees.

It was eerily quiet.

She turned in a circle, looking down on the valley below on one side, then the sharp wall of trees jutting upward on the other side. Her boots crunched on the fallen leaves underfoot. It was the only sound other than her breathing.

Feeling paranoid even as a tingle of unease crept up her spine, she pulled out her radio and turned it on. She needed to call someone—and realized that her batteries must have died. *No.*

Okay, okay, just head back home. Everything is fine. As she started back down the trail that would eventually take her home, she heard a low growl behind her.

All the hair on the back of her neck and arms stood up straight as she turned.

Four wolves with bright amber eyes appeared up on the edge of the cliff above her, growling low in their throats. One opened its jaws and snapped its sharp canines at her menacingly. All of them ready to pounce.

Her heart stopped for a beat, then she turned and ran.

CHAPTER NINE

Orion stepped into the house he lived in with the Robichaux sisters, tension pulsing through him as he shut the door behind him. Bowie was waiting for him, his dark tail wagging wildly as Orion crouched down and scratched under his chin. The pup's tail swung in even wider wags as he jumped up, placed his paws on Orion's shoulders and kissed his cheek.

He still wasn't sure how he'd come to have a dog—he was a fire breathing dragon. But this little beast had the heart of one. He'd found him in the woods one day and Bowie had simply followed him home. Had decided he lived with him and that was that.

"Come on," he murmured to his buddy. "Let's get this over with." He stood and followed the sound of female voices to the kitchen. He'd come to think of this place as home, or as much of a home as he would allow himself to have. But now he prepared to have to leave. He wouldn't abandon the territory, but he was ready for them to kick him out. It would hurt but he'd lived through worse.

Violet wasn't there, but the other three turned to look at him from where they sat at the little kitchen table, cups of what smelled like hot tea in front of each of them.

"Come here, boy," Rose murmured, patting her knees, and Bowie trotted over to her, sniffed her once, then placed his head on her lap for pets, his tail doing that "helicopter thing" as Violet called it.

"Should I move out?" he asked bluntly, not wanting to drag this out. The other humans had taken his "big reveal" about as calmly as he could have expected. Some had already known, or guessed, he realized. And they hadn't cared. But he'd been withholding information from the humans he lived with and that was a bigger deal.

"No, dumbass," Mari said on a snort, reaching out to join in the pets.

"Mari!" Laurel admonished. "Also, she's not wrong," she said, shaking her head at him in disbelief as he pulled out some homemade treats for Bowie from a ceramic container.

"Could you like, give us flights to places when we need it? If I get a callout late at night?" Rose asked. "That would be so cool."

"I...yes." Was she not angry with him?

"Do you take Bowie for flights? Like, does he ride on your back?" Rose continued.

"Ah, no." Bowie had enough issues without terrifying him that way. "Where's Violet?" he asked, needing to see her. She was the one he needed to talk to, but he was damn relieved that her sisters were accepting of him and didn't want him to go. If Violet wanted him gone, however, he would leave.

Mari and Rose looked at Laurel, who flushed pink. "She went for a hike. She just needed to clear her head. I don't think she's mad at you or anything," she said as she held out the treat and motioned for Bowie to sit—which he did, his gaze pinned on the dog biscuit in her hand.

Now he snorted. "You are not good at lying."

"I think she's hurt more than angry."

Aaaand that pierced deeper than anything. He'd rather her be angry. He'd never meant to hurt her. He'd wanted to protect her. And himself, if he was honest. "Do you know which trail she picked?" Not that it truly mattered; he would just track her scent.

Bowie hurried over to him and nuzzled his knee so he crouched down and picked up the beast. He was only about thirty-five or forty pounds, so easy to carry around. Though Bowie usually only let Orion carry him like this.

Laurel nodded and stood, putting her mug in the sink. "I do."

When it was clear she wasn't going to expand, he cleared his throat as his dog settled against him. The dog had been so fearful and traumatized when Orion had first crossed paths with him. It felt good to know he'd earned Bowie's trust. He wanted Violet's as well. "I apologize for not being more forthright about what I am. I should have told all of you."

Rose lifted a shoulder. "It's fine. I mean, it sucks that you didn't trust us, but I can only imagine what it's like to have to hide what you are to the world." She shot Mari a quick glance and he wondered if it was because she suspected Mari was a spy or because Mari liked female sexual partners and had hidden that part of herself until she was in her twenties.

Since awakening, he'd discovered that humans of this time had odd beliefs about sexuality and judged others harshly if they didn't fit into certain views.

"And I don't know that you even owed us enough to tell us. This is a situation I've never been in—so as far as I'm concerned we're good," Rose said.

He wasn't certain she was right, and his dragon agreed—he *had* owed them the truth.

"We just hope that you know this is your home," Laurel added. "You and Bowie both."

"I know that." He knew they'd keep Bowie anyway. Anyone would after seeing how far the dog had come, and how much he loved and trusted his people.

"Do you?" Now Mari stood, her expression dry. "Because you haven't changed one tiny thing in your room and you don't even call it *your* room. When you tell Bowie it's time for bed, you call it 'the bedroom.'"

Clearing his throat, he retreated a step. "I'm going to find Violet. Do you mind watching him? I don't want to bring him with me for this," he said as he sat Bowie on the floor.

The pup was already whining slightly, knowing he was about to be left behind.

"Of course not," Laurel murmured.

As he reached the front door, making a quick retreat, he heard Mari call out "Coward" as he closed the door behind him. She was right, but he wasn't going to talk about how he didn't even claim his own bedroom.

He ignored her and the other humans he passed as he hurried through the orchard. He could just shift right then and there but the humans *knowing* he was a dragon and actually seeing him in his beast form were two very different things. He wanted to give them time to adjust before showing his beast.

Please, his dragon sniffed. *They will want to worship me once they see how powerful I am.*

Once he was alone near the beginning of the hiking trail, he shifted to his dragon form, leaving his clothing in a neat pile by one of the trees. Then he took to the air, resisting that instinctual urge to camouflage himself. As soon as he'd discovered that he could camo himself as a child, he'd been invisible more often than not. Attempting to hide from his abusers. Though he'd been too small and untrained, too terrified of the ones who were supposed to protect him.

By now he was certain word had spread throughout the territory about him so he might as well help everyone get used to seeing him. That was what he told himself anyway.

But as he flew farther west, something in the air shifted and his beast immediately swathed his camouflage around him like an old, familiar coat.

Dipping lower until his wings skimmed the tree tops, he scented...*wolves*.

A pack of them.

Shifters. *Strangers*.

Something akin to malice hung in the air, an ugly scent that scraped over his scales as he followed the trail. Enemy wolf shifters were in his forest, his territory. *Not for long.*

A scream pierced the air. He recognized it instantly and his heart seized.

Violet!

He banked a hard left, rage consuming him as he dove through the trees.

As he plunged through the canopy, a red haze descended over his vision, his beast wanting to nuke the forest.

Violet was on the ground, a knife in one hand, a stick in the other as she struggled to stand—and she was surrounded by four snarling wolf shifters.

One of them must have sensed him or scented something off, because he turned, looked around above him.

Orion let his camouflage fall as he blasted a ball of fire at the male. Ash burst into the air against the growing blanket of leaves.

One of the wolves barked in alarm and they scattered, racing off in different directions like goddamn cowards. They'd pick on a lone human female, but didn't want to face him?

He only needed one of them alive to question.

Though he wanted to check on Violet, he couldn't scent any of her blood, just fear. And he needed to eliminate the threat to her immediately.

He attacked the nearest wolf, chomped down as the male attempted to flee, sliced him right in half before he turned, blasted another fireball at the one racing in the direction of the territory.

As the leaves below caught fire, the bright orange flames starting to creep outward, he slammed his tail down on it, extinguishing it before he flew up and out of the treetops. Wings pumping hard, he headed in the direction the final wolf had run, flying past it before he arrowed back downward and landed, shifted to his human form.

This one wasn't getting off so easily. This one would live.

For now.

Magic burst in the air as his human side took over. "If you keep running, I'll make this even harder on you," he growled at the wolf who broke through the clearing and skidded to a halt in front of him. "Shift!" he demanded, putting every ounce of his Alpha nature into the demand.

The wolf struggled on his feet, weaving back and forth, clearly fighting the order, but finally shifted to his human form.

A male with pale blond hair and icy blue eyes stood, glared at him for a fraction of a moment before he looked down, unable to hold Orion's gaze.

Twenty feet separated them now.

Orion stalked toward the male, his long legs and natural speed eating up the distance in moments. "You think it's sporting to attack a defenseless female?" The urge to kill him where he stood rode Orion hard. Only the need to find out what had caused this kept him in check. He needed to know if this male was following orders from someone or if this had been random.

"She isn't mated," the male spluttered. "And we weren't going to kill her, just have fun."

Orion knew what this male's version of fun would be. Without thought, he struck out, slamming his fist into the guy's jaw and...*oops*. The male's jaw and back broke as he flew through the air and slammed into a nearby tree, the crunch of bones breaking filling the air.

Not wasting another second on the incapacitated piece of trash, he raced back in Violet's direction, not bothering to shift. He'd pick the injured wolf back up later, but he needed to get to her first.

She'd already been through a lot and he didn't want to frighten her even more by flying at her as a fire-breathing beast.

As he reached where she'd been, he could scent her but not see her right away. He scanned the trees... "All but one are dead. You can come down," he said as he approached the wide oak that she'd somehow shimmied up.

Wordlessly, she closed her switchblade and swung down on the nearest branch.

He moved closer until he stood beneath her. "I'll catch you." *Always.*

She let go and he scooped her up in his arms, held her close, just inhaling her scent and wishing he could kill those males all over again. Slowly. Painfully. He wanted to go back and kill the final one, but needed him alive because Orion was going to get answers. Now those he could get slowly and painfully at least.

"Who were those...wolves?" Her voice was raspy, bringing him back to reality, but the acrid scent of her fear was ebbing.

He eased back and lowered her to the ground slowly, setting her on her feet.

But as he did, Violet winced.

Frowning, he crouched down in front of her, looking for any injury. "What's wrong?" he asked, even as he gently lifted her left calf. She wasn't standing on her left foot, so clearly...

"I think I sprained my ankle when I was running from them. They were so fast." Fear laced her words and he winced as he pushed up the pant leg. The bone was broken, not sprained.

"They'll never hurt anyone again," he said as he stood up. "I'm taking you to the New Orleans encampment. Darius says they have a healer with them," he continued as he called on his dragon, letting the shift overtake him. Maybe he should have asked, but he wasn't in an "ask for permission" kind of mood when the human he was obsessed with was injured and in pain.

Nope.

He could ask for forgiveness later. Right now he was going to make sure she got the treatment she needed.

He paused as she stared up at him, her eyes wide, her scent far too chaotic for him to read. When he went to scoop her up, she didn't flinch —or attempt to run in terror—so that was something.

In his claws, he gently held her close to his chest as he flew straight upward in a vertical liftoff. Ignoring the branches he broke on the way, he flew toward where he'd left the unconscious wolf, roughly picked him up in his other claws, then headed east in the direction of the newcomers' camp. The wolf was still unconscious and the most primitive part of Orion didn't care if the guy survived the flight.

He didn't think Darius had sent the wolves—their scent had been distinctive and he hadn't detected it on the air before. And they'd come from a different direction, the same one the vampires had been coming from. Still, he was going to find out for sure.

And if it turned out the newcomers *had* sent the wolves? He'd burn their entire camp to the ground.

CHAPTER TEN

"I can just splint this," Violet said to Orion as he crouched in front of her—still naked and, *just wow!*—and scooped her up in his arms. Pain shot through her ankle and she was pretty sure she might be in shock. Nope, she definitely was because she hadn't even been able to really think about the fact that Orion had shifted to a dragon in front of her.

A huge fire-breathing beast she'd only seen on television or read about in books.

And he was so stunning it made her brain hurt. His wings were glittering blues and purples that had seemed to almost flow and shift like water, the melding of the colors exquisite as they shimmered under the sunlight. He was truly a work of art.

Orion grunted and stepped around the unconscious wolf he'd basically just thrown onto the ground before he'd landed in a giant field of grass with her. The field was next to the New Orleans' people's encampment and they'd definitely seen Orion's huge form sweeping down.

"I need actual words, Orion," she snapped out through the pain lancing up her leg. She felt completely untethered to, well, everything. As if a breeze might blow her away in a million pieces, scattering her to the wind. She knew it was because she was having a difficult time processing what had just happened, what she'd seen with her own two eyes—acknowledging that the male she was obsessed with was really a dragon.

A fierce, sexy one who'd just saved her life.

He looked down at her in surprise even as a handful of shifters, including Darius and Hazel, raced across the field. "What?"

Shoving out a sigh, she didn't respond because it would sound pathetic to ask him to give her reassuring words, even if she did need them. Instead, she looked over as Darius reached them first.

"What's wrong?" he asked, narrowing in on her injured ankle.

"Four wolves breached our territory, tried to kill Violet. I let that one live. And I'm asking one of your healers to heal Violet." It came out more like a demand than an ask.

But Darius simply nodded, his expression concerned as he looked at Violet again. "Come on. We'll deal with whoever this is later," he said with a menacing look at the injured wolf shifter, motioning for Orion and her to follow.

"Does no one care that you're naked?" she murmured, the question popping out as she tried to breathe through the pain. It was difficult but no way was she going to have a breakdown. If she did, she wasn't sure she'd be able to get it back together. So no, she had to stay strong. She'd break down later, in the privacy of her own room at home.

He looked at her again in surprise. "We're shifters."

Ah. Right. The huge thing that she was still processing. Not to mention she'd seen the man she was just a teeny, tiny bit obsessed with turn into a huge, lethal beast, kill some randos who'd wanted to kill her, and then he'd flown her here in his claws.

Flown. Her.

As a dragon. And he'd been so gentle she could hardly believe it.

So what was a little nudity, right? Though there was nothing little about what was between his legs. She was going to be processing the image of *that* longer than the image of his dragon, that was for sure.

She let out a sort of manic laugh, but cut it off quickly when he gave her a look of concern, his emerald eyes flashing bright, his dragon looking out at her for an instant. "I'm fine," she murmured, staring at those beautiful, alien eyes, mesmerized. She felt like she was seeing him for the first time, and maybe she was.

An electric current sparked between them as they stared at each other. She knew that Orion was carrying her, could feel the faint movement, but even with the pain pulsing through her, all she could see or focus on was him and the way those dragon eyes were watching her so very intently.

Those dragon eyes were filled with heat and a little curiosity. Then, to her surprise, he leaned down, ran his nose along the side of her face and jaw. But when he looked down at her again, his eyes were human.

Oh, God. Just... She...needed to close her eyes. Or an entire bottle of vodka. Overwhelmed, she laid her head on his thick shoulder as he followed Darius into a large tent that was clearly a medical one. A couple cots had been set up and there was a table with medical supplies.

A tall male with kind dark brown eyes greeted them, his expression concerned as he approached. "What's going on?"

"She broke her ankle," Orion answered for her. "Fix it," he growled.

Normally she liked to be in control, but right now she was going to lean into this overbearing, overprotective male. Today had been a lot, maybe too much, and she didn't have the mental bandwidth to deal with much more. He wanted to be in control? *Yes, please. Just take over and fix things.*

"Are you hurt anywhere else?" the male asked as he motioned for Orion to lay her down on one of the stretchers that seemed higher than normal.

She realized it was to accommodate this man's height. He was almost as tall as Orion, but not as broad. "Ah, a few scrapes I think, but nothing big." She held out her palms, frowned as she saw the cuts on them from when she'd tripped over a fallen log. She'd tried to jump it when she'd been running, but had miscalculated in her fear-driven brain.

A shiver raked through her as cold fingers snaked down her spine. Her entire body started shaking as the doctor—or healer?—cut through the bottom of her pants and started easing her sneaker off. She winced at the pain of it, swallowed hard.

"You touch her only where necessary and you're not taking off the rest of her clothes. You will not see her in any sort of state of undress, and if you cause her any pain, I'll remove your head from your body." Orion said it with a sort of icy calm that was just as terrifying as his words, the deadly menace beneath them the thing of nightmares. She'd never seen this side of him.

"Orion," she snapped, his words bringing her world back into focus even as those cold tendrils of pain and fear continued to invade her. "You've got to dial it back eight hundred notches. He wants to help!"

"It's fine," the doctor said. "My name is Baris and I'm a healer. I'm used to dealing with obnoxious supernatural males. And females," he added, completely ignoring Orion, seemingly not afraid *at all* as he met her gaze with dark eyes. "I would like your permission to use my healing energy on you, to scan you to see where you're injured in case there's anything internal, and I'd like to heal your ankle if you'd let me."

She blinked as she digested all of this. "You can really just...heal me with energy?" She'd spoken to Luna last night about that—was it only just last night?—but hadn't expected to see or *experience* something like this so quickly after. Or ever.

"I can, but only with your permission."

Orion shifted next to her, clearly agitated, so she clasped one of his big hands in hers and held it to her chest as she nodded at the doctor— ah, healer. "Okay, yes, thank you."

The healer hovered his hands over her ankle, not even touching it, and she stared in surprise as they glowed a soft blue. She gripped Orion's hand tight as she felt a sort of warm energy infuse her, spread upward, immediately easing the pulsing pain and swelling in her ankle.

At first she'd thought it was a sprain, but the pain and swelling had been intensifying. Now... "I swear I can feel the bone knitting back together," she breathed out, awed.

The male looked up at her then with those kind eyes that made her want to tell him all her secrets. "It's rare to feel it, but I believe you," he said gently. "You also have a slightly lower than normal white blood cell count and a very minor temperature. It feels like the start of an infection," he murmured, moving his hands a little higher. "Nothing to worry about though."

"I was feeling a bit exhausted this morning," she admitted. When she glanced up at Orion, he was watching the healer with an unnerving intensity. As if, if the other male made one wrong move, he would pounce.

"Well I'm taking care of all of that now." He was looking down at her body now, an expression of concentration on his face.

She met Orion's gaze. "You know you can't actually hurt a healer, right," she murmured, not that she truly thought he would. Though…he had just massacred three wolf shifters in the woods and incapacitated another so completely and brutally she was still trying to process the violence. "It's the rules. Luna told me. No hurting healers or doctors."

He shot her a surprised glance, his expression softening. "I would never hurt a healer," he grumbled. "I'm just cranky."

"Thank you for saving me," she said, feeling like it needed to be voiced aloud. Because what he'd done had been incredible.

He blinked once, frowned. "You don't need to thank me."

"Well I am, so thank you," she said tartly.

He blinked again. "You're still mad at me? Do you wish me to move out of the house? Your sisters have said no, but—"

"Oh my God, Orion." Exasperation filled her tone, but she couldn't hold it back. She didn't love that they had an audience with the healer, but considering the things that had happened today she figured this was the least of anything she should be worrying about. "Did you seriously just ask me that?"

His posture was stiff. "I will move out—"

"Please stop before this kind healer has to heal a headache. Of course I don't want you to move out. If you try, I'll kidnap Bowie," she grumbled even as more warmth filled her, easing all the ache in her ankle. Wow, he worked fast. "And I can't very well stay mad at you after you just saved my life." Her voice caught then, as the memory of those wolves chasing her resurfaced. It had all happened so quickly, and they'd been so inhumanly fast. Seeing what supernaturals could do and had done on news feeds was one thing, but seeing it in person was altogether different. If Orion hadn't appeared when he had, she might be dead right now. Or wishing she was.

Orion crouched down next to her. "You may stay angry with me as long as you wish. I'm sorry I wasn't there sooner... I'm sorry this happened at all. I will make sure the last wolf suffers greatly when I'm done questioning him."

She stared at him in shock, at the serious tone of his voice. She was a doctor, didn't relish the thought of anyone in pain or suffering. I mean...she wasn't going to shed any tears if that last wolf suffered a little, not considering she was pretty sure he wanted to rape and kill her. "Orion," she whispered, reaching up to cup his cheek gently, not sure what to say to that at all.

That was when she realized her palms were healed. "Hey," she said looking back at the healer, a smile on her face as she held up her hands, free of scratches. "You work really fast."

He grinned down at her, had started to respond when the flap of the tent flew open and a tall, *beyond* stunning woman strode in and threw herself at Orion.

Violet stared as he...*didn't* push her off, but hugged the lithe, lean woman who had probably been a model before all the chaos of The Fall. Were her cheekbones even real? Oh my God, how could this woman actually exist outside of television or the big screen? Had she been Miss Galaxy or something? Wait, was that a thing...maybe Miss Universe. Ugh, Violet silenced her wayward thoughts. Her very jealous thoughts over the woman hugging a man who wasn't hers.

Feeling awkward lying down even though exhaustion was sweeping through her, she tried to sit up.

"You need to rest for a little longer," Baris said gently even as Orion turned toward her.

"Violet, this is Prima, a friend from long ago."

Violet tried to politely smile at the female even as lethargy and jealousy wound its way through her body. *Friend, huh? Ugh.* Then she felt a hand on her forehead, realized it was the healer.

"She needs rest, just for an hour or so as her body finishes healing," Baris said quietly.

"I'm not leaving her side." Orion's voice was dark and testy.

"No one said you had to." The healer's tone was patient, and Violet was pretty sure the guy was a saint if he regularly put up with people like Orion and anyone who acted like he was right now.

But the main thing she was focused on was the beautiful gray-eyed woman standing next to Orion. The woman who looked as if she'd be a perfect match for him in every way. And when Prima's eyes shifted to her animal side as she looked at Violet, it was clear she was a dragon or supernatural, not a human like her.

The woman was watching Violet boldly, as if she was trying to see inside her, to ferret out all her innermost thoughts.

Maybe that was why Orion had been holding back—because of this beautiful woman. Sure, he'd sniffed her on the way here, but...maybe that didn't mean as much as she thought it did? As the deepest sense of sadness swelled inside her, slumber weighing her eyelids down like bricks, she finally succumbed to the deep, healing sleep.

At least she wouldn't have to look at Orion and Miss Universe together anymore.

CHAPTER ELEVEN

"Is there anything I can do for her?" Orion asked the healer, keeping his voice down even though his Violet was asleep.

"Just sit with her, hold her hand," Baris said calmly. "She's healed, but her mind is catching up with her body and recovering. It's not just the physical trauma she went through, but a mental one. I felt it when I was healing her. She's a strong human, but she's still processing a huge thing. She'll be awake soon."

"I am sorry I snapped at you," he said, and did just as the male said and pulled up a chair next to Violet. He held her delicate hand gently in his, could feel the strength and energy pulsing through her. He could have lost her, and the thought…it was too much to bear. He couldn't live in a world without her.

The male's mouth curved in a wry grin and he gently patted Orion's upper arm. "I've heard much worse than your threats."

"Who has threatened you?" Prima demanded, suddenly at attention from the tent flap, her dragon in her eyes as she took a menacing step forward. Orion had kicked her out for a few minutes so he could speak with the healer alone. "I will tear them limb from limb."

The male sighed, patted Prima's arm as well and silently left without responding.

"He's exceptionally calm, even for a healer," Orion said once it was just the three of them. Violet's chest was rising and falling in a steady rhythm, her breathing even, her color good. He knew she would be okay. And that was the only reason he was remotely sane right now.

"Well, he is a panda." Prima lifted a shoulder as she jumped up on one of the beds across from Violet, stretched her long legs out and crossed them.

"What?" Orion stared at Prima in horror. The kind, handsome healer was a fucking panda bear shifter? He wasn't mated either because Orion would have scented it. So he had a similar profession to Violet, he was a *panda* and *slightly* good looking? And Violet already had an affinity for pandas.

She gave him a strange look. "You know, huge bear, sort of adorable, definitely the misfits of the bear shifters. They're either really sweet or really savage. So weird," she muttered, pulling out a sucker and sticking it in her mouth. "Must be some kind of DNA thing. And the fighters always look so cute when they fight, it's disarming." She was shaking her head now. "Maybe that's their secret to being such skilled killers."

"Don't tell Violet he's a panda," he blurted.

Which earned him another strange look. "How are you feeling? Were you injured in the fight with the wolves?"

"No. That was an easy takedown. They were pathetic. Where is the wolf who still lives?" Orion would not leave Violet's side but he wanted to be certain the male was secured and would not escape. Because he would be dying very soon, but not until Orion had answers. He'd left the wolf with Darius, knowing the other male would keep the wolf secured, but now he needed details.

"Darius has him being held in enchanted chains while Baris looks at him. He's not going anywhere."

"Not sure why Baris is going to bother healing him when I'm simply going to break his body again." His voice was all beast now and he knew his dragon was in his gaze.

Prima grinned, her dragon reflected back at him. "There's the male I remember. So. You are living here among humans. How long have you been awake? I have missed you, old friend."

"A little over a year, and I've missed you as well. Were you awake when The Fall happened?"

Her expression darkened and she nodded, setting the sucker aside. "I was. Stupid fools," she growled, likely referring to the dragons who'd thought to take over the world and had destroyed half of it instead. Or more than half, it seemed. At least the large cities around the world, according to Violet and what he'd seen during his flights. And that was where the majority of humans had lived.

"What do you think of King?" He kept his voice subvocal so no one outside the tent could hear. It soothed him on the deepest level to be close to Violet. He held her hand up to his face, breathed in her scent.

"He's a just, fair, Alpha. Truly. And his territory is one of the best in the world. There are others doing exceptionally well, and his is in the top five."

He nodded, looked back at Violet, who had the most peaceful expression. He wanted to cup her cheek, feel her soft skin, but resisted the urge. He did not have that right. *Not yet*, his dragon snarled sulkily. *She saw you in beast form and was impressed.*

You can't know that, he snapped back to his beast.

Of course I can, I am stunning.

"So, let's get back to you—are you going to claim your territory, or what?" Prima asked as he had an internal conversation with himself.

He looked back at her, bristling. "Why do you care?" he snapped, then felt like a dick. She was one of his oldest friends.

"Because I care about you."

He was taken off guard by her blunt statement, the truth rolling off her. Goddess, she'd always been like that: honest to a fault. The kind of warrior who would follow you into any Hell realm or Hell itself out of loyalty. "I've missed you," he murmured, his gaze once again straying back to Violet.

Her braid had come loose, her dark curls everywhere, and his fingers itched to slide through them.

Prima lay back on the other bed with a sigh. "There's so much you've missed out on—Reaper mated with a healer."

He blinked. "Reaper as in the Dragon of War?" It was unfathomable.

"Yup. Oh, and my baby brother and that little wisp Arya have three children now—and grandchildren. They're truly blessed," she said reverently.

"Thank the Goddess." He paused, looked at the sharp planes of his friend's face. There was a sadness that clung to her. "What about you, friend? How are you since awakening?"

She snickered and rolled over to look at him. "Do you mean is my mind whole?" She shrugged, fell back again, as if she couldn't sit still. "Some days I wonder," she murmured, staring at the ceiling of the tent. "But no, it is not like it was before, where my mind was fracturing and I was losing my tether to reality. I'm...devastated, Orion." Her words were spoken so quietly, but there was no mistaking them. "A single, pathetic word for the truth of how I feel, but it is the simplest."

The scent of pain popped in the air, sharp and cloying as it grew. "Why?" he asked.

"I have ended things with a male because I had to."

Not because she wanted to, but had to. "I'm so sorry, Prima." He wouldn't insult her by asking questions, and he hated that he couldn't ease her suffering. She had always been a faithful friend, one who knew the truth of his history, where he came from. The agony rolling off her was almost visceral, thick in the air, clinging to the walls of the tent. "I wish I could take away your pain."

She turned her head toward him, her expression sober. "I believe you would. So...tell me about your human. I don't want to dwell on my own pain."

"Violet is my friend." He turned back to his female. "She and her sisters help run this small territory. They're the kindest humans I've ever met. Too trusting," he added, because it was a constant source of frustration. "I've had to kill would-be violent newcomers in addition to the vampires who've been trying to infiltrate the territory." Something he probably needed to tell Violet about as well.

"She's just a friend?" Prima sat up, swinging her legs off the side of the bed.

"Yes."

"Then why can I not tell her Baris is a panda? Does she perhaps like pandas more than dragons?"

Orion shot her a cutting look, his dragon right at the surface. Until he saw the gleam in her gaze. "You're an asshole," he said mildly.

"I know." She slid off the bed and stood, a grin on her face. This was the Prima he remembered and missed. "If you claim this territory, or even if you don't, I would like permission to stay for a bit while I figure out my next move. I'd be happy to help out wherever needed—and Cale of the Cerrach clan is here as well. He is looking for a change. I know he and some others would jump at the chance to pledge loyalty to you."

Orion quickly searched his long memory banks, nodded. "If memory serves me correctly, he was one of the only decent ones of that clan."

"Your memory does serve," she said with a decisive nod. "His half-brother was part of the attempt to take over the world and humans. He is now dead and I fear Cale will never fully grow into who he can be if he stays in New Orleans. He's a solid male, but he needs a dragon for an Alpha. Needs to start fully fresh."

"You're a good female, Prima," he murmured, bringing Violet's hand up to his cheek again, holding it close. "Do you have any woodworkers here by chance? Artists traveling with you?"

"We do, I believe," she answered, not fazed by the change in topic. "Artists, anyway. I'm not sure about the woodwork part."

"Can you talk to one of them for me? Ask for something? I can trade."

"Anything."

After he told her what he wanted, his old friend left and he turned back to Violet, his female whether he could claim her as such or not. She was *his*, and he'd almost lost her today.

Something he would never allow to happen again.

He tried to will her awake, so he could see her pale gray eyes light up with life. But she simply continued to sleep, breathing in and out in a steady rhythm.

His entire world came down to this small human female in front of him. And until she woke up, he wouldn't be moving from his spot.

~

Violet opened her eyes and—saw Orion's face inches from hers, his head resting on the top of the bed she was stretched out on. His mouth was soft in sleep, the only soft thing about him. His bottom lip was full, kissable, but the rest of his face was harsh even as he slumbered. All sharp planes, and even his brow was slightly furrowed, as if he couldn't truly rest while asleep. She wanted to reach out, smooth out the furrow.

There was no more pain in her ankle and she felt wonderfully rested. Maybe she made a sound, or maybe he simply sensed that she was awake, because his eyes popped open suddenly. Bright emerald green staring right at her.

She sucked in a breath at the sight of them, couldn't stop that punch of heat that rolled through her. She wanted him with a madness she didn't fully understand. "Hi," she whispered.

"Hi." His gaze fell to her mouth, a flicker of heat in his eyes, but then he sat up, eyed her clinically, all hints of heat disappearing in an instant as he visually swept her body over—unfortunately still in that clinical fashion. "How are you feeling?" he asked quietly. "Did that healer do his job properly?" The question was a low growl.

There were sounds of life outside the tent—voices, laughter, an engine flaring to life—and she could see that it was later in the afternoon now by the shadows. "How long have I been asleep?" she asked, pushing up to a sitting position as she took stock of herself.

"A few hours. Longer than expected. And you didn't answer my question." He was still eyeing her like a doctor. Did she look like this to her patients? All frowny-faced and intense?

"I'm...good." She arched her back slightly, twisted to the side and back. "Really good, actually." Next she rolled her ankle around, couldn't believe that there was absolutely no pull or twinge of pain. Not even a hint of it. *Wow.* "Baris is incredible."

He made an almost scoffing sound, but not quite. "What you do is harder. He depends on his magic."

She eyed Orion curiously as she shifted her position, swung her legs off the side to face him better. "That sounds pretty ungracious to the man…or male, who just healed me." While Orion might be "hella bossy," to quote Laurel, he was never unkind. Or not that she'd seen.

Orion had the oddest expression on his face as he lifted a shoulder. "Perhaps."

She blinked at him. "What's going on with you?"

"Nothing. I have a present for you."

She blinked again at the abrupt change, her tired brain trying to catch up. Her body felt amazing, but there was a bit of a fog resting over her as she struggled to wake up fully. "Oh…thank you."

He reached into one of his pockets and she tried not to stare at his long, thick fingers and wonder what those callused fingers would feel like roaming over her body, pushing inside her…

She forced the thoughts away as he held out a little carved figurine of a panda. It was wood, teak maybe, and very detailed. "This is adorable," she breathed, tracing her fingers over the ears and face. "Where did you get this?"

"I didn't actually leave your side, but I asked a friend to make a trade for me." He pulled out a slightly larger figure, this one a small wooden dragon with intricate carvings along the wings. "I thought you might like a dragon too."

Ohhh. Her heart skipped a beat as she looked up at him and saw something almost like yearning in his eyes. But she was too afraid to hope it was real.

"I love it, thank you." She clasped the dragon to her chest, not caring if she looked foolish. This gift mattered; she could see it on Orion's face clearer than she'd ever seen anything. It was like he was showing her a new part of himself. She was afraid to hope that this gift meant more than she thought it did. "I'll put it on my nightstand so I can see it every night."

He blinked, and for the second time, his dragon looked back at her. She had so many questions—Did his dragon side like her? Were they separate entities? How old was he? Did he want her?—and the science of it was beyond fascinating. But right now she really, really wanted to know what he would do if she leaned over and kissed him fully on the mouth. It would certainly answer the last question.

Because for the first time since she'd met him, he was staring at her as if he could eat her up. And that low growl in his throat was sending little shivers of heat curling through her, hitting all the right places. Oh, she was definitely going to kiss him, then just claim exhaustion or something if he rejected her.

Suddenly the flap to the tent flew open and the spell dissipated.

Disappointment punched through her and Orion started growling, the sound rising in intensity as he turned on the newcomer.

But then he stood, frowning at the female from before. Prima, Violet remembered. The supermodel.

Insecurity flared to life inside her, the wildfire spreading out everywhere. Because next to this woman she felt like a lumpy potato.

"Hello, Violet. It's nice to see you up." The female nodded at her like a soldier, her body long and lean, her arms perfectly muscled. "A beautiful name for a beautiful female."

"Oh...thank you." Suddenly disarmed, she smiled tentatively at the intimidating woman, who had to be a dragon. Right? She'd seen those eyes before and this woman had such a tall, strong frame.

"I'm a dragon," the female said, "In case you were wondering."

"Do you read minds?"

The female shook her head, her jet-black hair the only thing messy about her. It had come out of her lopsided braid. "I just figured you were curious. Dragons are the best of all the shifters, you know. Even better than pandas," she said conspiratorially. Then she shot Orion a mischievous look that told of a real friendship.

Also...why was she bringing up pandas? Violet tried to squish the jealousy that wanted to surface. Okay, that *did* surface and wanted to totally suffocate her.

"Did you need something?" Orion demanded of Prima, his tone annoyed.

Which made Violet feel better than it should have. He'd never sounded annoyed with her.

The female just smiled, and that turned her from beautiful to the actual Miss Universe. "There's another pretty human here, also named for a flower. Marigold. She wants to see her sister and she told me that if I didn't bring her to Violet immediately, she would make me sorry I was born."

Oh God.

Prima seemed amused, however, as she continued. "I like that human. I might keep her."

Wait...what?

Orion rubbed a hand over his face. "You can't keep humans."

"I don't mean like that. I mean I might train her. She's quite stealthy. I didn't even scent her when she walked up behind me. She'd make a fantastic spy. She's small and unassuming and—"

"Stay away from my people," Orion growled low in his throat.

Something about the way he said "my people" warmed Violet even as impatience surged through her. "Can I see my sister?" Violet asked, her head starting to hurt at their back-and-forth. Also, she had to pee and needed to run off into the woods for privacy. Or go home—that was what she really wanted.

"Yes, of course." Prima stuck her head out of the tent, and Baris and Mari strode in, one after the other.

Mari shot Prima a dark, threatening look before focusing on Violet, her expression worried. "How are you?"

"I'm good," Violet said.

"Prima, out," Baris said mildly.

And to Violet's surprise the dragon female nodded, but not before she gave Orion a hard look. "Claim the territory now, Orion. If you don't, someone else will make a play for it."

Alarm punched through Violet, but she tabled it as Baris approached, a kind smile on his face. He looked slightly surprised at the two figurines on the bed next to her, but then he held up a hand over her head and just hovered, that blue glow emanating off him in gentle waves. "Well, you're good on my end, but how do you feel?"

"Amazing," she said, still stunned and wondering if this was some strange dream. "Why did Prima tell Orion to claim the territory?" she asked the doctor, even though Orion was right there with Mari, mere feet away.

She wasn't sure if Orion would be totally honest with her, not after he'd kept something so huge from her, and she wanted the truth. Something told her that Baris would be forthcoming.

"The majority of supernaturals live in a pack, or clan or pride, or whatever," the healer said. "And an Alpha runs those packs, etc. Even before The Fall, an Alpha claimed a territory for his or her people. Supernaturals of all kinds lived side by side with humans in secret, but they still claimed territories. It's simply the way of shifters. If a territory remains unclaimed, it's essentially up for grabs."

"But...we all live here. This is our home. Our territory."

The healer lifted a shoulder. "I'm not saying it's right or wrong, simply the way it is. In this new world, an Alpha has to hold on to their territory. That Alpha can be human, theoretically. But they have to be able to withstand challengers and show enough power so that there aren't any more challengers eventually. They have to be strong enough that there is no reward for attacking their territory. Only pain and death and massive casualties. If Orion doesn't claim the territory your community lives in, then eventually someone will try to take it for their own. It will likely be by force and blood will be shed, unfortunately." His words were so matter-of-fact.

Violet looked at Orion, who simply nodded, his dragon back in his gaze. "The healer is correct."

Oh, she definitely had questions. And he would answer them, but she would wait until they were alone.

"Speaking of community," Mari said into the brief quiet. "The families want to talk to both of you. We heard what happened though, so I was sent here to check on you and get more details. Are you sure you're okay?"

"I am, I swear. I'll come home with you now." Violet slid off the bed, ignoring her bladder for the moment. She could last until they got home.

"I need to stay here longer." Orion's expression was unreadable now, his eyes human once again.

"Why?"

"I need to deal with that wolf." His words came out in that same scary tone as before.

90

Oooh. "Okay, then I guess…I'll see you when you get back?"

His expression softened. "I won't be long. And you will take an escort."

Violet's eyebrows rose even as Mari coughed to cover a laugh. "I didn't hear a question in there."

Orion stared at her for a long moment. "I'm going to send one with you regardless. Asking seems disingenuous."

Now Mari just laughed out loud, not bothering to hide it.

Violet stared at Orion, at his earnest expression, and wasn't sure if she wanted to smack him or kiss him. Maybe both.

Definitely both.

CHAPTER TWELVE

"I hope Orion makes that wolf suffer," Mari said as Violet stepped into the kitchen, her medical bag in hand.

She blinked at her sister's violent sentiment. "I'm trying not to think about what he's doing right now." After she and Mari left the encampment, she'd realized that he was staying to torture that wolf for information. Something that was...a lot to think about. So she wasn't going to. Her feelings on the matter were complicated enough.

"The Pappas family are waiting by the barn with the Héberts and Fontenots. I think Cassandra brought some of her baklava." Mari rubbed her hands together like a cartoon villain. "And I plan on sneaking away with some of them."

"Were you a spy?" she asked her sister bluntly, hoping to catch her off guard.

Mari blinked, paused, then lifted a shoulder. "More or less, yes."

"Is that how you know how to kill vampires?"

"Also, more or less...yes. I was aware of some supernatural existence before The Fall, but not the full scale of beings out there."

"And you knew Orion was a dragon?" Violet tried to keep the hurt out of her voice, to ask the question as neutrally as possible, but she was pretty sure the hurt bled through because Mari's expression softened.

"Well, I knew he was a supernatural and I guessed what he was. I never actually saw him in dragon form before."

"Why didn't you tell me?" She leaned against the countertop, setting her bag down. The others could wait because she needed these questions answered.

"At first I thought you might already know. Then, it was clear he was keeping secrets because he wanted to keep all of us protected. I think it was stupid of him to, but...I get having to hide part of yourself." Mari was a lesbian so Violet assumed that was what she was referencing. "And it didn't seem my place to out him, you know? It just felt wrong to do it."

"Yeah, okay. I get that. I'm just hurt he didn't tell me," she said honestly. "I thought we were closer than that."

"I don't think him not telling you or any of us has anything to do with how much he trusts us or even how close he feels to us. You specifically."

Violet wasn't sure how to respond to that last bit. Because she'd thought that she and Orion had something special, at least a solid friendship, even if she wanted more.

Mari continued, cutting into her thoughts. "At its very core, keeping a secret like that is a defense mechanism for anyone to keep themselves from feeling vulnerable. And the reasons for that are as vast as the galaxy."

"Ugh. I know you're right. And I feel stupid being hurt." She bit her bottom lip, then said, "So Prima was gorgeous, right?"

"Oh, holy shit, yeah. Like, wow." Mari fanned herself slightly, a grin on her face. "And your man is not interested in her if that's where this is going. There were no vibes between them at all. Other than friendship."

Violet ignored the "your man" comment because she couldn't deal with it today and grabbed her bag. She liked to do the healthy thing and ignore shit she didn't want to think about. "Let's go."

"Oh my God, you and Orion both love to ignore things you don't want to talk about. Has anything happened between you two?" Mari asked as they stepped out onto the back porch, heading toward a conversation Violet wasn't sure she wanted to have with other families in the territory.

"No," she murmured, glancing over toward the orchard and around their property. Solar lights illuminated the yard and beyond, including their growing pods, which currently had heated lamps covering the winter crops. There was no one nearby but she still didn't want to talk about Orion where anyone might overhear.

As they reached the other side of the barn, she saw that yep, all the families that provided most of the food in the territory were there, sitting around tables talking quietly. Rose and Laurel were sitting with the Pappas family.

Cassandra, one of the most outspoken people in their community, stood as Violet and Mari approached and held out her arms for Violet. Cassandra's parents had emigrated from Greece, eventually settled in Baton Rouge, then later moved here and had the only Greek restaurant in town. The restaurant had long since closed but Violet had helped deliver two of Cassandra's grandchildren in the last year.

"We were so worried about you." Cassandra hugged her, then cupped her cheeks in her callused palms gently. "Orion sent word you'd been attacked but the information since then has been scarce. How are you?" She looked her over much like how her mom would have and Violet had to fight off a wave of tears. God, she missed her parents. Facing the world was always a bit harder without them, no matter how old she got.

But being back here with her neighbors and family released the tension that had been building inside her. "I'm...okay. It was terrifying," she said honestly, looking out at all the familiar faces. There were about twenty of them who had showed up and they'd all quieted to listen.

"Please sit and tell us." Cassandra motioned for her to sit at one of the benched tables. "I made you some melitzanosalata too. Enough to take home if you're not hungry now."

She actually was hungry, but wanted to get all this out first. So she told them about the wolves chasing her, then Orion saving her—leaving out the details of violence—and how he'd brought her to the healer. As she told that part, she stood and rolled her ankle for everyone. "It's like I was never injured. I'm grateful to them, and they've made it clear that no matter what happens they'll give us some medical supplies and machines."

"Why would they do that?" John, a nearby farmer asked, his expression skeptical as always.

His nephew, Thomas, nudged him in exasperation. "Uncle John—"

"It's fine," she said, nodding at John. "It's a good question. And I think the answer is because it's the kind thing to do. Supernatural healers are a lot like doctors and play by their own rules, I think." She smiled slightly as she recalled everything Luna had told her. She also answered more questions about what the New Orleans encampment was like and anything they asked. And the questions were a whole lot, not that she was surprised.

"So what do you think about an allyship?" Cassandra asked once she was done.

Violet glanced at Mari, before looking at the others. "I think it's a good idea. I wasn't aware of the scope of vampire attacks before, but even without those, having friends and allies from a nearby territory is a really good thing. I'm only one person, one doctor and…what happens if something happens to me?" she asked into the quiet, not really needing an answer.

Some days she was able to help out with the crops, or actually hike or rest. But on others, when there were multiple medical emergencies, she only got a few hours of sleep and often had to just do what she could and pray for the best because she couldn't be in two places at once.

"We've been doing so well here but we need more doctors. More teachers. And we definitely need to shore up our security." Orion wasn't there so she couldn't speak for him, but she glanced at Mari, hoping her sister would pick up on that thread.

Mari stood, petite and unassuming as Prima had said, but her sister had a very assertive air about her, and when she spoke, people tended to listen.

As Mari launched into an explanation about their security needs and what she and the brothers—who weren't there because they were currently patrolling the border—had been doing to keep the territory safe, she could sense another shift in the air. A good one.

When Mari was done she sat next to Violet, and almost immediately Cassandra stood, looked out at everyone. "I'm with the Robichaux sisters. And Orion, though he's not here. I think an allyship is the best thing for all of us."

Then to Violet's surprise, Cassandra sat instead of launching into all the reasons it was the right decision.

Everyone else looked around at each other, then they all slowly nodded, even John, who simply said, "I'm fine with an allyship for now," in his grumbling tone.

"We'll need to tell the rest of the community, call a town meeting," Violet said, standing once again, but staying close to her melitzanosalata —because that was definitely coming home with her. It was basically baba ghanoush but creamier and she was obsessed with it. "We'll need to explain fully what it means to have an Alpha, and that if we want to survive, we're going to adapt." She figured there might be a few hold-outs, but at the end of the day it didn't matter. The safety and security of all of them was what was important.

"I can organize that," Laurel said, jumping up. "Put all those former event planning skills to use." Her tone was self-deprecating, making everyone laugh.

Even Violet, though she found herself annoyed that her sister constantly put herself down even in subtle ways. Laurel was amazing, but didn't take compliments well and always tried to downplay how much she contributed. She wished her sister could see herself the way she and others did.

Shelving that for now, she smiled as John approached her, no doubt wanting to tell her all the things he thought could go wrong with the allyship. But in the end, Cassandra headed John off and Thomas approached her, a rueful smile on his handsome face.

"Sorry about my uncle. You know what he's like," he said quietly.

"It's fine, seriously. I'm glad he has questions." She had a lot too, but for now her gut was telling her this was the right move. And even though she was a little scared about all the changes in the air, it was a good kind of scared. Not the kind she'd experienced when being chased by psycho wolf shifters.

"Where's Orion? I thought he'd be here."

"Oh, he's on security right now." A teeny lie, but she didn't really feel guilty either.

"I'd like to talk to him about helping out with patrols or at least helping out with the borders."

The offer surprised her because Thomas had always struck her as sort of softer, but he did help his uncle out on their farm and he was in shape so maybe she shouldn't be. "Definitely. You can probably just talk to Mari," she said, nodding at her sister who was talking to another neighbor.

Cassandra moved in then, smiling at Thomas. "I think your uncle is ready to go."

"Ah, okay." Thomas nodded at both of them.

"I have more questions," Cassandra said. "But I didn't want to dominate the meeting with a bunch of follow-ups. I trust you guys, I just want to clarify some things."

"Of course. And since we're here, I want to take some of your vitals. We can do it back at my place." Cassandra had missed her last couple scheduled checkups.

"Oh, I'm fine."

"And I'm not asking."

Cassandra grinned at her tone. "I can never say no to you. Fine," she sighed. "Let's get it over with."

As she headed back to her family's house with Cassandra, who'd already started asking questions, Violet wondered what Orion was doing, if he'd gotten the information he'd wanted from that wolf.

She always wondered what Orion was doing if they weren't together, but she was also wondering who the heck those wolves were and why they'd attacked her.

She also realized how lucky she and the community were that

Orion, the broody brothers and Mari had been keeping watch over all of them without their knowledge.

And how differently things could be if the community hadn't had their guardians looking out for all of them.

CHAPTER THIRTEEN

L aurel double-checked the whiteboard she'd set up in the back room of the house, then compared it with the notes she'd made in her notebook. In her "before" life, as she sometimes thought of it, she'd planned parties, organized meetings and been a type A planner in all parts of her life.

That had bled over into her "after" or current life. There were only about seven hundred people in the community and she'd planned parties with more people than that. The biggest wedding she'd handled had been about five hundred but it had been ridiculously complicated. So dealing with something this big was doable. She just needed to make sure everyone was reached about the upcoming community meeting.

And that they knew what it was about, how important it was. "I can have someone courier messages to those who don't have radios," she murmured to herself, then looked down at Bowie, who was sitting up straight, watching her work on the whiteboard as if he understood exactly what she was doing. "What do you think, boy?"

He barked once in response.

"I knew you'd agree." She reached into her pocket, pulled out one of the peanut butter treats she'd made him.

His mouth opened slightly and she swore it looked as if he was smiling as he sat up even straighter. His tail was helicopter wild but then he froze, turned away from her and raced out into the hallway, then out the doggy door, a growling low in his throat.

She frowned, hurrying after him. As she swung open the door she nearly tripped over a man crouched down and giving Bowie scratches behind his ear.

"Who are you?" she demanded, never having seen the guy before.

The male stood then, his pale green eyes almost glowing as he looked down at her. Whoa, he was tall, probably as tall as Orion. Or maybe not, but close. But they weren't related, or she didn't think they were. The male had bronze skin, dark, slightly tousled hair, and a charming half smile.

"Hello, human. I'm looking for Orion and got turned around."

She blinked. "Hello human?" He grinned slightly and oh God, her knees actually went weak. *What. The. Hell.* She'd never been charmed by a pretty face and wasn't going to start now.

"Apologies, I am Cale of the Cerrach clan and I am looking for Orion."

"Oh...I'm Laurel."

"Ah yes, one of Violet's sisters. Prima has told me of her. And I met your other sister, Marigold." He held out his hand even as Bowie nudged his leg, looking for attention and pets. Even over her treats. That told her a lot about this man.

She held out her hand, found it engulfed by his much bigger one. And though it sounded crazy, even in her head, she swore she felt sparks. "You called my sister Marigold? To her face?" She was just Mari unless you wanted Nair in your shampoo.

"I thought that was her name." He frowned ever so slightly and didn't let her hand go, but held it tight. Not hard, just firm as he lifted it to his face.

What the hell was he doing? And why did she kinda like it when the weirdo started to...*sniff* her?

Yanking her hand back, she frowned down at Bowie. "We don't even know if he can be trusted. I think maybe you're not a good guard dog." Even if the guy was ridiculously gorgeous, he could mean trouble.

Bowie stared up at her, tongue lolling out with a goofy smile. *Nope, definitely not a good guard dog.*

"I'm trustworthy! And of course he likes me. He's a good boy." Cale leaned down again and started petting Bowie, who was now on his back, legs spread without a care in the world.

"He's the *best* boy," she corrected. He might not be a great guard dog but he was the sweetest dog who'd ever lived.

For some reason her words made Cale smile broadly, and for a moment her mind went utterly blank. How was it possible that someone was this handsome?

He looked back up at her. "You smell like peanut butter. Do you have food? I'm hungry."

Maybe that was why he'd been smelling her hand? The guy was kind of a weirdo but Bowie trusted him, so… "Yeah, come on. I've got some human…ah, or non-dog peanut butter treats. Because what you're smelling are Bowie's treats." Which technically humans could eat too; she'd made them with all natural, basic products. All they could get now anyway, since she couldn't run up to a grocery store anymore. "Are you a dragon too, like Orion?" Huge news they were all adjusting to.

Though after the world had gone mad, she'd found that she adjusted to things a whole lot faster now. You either adapted or you didn't survive. Simple as that.

"I am," he said, following after her into their kitchen.

It was a little odd to have a stranger in her home, or a man at all other than Orion. But her gut was telling her this dragon wasn't a threat. If he was, there really wasn't much she could do about it anyway. And Bowie clearly trusted him, was trotting after them, still smelling the guy as if he had drugs on his pants.

"So why do you want to see Orion?" She opened up a container of peanut butter cookies she'd made the day before using a new recipe, held it out to him.

He inhaled, his expression one of bliss, and when he bit into one of them, the sound he made was sort of orgasmic in nature.

Oh God, why did she like that? Heat pooled deep inside her as she listened to that groan and she had all sorts of thoughts then. Mainly she wondered if he sounded like that when he came. And what would he look like all naked and sweaty... Oh sweet peanut butter balls, why was she lusting after this stranger with the nice smile? This was so not like her. Not even in the same realm of what she was normally like.

"You smell amazing," he murmured, setting the half-eaten cookie down on the plate she'd set in front of him.

She blinked in surprise. "Ah, pretty sure that's the peanut butter."

"No, Laurel, it is definitely you."

She felt her cheeks heat up and glanced away from him. "So," she said, pouring both of them a glass of water. "You never answered my question."

He was silent, and when she turned around, he was still sitting at the kitchen table but his dragon was in his eyes.

Yelping, she dropped the glasses but he was so fast she didn't even track him, snatching them out of the air before they hit the ground, only a little water sloshing over the edge.

Her heart beat erratically in her chest as he set them gently on the table.

"I apologize, I did not mean to scare you." He was no longer smiling, his expression concerned.

"No, no, it's fine." But she couldn't get her heart rate to slow down.

Bowie whined softly now, nudging his head against her calf.

"Obviously it's not," Cale murmured, urging her to sit in the chair, his movements slow and gentle.

She thrust her fingers into Bowie's fur, petting him even as he soothed the edges of her weird panic. "You just surprised me, that's all. I mean, I know about supernaturals, obviously. And now we know that Orion is one... I've just never met one up close. Not that I know of anyway. And I'm rambling," she said, feeling so foolish. And a whole lot embarrassed.

He sat too and scooted his chair closer to hers. "I can imagine it's a fright to anyone and I didn't mean to startle you. It sometimes just happens."

"Can I see it again?" she asked, then wondered if that was rude. She didn't know any rules when it came to supernaturals.

"You're sure?"

"Yes."

As soon as she said yes, his eyes changed again, the beast staring at her, his dragon eyes the same shade of pale green as the man's. "Your eyes are beautiful," she whispered, staring into them, mesmerized instead of scared now that she'd been prepared for it.

To her surprise, he made a low sort of purring growl sound, then his eyes were human again. "Thank you. So are yours."

His voice had dropped a couple octaves now, and oh, she recognized that tone. And she liked it. Way, way too much. Was he...attracted to her? Heat detonated inside her as he leaned a fraction closer, the dark, masculine scent of him going to her head.

She'd cleared her throat, not sure what she was going to say, when she heard the front door open. She wasn't sure if it was relief that punched through her or something else. Perhaps...disappointment?

Moments later Orion was in the doorway, glancing between the two of them. "Cale, what are you doing here?"

"Looking for you."

Orion nodded, his expression fairly neutral except when he looked down at an adoring Bowie. Then his hard face softened as he greeted the dog. His face also softened whenever Violet was around, but those two had cornered the market on ignoring their feelings for each other.

Laurel and her sisters had a friendly wager on who would make the first move—and when. Unfortunately Orion and Violet were the king and queen of playing ostrich so she and her sisters had needed to re-bet once all their original dates had flown by with no hint of either of them acknowledging their mutual attraction.

"Laurel, do you know where Violet is?" Orion asked, and yep, his face did that thing where his eyes crinkled as he asked about Violet.

"Ah, she was here not too long ago with Cassandra but they left. Also, since you're here I wanted to let you know that I've got a game plan for getting messages to the whole community about the town meeting. And instead of having the meeting tomorrow I think it should be Friday instead. It'll give me enough time to make sure everyone is aware of the details."

"Of course. Thank you for setting everything up."

She nodded and stood, needing to get some distance from the strange, unbelievably sexy male in her kitchen. "I'm going to get back to it, then. Nice to meet you, Cale."

He nodded and murmured something barely audible, but his gaze was heated, tracking her as she hurried from the kitchen. Only then could she breathe clearly again.

Instead of heading back to the room she'd been working in, however, she stepped out the back door and breathed in the early evening air deeply. Trying to calm her racing mind.

The blast of cold cut through her, grounding her even as her mind strayed to the virtual stranger in her kitchen who'd watched her as if he wanted to see what she looked like naked.

The feeling was very much mutual but...he was a supernatural. A dragon shifter. She wasn't sure how any of that worked and...she was getting ahead of herself.

Shaking her head, she stalked away from the house, deciding to take a ten-minute break and clear her head before she jumped back into planning everything.

She hadn't been with anyone since The Fall—and even before, she'd only had fairly bland relationships. Ones that she was pretty embarrassed about now.

Cale was larger than life, however. But she couldn't help wondering if he'd be interested in maybe a fling or...something. *Hmmm.*

When she ran into him again, if she did, she was going to test the waters. See if there really was an attraction or if she was just imagining it.

CHAPTER FOURTEEN

"You were supposed to meet me by the barn." Orion eyed Cale of the Cerrach clan suspiciously. Because he'd seen the way the ancient male had been watching Laurel and he wasn't sure how he felt about it. Laurel was like a sister to him and incredibly important to Violet.

"I got turned around."

"You're lying."

"Fine. I smelled Laurel and followed her scent."

"She's off-limits."

Cale, who was almost as tall as him, but not as broad, stood. "Why?" he demanded.

"She is like a sister to me."

"Good thing it's not more than that," the other male growled low in his throat, his tone possessive.

Orion's beast shoved to the surface and he stepped forward until they were inches apart. He didn't put hands on the male, mainly because he didn't want to fight and destroy Violet's kitchen. It would upset her and that was unacceptable. But his dragon was barely being leashed. "And why is that?"

"Because she smells like mine. My mate."

Oh. Oooooh. Orion scrubbed a hand over his face and stepped back. "She's a human and under my protection. Never forget that." Laurel made her own choices. He could not and would not stop her if she was interested in Cale, a male who was an honorable warrior. But...his over-protectiveness swelled up, especially since she was Violet's sister. And he had not been lying—he viewed her as a sister as well. "I will remove your head from your body if you harm her."

Cale rolled his shoulders once, his dragon disappearing from his gaze. "I would never hurt her. Or any human."

Orion didn't want to discuss any of this so he shifted subjects to something much safer. "Are you ready to do an aerial sweep?" Orion had asked Cale to meet him so they could fly over the territory. Cale's reputation was solid, and many, many years ago Orion had seen the male in battle, knew he was a skilled fighter. But he wanted to see if Cale had the right kind of eye for security, what he thought of the perimeter, and where he would shore things up.

Cale stood at attention, nodded once. "Yes."

"Let's go, then."

The male grabbed a couple cookies, a grin on his face, and followed after Orion, Bowie trailing after them. Unfortunately the pup couldn't go with them, so Orion left him behind with soft words and a pat on the head.

Outside the night was quiet, but chilly and they waited until they were in the forest to shift and take to the air.

Orion was surprised by how natural it felt to go flying with another dragon after so long—and wished Violet was with him to enjoy this. The first time he'd taken her flying had been out of necessity, because she'd been injured. He wanted her to ride on him, to see the world from the same position he did.

And he wanted to be with her now, taking care of her even if she was healed. By a dumb panda.

As he and Cale surveyed the perimeter, dipping low, scenting along the western border more than anywhere else, he allowed himself a moment where he accepted the idea of having a clan again. Though this time it would be more humans than supernaturals.

This was a new world and his people were softer, but they had many skills when it came to building up a territory. He knew he could make it work, could keep everyone safe while they fortified their home, but deep down that fear of losing people hit hard.

He didn't think there was a way around it, however. It was the price one paid for being part of a society, a family. You got hurt because you cared about others. *Ugh.* Hibernation had been so much easier.

Hours later, Orion landed back near Violet's home—*his home*, he forced himself to acknowledge—keeping himself camouflaged until he was in his human form. Cale had already headed back to the New Orleans encampment and it was time for Orion to get a few hours of sleep.

But he needed to talk to Violet first, was desperate to see her.

The closer he got to the house, the more tension ratcheted up inside him. She'd already told him she wasn't angry at him, and she didn't seem afraid of or disgusted by his dragon side, but they hadn't had time to talk before she'd headed back here and spoken to all their neighbors.

And he knew she'd have questions—likely about the now dead wolf who hadn't given him much before taking his own life. That bastard had taken a poison silver pill rather than be tortured. *Pathetic.*

Orion might want to avoid answering some of her questions, but she deserved the truth. She deserved everything she wanted.

He could see lights on in all the rooms from outside so he knew she had to be home.

Instead of going to his room, he headed for hers first, but it was empty, surprising him. Not liking that she wasn't back yet, he headed downstairs again—and paused outside his room.

She was inside.

Far too eager to see her, even as he dreaded her looking at him differently now, he opened the door and sure enough she was sitting up on his bed, lying back against some of his pillows.

"Hey." She straightened, blinking slightly as she set a book to the side, looking as if she might have been dozing and not reading.

Bowie was definitely dozing, was already in his bed on the floor, one of his paws covering his face. He peeked up at Orion, but then covered his face again and made a whining sound that clearly said—*it's bedtime*!

"I hope it's okay that I'm here," she whispered, sitting up straighter and crossing her legs.

"Of course." He sat on the edge of the bed near her, turned to face her. He wanted her here *all* the time. Heat curled through him now that they were alone. As it always did. When he was near her, something inside him flared to life. It had been like that from the moment he'd seen her, caught her scent. "How are you feeling?"

"Completely healed." There was a touch of awe in her tone.

"I'm glad." Even if it had been a panda who'd healed her.

"You saved me. And I know you said not to thank you, but I'm doing it again anyway. If you hadn't been there…" She shuddered slightly and he could see fear flicker in her gray eyes.

On instinct, he took one of her hands in his, was glad when she didn't pull away. He was careful about touching her, didn't do it too often. Because the more he did, the more he wanted. Touch and wanting touch were a weakness—that was what he'd been taught growing up. On the deepest level he knew it was bullshit, but that had been drilled into him with violence. The only touches he'd gotten for so long had been ones delivered in anger. Or worse, with complete calm, but still ended with his broken bones.

She laced her fingers through his, tightened her grip as she scooted a little closer, her knees touching his. "I have a lot of questions."

He braced himself and nodded. "Ask anything you want."

Violet took a breath, then gave him a half smile. "I'm trying to decide on just one. Okay so…can you explain more about the Alpha thing? I feel like we've made this huge decision to have an Alpha run our territory because of everything that's been happening but…I want to make sure I actually understand. I think I do, since Baris explained some, but I want to hear it from you."

"In packs, or clans in my case since I'm a dragon, there's always an Alpha who is in charge. More often than not, like Baris said, that Alpha is physically the strongest. There are exceptions and that's usually when the strongest is devoted to whoever is in charge. They are essentially the tip of the spear and will do whatever the Alpha asks. And in that case, usually most of the physically strongest members in a clan support a physically weaker being because they trust them to make the best decisions. Because that being is an Alpha and has that gene that drives them to take care of everyone. Even if they don't have the physical strength."

"How do you know if you're Alpha? Is that a weird question?" She winced as she asked it.

"No, it's not weird, but I accept all questions, weird or not." He was just glad she was talking to him. "And it's an inborn thing. Usually your pack or clan will know what you are from the time you're young."

"Did your clan know? Like your parents, I guess?"

He froze, not having expected the question. He never talked about them with anyone. Prima and her sister Mira were the only ones from his time who even knew of those evil dragons.

"You don't have to answer," she rushed out, maybe reading something on his face.

Normally he was good at keeping his emotions in check, but with Violet he sometimes let his guard down, let her see the heart of him. He didn't even mean to. "When I was older it was clear that I was an Alpha. And for the record there are those who are alpha in nature, but not necessarily born or built to run a clan or territory. Like Darius. He's a good leader, definitely an alpha wolf, but he'll never run a territory."

"Fascinating," she murmured, all her attention on him.

Having Violet's attention on him was unnerving, but his dragon half certainly loved it, wanted to shift and strut around for her. "Did my dragon side scare you?" he asked, wanting answers of his own.

She blinked, then grinned. "That whole situation scared me. But you? No, your dragon is quite literally the most stunning thing I've ever seen in my entire life. And I've seen the aurora borealis. You've got that beat, hands down. You were so beautiful it almost hurt to look at you, and I definitely want to see you again."

There was so much adoration in her tone, he froze, looked away for a moment. *Told you*, his dragon purred. *She likes what she sees—she likes us. It is time to shed the past and make a move on her.*

If only it were that simple. But he couldn't stop the ache in his chest, the one that made him want to reach for her fully, to take her in his arms and claim her forever. "You honor me with your compliment."

She squeezed his hand once, and still didn't let go. "Just stating the truth."

He looked back at her, resisted the urge to cup her cheek—or pin her beneath him the way he was dying to. The way his body called out for.

"So...how does, like, electing an Alpha work?"

He snorted at her question, a smile tugging at his lips. "Supernaturals don't elect. That is a human concept. It's more of a... I'm not certain how to explain it correctly. Our animals recognize who is in charge and automatically want to follow the strongest, but also smartest. The one who will keep us safe and protected, as well as our children. And I'm speaking more in a general sense now, but it is part of who we are at our core. There are always exceptions of course. Some dragon clans alternate Alphas because of the way my kind goes into Hibernation. It's a necessity."

"This is the most I've heard you speak at once, ever. So no complaints from me." She gave him a soft smile that wrapped around him, made him feel things he wasn't sure he was ready to accept.

Made it difficult to breathe as he looked into her gray eyes. Her dark hair was pulled back into two braids tonight, making her look younger than what he knew her to be. "I'd never lived with humans before coming here so I assumed saying less was better than giving myself away."

"Oh, Orion." She took his hand and held it up to her chest, her expression intense as she watched him.

He loved the way she touched him so freely, so gently. It was a balm to his soul.

"I hate that you felt you had to hide who you are—and that's not an accusation or anything. I was hurt that you didn't tell me and my sisters that you're a dragon. But that's just because I care about you. I consider you family and I hope you consider all of us your family too."

Throat tight, he didn't know how to respond, so he nodded. She stripped him bare without even trying, with her simple honesty. And if he was being honest, he wanted more than to be her family. He wanted to be her everything.

"So, if Alpha's aren't elected...what exactly are we setting up for Friday at the community center?"

The slight change in topic released that tight grip on his throat. This was better, a safer topic. "I honestly don't know if it's the right choice, but humans are different than shifters and I believe they will need this election." His tone was wry.

And she smiled.

"I'm going to outline what's been happening and explain what it means if I'm officially their Alpha. Because there won't be any going back after that. There won't be another 'election' or whatever humans do. I'll either step down for another Alpha to take over or be challenged to a fight to the death—that is how Alphas change leadership, in case that was your next question."

"Ah." She bit her bottom lip for a moment, still idly holding his hand in her lap as she ruminated over his words.

He wondered if she was aware of still holding his hand, because he was aware of every moment her gentle fingers were on him, stroking over the top of his hand.

"Well no matter what happens, my sisters and I have your back. As do the rest of the families who were here earlier tonight."

Her words humbled him in a way he hadn't expected. But then again, he'd never expected a woman like Violet. Had never expected to fall for someone so kind and gentle. And a human. "I'm sorry I withheld what I was to you," he said into the silence, needing her to know he hadn't set out to deceive her long-term.

She blinked in surprise. "I don't know that you owe me an apology, but thank you. I hope I've earned your trust enough by now."

"And I hope to earn your trust back."

She sighed, squeezed his hand again, and the scent that trickled off her was interesting. "You have my trust. Since leaving Baris and their encampment, I've been trying to put myself in your shoes. I can't imagine what it was like to wake up into a strange world and not know anyone or who you could trust—oh, later I want more details about the whole Hibernation thing. So we're good, I promise." She cleared her throat. "Hey, is that why you were naked the first time I met you?"

"Ah, yes. I'd literally just woken up, hours before. I'd clawed my way out of a very deep resting place."

"How old are you exactly? And how long were you in Hibernation?"

He didn't respond, just watched her carefully for a long moment.

"What? Oh, should I not have asked that?"

"It's not that. I don't want to frighten you."

"Ah, okay, now you're sorta frightening me," she said on a laugh, no actual fear rolling off her. "Come on."

"I don't know the answer to either of those. A very long time. Millennia perhaps."

She blinked. "Whoa." Taking him by surprise, she reached up and brushed her fingers at his temples. "I don't see any gray at least."

Heat slammed into him at the soft touch, the gentleness. Goddess, he wanted to lean into her touch, but he remained frozen where he was and she dropped her hand.

She watched him wide-eyed, and now he was certain he scented lust. But…he was inexperienced with humans. Or softness in general. And this was Violet. He did want to claim her, was desperate for it, but wasn't sure he deserved her. Even if it was clear that she wanted him. What if he screwed up, was too rough?

"I know I have more questions," she said around a yawn. "But I think you answered the basics. Are you going to be sneaking off for patrols later?" she asked, glancing over at the clock. It was one now.

"Maybe, but I won't sneak around anymore."

"Good." She looked as if she wanted to say more, but then simply gave a short nod.

There was so much he wanted to say to her, to admit—namely his ever-present obsession for her—but there was a noise outside that made him pause. And a scent.

Bowie must have sensed it too, jumped out of his puppy bed and moved to the window, trying to shove the curtains out of the way with his nose.

"What's wrong?" Violet was off the bed with him, following close behind as Orion hurried out of the bedroom and into the kitchen.

He scented who was on the other side of the kitchen door before he opened it. Bentley—who should be out patrolling. This was not going to be good.

"There's been a fire. And..." The wolf glanced behind Orion at Violet, his expression grim. "A murder."

CHAPTER FIFTEEN

Orion wanted to shield Violet as they stalked up to the house, but that was just his mating instinct riding him. As soon as Bentley had told him about the fire and murder at a neighbor's house, they'd changed clothes quickly and he'd flown here, with Violet riding on his back this time. Not the way he'd wanted to introduce her to riding on him.

The scent of burning embers drifted on the air as they raced up to the smoking one-story home of the Thatcher family. People he genuinely liked. Kind human artists who lived on the outskirts of Violet's land.

"Is that…" Violet stumbled slightly in the grass as they neared the home, saw three still bodies in the grass. One of them very small.

Bentley's two brothers were standing back about ten feet, their expressions grim. Tyler looked murderous.

Orion nodded at them and they joined the brothers. "Tell me what you know." Bentley had only said that there were three bodies and a fire they'd managed to get under control. Orion had also sent Mari on a mission to find Prima and ask her to meet them here.

"They were killed before the fire," Tyler rasped out, glancing away from the bodies. "There are vampire bites on their necks and wrists. They appear to have been drained."

"I'll check for sure." Violet's voice was hoarse, her expression shocked, but he didn't think she was going into shock. "And we'll need to transport them back to our land and make sure..." She cleared her throat.

"What exactly happened? Give me exact details," Orion said.

"This was my patrol area," Tyler answered again. "I wasn't late or anything. I found the house on fire, called it in to my brothers. And then I headed inside, found them..." He cleared his throat. "They were in the kitchen at the table as if they'd been posed. I knew I shouldn't move the bodies but I wanted to get them out before the flames took over."

"By the time he got them outside, we'd arrived," Bentley added. "Using fire extinguishers and blankets we managed to stop the spread of it. I'm just glad the extinguishers worked," he murmured, glancing at what had been a carport area but was now crumbled ash.

As he spoke, Violet broke away, headed for the still bodies, and he didn't attempt to stop her, but Orion kept her in his line of vision as she crouched by the closest. Greta, he saw. The mom. Young, in her thirties. Wait...where was—

"Where's Lucy?" Violet stood, looked at Orion as he had the same thought.

"Who's that?" Bentley asked, glancing between the two of them.

"The oldest daughter," Orion answered, stalking over to the bodies, rage consuming him to see Leah so still, so small and fragile under the moonlight. He couldn't see any bruises on her small body, just the puncture marks on her wrist.

It didn't make it better, but it would be a small comfort if she hadn't suffered. He inhaled deeply, taking in all the scents, searching for the ones who'd done this. They would die.

"There was no one else here or in the house. I didn't realize anyone was missing, I'm sorry," Tyler said.

Orion squeezed his shoulder once, then headed for the house, still inhaling as he went. There were multiple scents here, the family's and a single vampire. The scent of vampire was faint, so faint he almost didn't pick up on it. But it was there, an undercurrent of darkness.

"This was only one vampire," he murmured. "And we need to find Lucy." He looked back at the others, didn't want to leave Violet.

Wouldn't leave her. Not with a killer vampire on the loose and her in such obvious pain. He also hated the thought of bringing her with him as he hunted down said killer.

"What?" she asked, stalking up to him. She'd changed into jeans and a sweater, but her hair was still in the braids and she looked so innocent and sweet staring up at him. He wanted to protect her from all the darkness and evil in the world.

"We need to find Lucy if she's been taken." That was the main priority. "I can't leave you here—"

"I'll ride on you again. It's fine."

Though it went against his instinct to bring her into danger, he nodded, then looked at the brothers. "I've got her scent."

"Her?" Bentley asked.

"A female vampire did this." He wasn't sure how he knew, but that primitive part of his brain he never ignored was certain. "She's old and dangerous. I can feel whatever imprint she left behind. And anyone who can kill a child…" He didn't finish. He didn't need to. "I'll take to the air, you follow below. Watch your backs. I don't think she's like the ones we've been killing." Those vampires had come into the territory so sure of themselves, a pack of wild animals intent on destruction.

They all nodded and he stood back, shucked his pants once again and called on the change, his dragon taking over in an instant. Prima and Mari would be arriving soon, and he had no doubt that Prima would come to the same conclusion as he had, would scent the predator vampire.

Orion couldn't waste any more time than they already had. If Lucy was still out there, they would find her and save her.

Violet gripped Orion's scales tight as he flew over the treetops, his body a shimmering mirage of color beneath her. He'd explained to her that he'd be in camouflage as he followed the scent of the vampire, but it was strange to see it up close.

On top of him like this, she could make out the outline of his large body, but it was still strange to be flying like this—or flying at all.

And she was still trying to comprehend that the Thatcher family had been murdered in their home. That Lucy was missing and potentially being held by some murderous vampire who'd killed a girl under ten.

But Violet wasn't going to lose her shit over this. Not now anyway. Oh, she'd cry later in the privacy of her shower or room, but Lucy was depending on them. And so was their community. And if Lucy was injured, she was damn sure going to help her.

Still, she could see the bodies of her friends in the back of her mind, especially Leah...

Whoever had done this needed to pay. As a doctor she'd never had violent urges or tendencies, but right now a slow rage was building inside her, starting from her toes and spreading to her head. The senselessness of it all, the quiet savagery of wiping out an entire family, was incomprehensible.

And it was easier to give in to the rage than— "Orion," she called out, hoping he heard her over the wind. "To the right. Ah, down below, through—"

Oh, he definitely heard because he banked right and dove downward. Violet had seen a flash of something, then realized it was someone walking.

Lucy! Her dark hair was pulled back by a sparkly headband, that was what had caught Violet's eye.

The girl looked upward as Orion breached the trees and let out a scream as he landed in front of her, staring in shock as Violet slid off him.

"Lucy, are you okay?" Violet hurried toward the teen as Orion shifted to human behind her.

"I...am I in trouble?" She stared wide-eyed at Violet. "Did my parents call you? I just went to see my boyfriend, I didn't think anyone would wake up—"

Oh God. "You're not in trouble." Violet's throat clenched as she realized that Lucy had just snuck out, she hadn't been taken. She was lucky to be alive, but... Oh, this sweet girl had lost so much. "I need to tell you something. It's about your family."

Lucy blinked, then a sort of dawning must have hit her because Violet saw something like understanding flicker in her eyes. "No."

"I'm so sorry to tell you this, but they..." Her voice broke, but Orion placed a steady hand on her shoulder, giving her the strength to continue. "Your parents and sister were killed earlier tonight."

Lucy stared at her in pure horror before a sob tore from her throat, long, wrenching cries of pain filling the night air.

CHAPTER SIXTEEN

Violet stepped into Cassandra's kitchen, Rose with her. Orion was off with the Bentley brothers trying to track the vampire who'd killed Lucy's family. "How is Lucy?" Violet asked as Cassandra motioned for them to sit at the island top.

John, another neighbor, and Emma, were already there waiting, coffee mugs in hand. It was early but she knew John was always up before sunrise so she wasn't surprised to see him here.

"Sleeping, last I heard," Cassandra said. "Sofia said she finally got her to doze after making her some tea. She's going to be grieving for a long while. And fighting guilt for not being there." Cassandra set two mugs in front of her and Rose—who'd sat next to John.

John was one of the grumpiest people she'd ever met, but he liked Rose. Probably because she was the vet for his animals and didn't take his shit.

"Yes she is," Violet murmured, accepting the coffee in appreciation. "I still…" She swallowed hard as the images shoved up in her mind. "I can see the three of them." She rubbed her eyes with her hands, as if that could banish them. "Jesus. Leah was so young." Blinking back the deluge of tears she knew were just waiting to be unleashed, she mentally shook herself.

"Orion will get whoever did it," John said into the quiet, his tone somber.

Which kind of surprised her, considering his normally surly attitude. "I think he will too." And the healer side of her, the doctor, didn't care that the vampire who'd committed those heinous murders would die. Because there would be no trial or second chance for something like that. "Right now Darius and his people have started to secure our territory more while Orion, Bentley and his brothers are out tracking. They said that unless the vampire is a bloodborn"—another concept that was new to her—"that she'll have gone to ground or returned to her territory. They said they'll know more when they see how far they can track her."

Which was something else totally foreign she was digesting. Orion and the other brothers could track based on scent, and had said that the killer's scent would be forever imprinted on their brains. So if they ran into her years later, they'd know it was her.

"Laurel's set everything up for tomorrow," Rose said into the quiet. "And I don't like changing the subject, but we need to. Because this all ties into what's happening. We need Orion to be our official Alpha and we need the community to understand why." She gave John a sharp look. "I expect you to talk to all your buddies—"

"I already have. They're on board." John might be grumpy, but before The Fall he'd been a long-standing member of the local Rotary Club. His main concern had always been the environment and sustainability.

Rose nodded once and Violet turned back to Cassandra. "I'm going to be visiting neighbors today to tell them more about tomorrow so they have a better understanding of what to expect. I know it's a lot to ask, but will you help?"

Cassandra made a scoffing sound. "Of course. And you know the others will too. We can break down different areas and cover more ground that way."

Violet had known Cassandra would pitch in, but now she needed to bring something else up. Something more delicate. She geared up for pushback as she said, "I kind of figured you'd say yes...and Orion wants all of us to have escorts today. I know you're independent and—"

"It's fine. See if you can get one of those hot older shifters to be my escort. I saw some of them and—"

"Jesus, Cassandra." John groaned, but his mouth was curved up slightly.

Cassandra just gave him a tart look, then looked back at Violet. "Whatever you guys need, we're in. What happened was a tragedy and we don't want to lose anyone else. I don't mind having an escort."

Violet nodded, and as she did, Rose slid off her stool and clapped John on the shoulder once. "Good, then. You'll be taking the northwest quadrant. There should be someone to escort you in an hour. They haven't arrived yet, but when they do I'll send one your way. I'll try to find someone you'll like." She laughed lightly, even with the heavy weight on her chest.

Violet was still reeling from what had happened to Lucy's family, but she still had to work, had to get out there and make sure the community was informed.

Because she refused to let this kind of tragedy happen again.

Laurel stalked back toward the house, beyond exhausted. Everyone had been out all day talking to all their neighbors, herself included. She'd organized everything at warp speed, then about fifteen of them had split up and gotten to work. She'd just left her wolf shifter escort when they'd reached the orchards—it still felt kind of strange to think about so many supernaturals in their territory now.

And she was trying desperately not to obsess over Cale, the dragon from yesterday. She hadn't seen him all day and she hated to admit that she'd been hoping to maybe be paired up with him. Which was stupid. He wasn't her type at all.

He was too charming. Too handsome. Far too big.

Aaaannnd he was currently walking *right* toward her, his long, muscular legs eating up the distance as he broke into a jog. Where the heck had he come from? It was like he'd appeared out of nowhere.

"Hey, Laurel." That affable smile firmly in place, Cale fell in step with her so casually. "Are you just returning home so late?" He frowned a little as he sniffed the air.

"Ah, yes. What's wrong? Why are you sniffing... Oh my God, are you smelling me?" Did he think she smelled bad or something? She'd been out all day, maybe she was ripe. The thought was beyond mortifying and she started to take a step away from him, even though he was walking next to her.

"Who were you with today?" he demanded instead of answering.

She blinked up at him, then snorted. "Excuse me, do you think I answer to you or something?"

He cleared his throat. "Ah, I meant...who were you with today?" His tone was slightly less accusatory, but it was still the same question.

"Why does it matter?"

"I smell...wolf. A supernatural. Are you seeing someone?"

She eyed him curiously as they reached the bottom step of her family's porch stairs. "Again, why does it matter?"

"Because I like you."

She blinked, surprised by his bluntness. *Oh.* "Would you care if I had been with someone today? A boyfriend?" Which seemed like an absurd word for some reason.

"Of course I would care." He growled low in his throat and leaned down slightly. "But it won't deter me, if that's what you're asking. I want you, Laurel, more than I've ever wanted anyone. Ever. You smell like sunshine and sweet, ripe peaches."

The growl that emanated from him sent a shock wave of hunger rippling through her.

And he was just putting it out there, no games—he wanted her. She'd never had a one-night stand before. Never been a risk-taker. Never broken any rules. Had always dated boring analyst types. Then the world had fallen apart and she'd run home, so damn thankful to be alive and that her sisters had made it too.

But she had regrets from her previous life. And in the end, the world had gone mad and there was nothing she could have done to stop it. Certainly not living safely. As she looked into Cale's vivid, beautiful pale green eyes, she knew without a doubt that she was taking a risk right now. Or hell, maybe it wasn't one—he seemed like a sure bet and he'd be returning to New Orleans soon enough.

She was going to force herself to be brave and just ask for what she wanted. Especially since her sisters weren't home yet and wouldn't be for some time. "I'm going to take a shower, and when I get out, I would like to have sex with you. I've never had a one-night stand and I would like to have one now. With you." Did she care that they hadn't kissed yet? Nope. Something told her this man would be incredible with his hands and mouth. And hopefully his cock. "Does that sound like a good plan to you?"

Now he was the one to blink, his mouth falling open ever so slightly before he moved supernaturally fast, reaching out and scooping her up in his arms. So, apparently his answer was yes.

She let out a slight yelp, but he was inside the house and up the stairs before she'd had a chance to really process that yep, this was totally happening. And she was so ready for it. Ready to just not think and do what felt good.

Heat rushed through her as he barreled through her bedroom door like a dragon possessed.

"How'd you know where my room was?" she asked, a little breathlessly because this was happening so quickly, even if she'd been the one to initiate it.

"Smells like you," he growled as he kicked it shut behind her then set her down on her feet, his movements a little slower and gentler. "And anytime you want to stop, we stop," he murmured, cupping her cheek with his big hand, staring down at her as if she was the only person who existed.

And talk about a heady sensation, to be the focus of such intensity... Her nipples beaded tight against her bra cups and she wished she had some sort of magic right now to just will her clothes away.

"I should be a gentleman and—"

"I don't want a gentleman." She grabbed the front of his shirt, intending to pull him to her, but he took over with no hesitation, pulling her flush against his hard body.

He crushed his mouth to hers, his tongue teasing against hers, invading and taking over in the best way possible.

As he devoured her mouth, she refused to second-guess herself, even if this almost felt like an out-of-body experience. Except she was going to remember all of this, especially the feel of his thick length pressing against her. Hoooly shit, was that real?

Feeling bold and more turned on by the second as he teased his tongue against hers, his strokes demanding and sensual, she reached between them and ran her palm over his covered erection. Yep, as big as it felt against her. Maybe bigger.

Heat rolled through her as she thought about how he would feel pushing inside her.

He sucked in a breath at her touch and pulled his hips back slightly. "Sunshine, you've gotta keep your hands to yourself," he rasped out.

Oh no, that wasn't happening. She wrapped her fingers around him through the material of his pants and he sucked in another breath before he grinned, slow and wicked.

Grasping her wrist, he guided her hand away from him even as he backed her up against the bed. "I like that you don't listen to me," he murmured. "But I might need to restrain you."

That sounded far, far too hot for words. She'd never been tied up or anything but the idea of him restraining her had another punch of heat curling through her.

"I need a shower first," she protested when she realized that he meant right now.

But he simply pinned her to the bed, caging her in with his big body. "I want to make you come first. You smell amazing. Let me taste you." There was a sort of desperation to his words, mirroring the way she felt right now.

Ooooh. Yes, please. And the last four words out of his gorgeous mouth sent a scorching punch of fire through her.

"Oh, you like the thought of that, don't you?" he murmured, nipping her bottom lip with his teeth.

She swallowed hard, nodded.

"Say it. No one's home, no one will hear you. Tell me you want me to make you come."

"I want you to make me come," she whispered. She couldn't believe she was being so vulnerable with a virtual stranger but she was grabbing onto life with both hands tonight. And the way he looked at her, as if she hung the moon, was a heady aphrodisiac. "And I want to make *you* come."

He closed his eyes, a groan tearing from him as he laid his forehead against hers and dragged in a breath. And that was when she realized he was kind of glowing. She blinked, staring at the blue lighting up the room. Maybe it was a dragon thing?

They hadn't turned on the lights in her room and he was *definitely* glowing, sort of a bluish haze. Not too strong, but the man was illuminating the entire room. She stared in surprise, and when he opened his again, he seemed to realize she was staring in shock this time.

"It's a dragon thing," he murmured, before he reached for the button of her jeans, and dragged them down her legs. "Just ignore it."

Then he shredded her panties—

"Hey, no destroying clothes," she hurried out, quickly shucking her shirt and bra.

And he just stared at her as she sat on the bed, her feminine things surrounding them, him very much out of place in her space, yet...also perfect.

He knelt down on the edge of the bed, hovering over her like a predator who wanted to devour her. "I'll tie you up later, but for now..." With his big, callused hands, he spread her legs, pushing insistently against her inner thighs as he lowered his head between her legs.

Ribbons of heat curled through her as he inhaled then shuddered as if she was the sweetest thing ever.

She stared down at him, her nipples hard points that were almost painful now, but she was so wet and turned on and he was just—

He swiped his tongue up the length of her folds and she jerked off the bed, her hips rolling up hard at the shock of sensation.

He slid one big hand up and palmed her abdomen, holding her in place as he continued teasing her folds, very carefully avoiding her clit, as if he knew exactly how crazy he was making her. Because of course he did, this male with the wicked mouth and knowing smile. He knew what he was doing.

She tried to lift her hips but he held firm, maddeningly keeping her in place with an impressive show of strength. The lack of control was oddly hot and sent more heat curling through her. "I need more."

He growled against her clit, the reverberation sending a little shock wave through her, but then he flicked his tongue against her clit with increased pressure and she jolted again.

As he sucked on her clit, increasing the pressure of his tongue against her sensitive nerves, she could feel the impending orgasm, the building tension in her core as he drove her crazy.

She couldn't believe this male who she barely knew had her so turned on, so close to the edge of climax already. And this felt like an appetizer to the rest of the night—she hoped there was more after this, hoped he joined her in the shower. If she was having a one-night stand, she wanted it to be all night long.

She held on to his head as he continued to tease her clit, the pressure intense when he sucked again, harder than before. That pushed her over the edge, her orgasm surging through her, her inner walls clenching around nothing.

Even as pleasure rolled through her, as she rode out the wave, she wanted to be filled by him, to feel that thick erection pushing inside her and easing that ache.

As if he'd read her mind, he raised his head, his expression primal as he looked up at her.

Her breathing was shallow as she stared down at him, her body spent but also keyed up, ready for more of him. "Join me in the shower?"

In response, he leaned back and stood, six feet plus whatever of pure, powerful male as he slowly lifted his shirt from his body.

It was like he was moving in slow motion as he eased the cotton off his body, up, up, and over his head. As he tossed it to the ground, she sat up, her gaze tracking every inch of the muscular planes and striations of his chest and abs. And arms! God, he might as well be carved from granite. She wasn't sure where to look, wanted to memorize every bare inch of him.

When he shucked his pants, she forgot to breathe as she stared at what was between his legs. Blinked a couple times.

"Uh...maybe I'll just shower by myself," she said on a laugh as she slid from the bed. "Because that's not fitting in me."

He laughed, the easy sound sending another rush of heat through her. So apparently everything he did got her hot.

"Oh, I'll fit," he murmured, scooping her up again, his words a delicious promise as he stalked toward the door.

"Are you planning on carrying me everywhere?"

"I like the feel of you in my arms," he said as he stepped into her little bathroom and flipped the light on. That bluish glow was still emanating off him, lighting the way so she wasn't sure why he bothered.

And that was when she realized... "The shower might be too small for us to, uh...do anything."

He shrugged and pulled the curtain back, the hooks making a jingling sound. "We can still shower together," he said as he turned on the water.

They were on a well system, something she was grateful for.

Once steam started billowing out, he stepped in first, then pulled her with him. And sure enough, he was too broad to fit in the shower comfortably. Her room and bathroom were in the loft area of the house and the roof was at an angle, which had never been a problem since she was five foot five.

None of that seemed to matter as the water rolled down around them. She wrapped her arms around his waist and laid her head on his chest, his broad shoulders blocking most of the deluge, even if his head was taller than the showerhead. "I can't believe we're doing this and I don't even know anything about you." You know, other than he was built like a god.

"I'm part of the Cerrach clan, a couple thousand years old, I like a very pretty blonde human and my favorite color is now gray."

Gray? It took her a moment to realize he meant that because of her eyes, and butterflies launched inside her. She looked up at him, smiled softly. "That's a good line."

"Not a line, sweet Sunshine," he murmured as he ran his hands all over her, up and down her back, over her ass, between her legs…

She sucked in a swift breath as he cupped her mound, still sensitive from her recent orgasm.

Since he was rock-hard, his erection thick between them, she reached between their bodies, wanting to touch him as intimately as he'd touched her. And she wanted to bring him as much pleasure, to watch him lose control.

As she wrapped her fingers around his thick length, his eyes changed, flickering once to his dragon, then back.

So she stroked him soft at first, then harder as he sucked in another harsh breath. She wanted to know what he liked too. As she stroked him, he cupped one of her breasts, lazily strumming his thumb against her hard nipple. The sensation almost overloaded her, but she continued working his cock, watching the way his eyes changed, his rapid intake of breath as she squeezed harder. So he definitely liked it a little rougher.

And when she ran her thumb over the thick crown of his cock he shut his eyes completely and groaned, the sound wrapping around her like a lover's caress.

Ridiculously turned on and feeling more powerful than she ever had, she went down on her knees without warning.

"Oh Sunshine," he growled as she took him in her mouth, sucking him deep.

Barely able to move, he slightly shifted on his feet as a low growl rumbled from him. "It's not going to take me long, darlin', but I rebound fast." The last part was a dark promise.

One she hoped he fulfilled as she cupped his balls, massaged them.

Aaaaand that set him off. He slammed his hand against the wall of the shower and cursed again. "I'm about to come.."

She wasn't sure if he was trying to warn her so she could move, but no way was that happening. Tonight was all about pleasure for the two of them, of making the most of their time together. That was what one-night stands were about, right?

She sucked him deep, could feel the moment before he was about to let go. When he did, she didn't move, wanting to taste all of him as he came in hard, shuddering strokes.

And when she stood and looked into his lust-hazed green eyes, she'd never felt more powerful or alive in her life.

He tugged her close so that her nipples brushed against his hard body, the stimulation sending little waves of need pulsing through her. Then he surprised her by grabbing a bottle of shampoo. "You are a goddess," he murmured. "Thank you."

She didn't know how to respond so she turned around as he started working his fingers through her hair. And was surprised by how normal this felt, to be letting Cale wash her hair as if he'd done it before multiple times.

As he massaged her scalp, she let out a little moan and—yep, he was getting hard again, his cock right against her back as he continued working his fingers down to the ends. He hadn't been kidding about rebounding fast.

And in that moment she wondered what she'd been thinking. Because one night wasn't going to be nearly enough.

CHAPTER SEVENTEEN

Curled on her side, Laurel opened her eyes as a big, warm hand slid down her abdomen, slowly, before cupping her mound. And the man who the hand belonged to was plastered up against her, his erection heavy against her back.

She'd heard him get up about fifteen minutes ago, but had thought he might have left. Instead he'd slipped back into bed and...she was ready for him again. Which shouldn't be possible after the night they'd had.

She'd heard her sisters come in eventually but thankfully no one had bothered her—though she had locked her door just to be safe.

Wordlessly, he nipped her earlobe as he started strumming her clit, and she sucked in a breath.

"You've gotta be quiet," he murmured, pressing down on her lobe. "Got a full house this morning."

She let out a whimpering sound when he gently pinched her clit. He'd learned her body quickly last night, had given her the kind of pleasure she'd only read about. The male had a ridiculous sex drive and this new Laurel was here for it.

Telling him what she wanted, she lifted her left leg slightly, the angle a little odd, but then he pulled his hand back and pushed it between her legs from behind. Yep, he understood what she was asking for. She shuddered as he slid a finger, then two inside her. When she'd woken up and felt his reaction, she'd gotten wet instantly, her body apparently attuned to his already.

Or what his could *do* to hers. Oh God, it was like someone else had taken over her body.

Moaning softly, she let her head fall back against his chest, could feel the steady beat of his heart against her back. "I want more than your fingers," she whispered. It was so hard to be quiet with him.

He let out a low growling sound and nipped at her ear again, but withdrew his fingers. And as he slid his cock inside her, she sucked in a sharp breath.

It wasn't that she'd forgotten how big he was—she was still tender between her legs—but it was a shock nonetheless. "It's not going to take me long." She kept her voice low as her inner walls clenched around him, savoring the now familiar feel of his thickness inside her.

Maybe they could have more than one night after this?

Oh God, she sounded like an addict, even to herself. *No.* One night was it, and this morning was still technically part of last night. So it didn't count.

When he pulled back, her inner walls automatically tightened, wanting him deep again.

"Goddess, you take me so good," he growled against her ear, his words setting off a burst of need inside her.

She reached between her legs but he took over, batting her hand away as he slid inside her again.

He started massaging her clit as he said, "That's my pretty pussy."

And she almost combusted. Her nipples tightened even more at his words and the feel of him still thrusting inside her. A moan was building inside her so she turned her head into the pillow, bit down on it so she wouldn't cry out. She couldn't hear anyone moving around downstairs but that didn't mean they weren't awake and might hear her if she didn't stay quiet.

"Hell yeah, sweetheart, come for me, you're so close." His words were a dark whisper against her ear, a sensual promise of all he could give her.

And as he put more pressure on her clit, she let go, that tension building inside her releasing in a sharp, toe-curling climax.

She bucked back against him, meeting him stroke for stroke as he thrust into her. The angle might be slightly awkward, but she didn't care because right now it felt amazing.

"Goddess," he growled out, his thrusts growing wilder as he pounded into her.

But suddenly he pulled out, coming all over her back and ass. Then he surprised her by rubbing his come into her. Was that a shifter thing? Whatever it was, it was hot.

"I want my scent all over you. Don't wash it off," he demanded as if he'd read her mind.

And she really, really shouldn't like his demanding tone so much, especially since this was just a one-night thing, but found herself nodding drowsily. "Okay."

He rolled her over, took her mouth hard, as if he was actually claiming her, his tongue teasing hers, his big body pinning her in place. And she felt as if she was holding on for dear life as he kept her pinned against the bed.

Finally he leaned back, breathing hard as he stared down at her. "I hate that I've gotta get back this morning."

"It's fine. I've got to get up anyway. I've got a ton to do today." Because today was the big community meeting and she was organizing everything. And she didn't want their goodbye to be awkward. She wanted to end her one-night stand easily, with no fuss.

Sighing, he kissed her again and grabbed his clothes from the ground, taking his time as he slipped them back on.

It took all the self-control she had not to ask for one more round, but she had to keep it together. This had been *one* night. They'd never talked about anything else. Well, that wasn't true. They'd talked last night and she'd learned about his family—his clan—his current home, and some other random things that she'd soaked up. But she'd made it clear that this was one night from the start and he'd been on board with it.

Except now she wanted more. Well, she couldn't change the rules, could she.

Once he was dressed he kissed her again, this time softer, sweeter, before he pulled back with a groan. "Today can't go by fast enough," he murmured.

She laughed lightly and forced herself to get out of bed as he quietly slipped out of her room. A sense of sadness invaded her, but she tried to ignore it. She couldn't be all emotional after she'd gotten exactly what she wanted.

Once he was gone, she grabbed her robe and slid it on, her breasts overly sensitive from his kisses. In fact, she was tender everywhere, it seemed. But totally worth it. Even if the strangest sense of longing had invaded her as she remembered all his kisses, touches.

Ugh, whatever. She was just all up in her head because it had been an eternity since she'd had good sex. And never sex like that.

After brushing her teeth, she headed downstairs and found her three sisters at the kitchen table, Orion leaning against the countertop by the refrigerator.

"Soooo," Rose drawled, a grin on her face. She was the only one not in her pajamas, but work-worn jeans and a button-down flannel. Because of course she was. She'd probably already fed her horse and done ten other things before the rest of them had managed to get out of bed. "We just saw tall, dark and delicious sneaking out the front door."

"He wasn't sneaking," Mari murmured, a grin on her face. "He seemed quite proud of himself. Even saluted us as he left."

"He *should* be proud of himself after last night," she said, the words out of her mouth before she could think about censoring them. "And this morning."

Violet let out a snort-laugh, nearly spilling her coffee, and Orion looked...soooo uncomfortable. He'd no doubt known Cale was here anyway, what with his dragon senses, but right about now he looked like a dragon caught in headlights. He wanted to be anywhere but where this conversation was happening. Which was sort of hilarious.

"I have...things to do." He shot Violet a look of, yep, horror, then basically ran from the room, Bowie hot on his heels, his little nails making clicking sounds on the hardwood floor as he ran after his best friend.

Which just made Laurel laugh. "Apparently Orion is a prude?"

Her sisters all giggled, but Violet shook her head through her laughter. "I think he's fighting that big brother instinct right now. So...how was it with a dragon?" she whispered. "Anything weird or..."

She lifted her eyebrows and Laurel realized all of her sisters were watching her, waiting for an answer. She wondered if Violet wanted to know because her big sister was totally obsessed with Orion, or if she was just curious.

Laurel had never had any sex worth talking about, and while she didn't want to talk about last night in detail... "He has a lot of stamina. A ridiculous amount, in fact. Best one-night stand ever." She wasn't going to get technical and point out that it was her only one.

"One-night stand, my ass. He'll definitely be coming back for more," Rose said around a yawn as she stood. "And I've got a stop to make before heading out. But I'll see you all at the high school?"

Everyone nodded and Laurel started pouring herself a cup of coffee. They'd decided to use the high school football field as the meeting place for the community. It was big enough and everyone knew where it was.

And Laurel needed to keep her head on straight and not obsess about last night because she had work to do. Even if she was more than a little hopeful that maybe they could turn one night into just a couple more. But nothing more.

She wasn't going to do something stupid and fall for a dragon who was heading back to New Orleans soon.

CHAPTER EIGHTEEN

"Do you know what you're going to say to everyone?" Violet asked Orion as they waited on the edge of the ten-yard line of the high school's football field as Laurel finished setting up the speaker system.

The field was normally unused as far as anything organized, but parents with young kids had been bringing their families here on and off over the last year for different sports and games. Right now most of the community was up in the stands, though some had brought fold-out or camp-style chairs and were sitting where the players normally sat as everyone waited for Orion and her to address them formally.

"I don't know what to say. Humans are different than shifters. And after yesterday..." He shook his head, clearly frustrated with himself.

Violet placed a gentle hand on his forearm and left it there, wishing that they were more than friends. His muscles slightly flexed under her touch, unconsciously, she thought, and she couldn't stop the slight stroke over his arm. She wanted to comfort him, to be everything for him. "You tracked that vampire all day."

"And I have nothing to show for it." It was clear he was beating himself up over it. "And I still don't know why those wolves were in our woods. Something's brewing, I can feel it," he said, quiet enough for her ears only. "On the horizon. Dark and nasty and…" His jaw was clenched tight as he eyed the community. Then he looked down at her, his expression more open than it had ever been. "What if I can't protect everyone?" The words were so low she almost didn't hear them.

There was such a raw vulnerability in his expression, in his eyes. She moved on instinct and turned into him, wrapping her arms around him tight. She'd never seen him anything close to worried or unsure until now.

He was stiff for only a moment, then he hugged her back, setting his chin on her head as he basically caged her in with the best hug ever. She melted into him, wished that this was more than a hug of comfort, friendship. She wanted him with an intensity she'd never thought possible. Her parents had been ridiculously in love, but she hadn't thought that kind of thing would exist for her. Especially not in this new world. Then Orion had walked into her life and she was a goner.

"I've got your back no matter what," she murmured into his chest.

"And I have yours. Always."

She felt those words right to her core and had to cage the butterflies inside her, lock them down as he stepped back and headed out to the fifty-yard line, all the muscles in his body pulled tight.

Laurel had found a microphone for them to use and had hooked it up to the speaker system. Orion nodded once at her as he reached the middle of the field, and as he did it was like he'd unleashed something in the crowd.

Everyone started talking at once, shouting questions. *What the hell?* Violet glanced at Mari and Cassandra, as well as the others who were waiting with her at the end zone.

But Orion held up a hand, didn't even say a word into the microphone, and everyone immediately silenced. His Alpha nature was so obvious she couldn't believe she hadn't noticed it fully before. She'd known he was a leader, the type of person others intrinsically listened to, but he was in his element now. And it was on full display as he faced everyone.

"By now you all know why you're here. I don't have much to say other than I'm grateful for the home your community has given me over the last year." He glanced in Violet's direction as he spoke, then looked back out at everyone.

She knew in that moment that if the community tried to drive him out, or if he decided to leave, she'd go with him. And *that* shook her to her very core. She would go anywhere that dragon went.

He continued. "I know some of these changes will be a shock to you, but as Alpha I'll do whatever it takes to keep this community safe. I care about this place and everyone in it."

"What do you want in exchange for your protection?" someone shouted from near the front.

Violet zeroed in on the man, vaguely recognized a drunk asshole she sometimes had to deal with when he injured himself after drinking his homemade moonshine. Feeling her hackles raise, she started across the field, wanting to back Orion up in a more figurative sense than anything and give this asshole a piece of her mind. Because she *would* have Orion's back.

Orion gave the guy a look she could only describe as dismissive and disdainful at the same time. Then he spoke clearly into the microphone, his deep voice carrying. "I've never asked for anything since settling here and that's not changing. And I would never ask for blind loyalty. I expect you all to treat your neighbors with respect, the way you would like to be treated. To never put anyone in danger—and to always come to me with a problem. As Alpha, it's my job to keep you all safe. And right now our territory is under siege from vampires. It's been happening for months and I, along with a few others, have been keeping you safe from them—and let me spell out what that means. I'm killing vampires. Anyone who means harm to this territory will die. Simple as that. I want you all to be crystal clear on what you're getting with me as an Alpha. I'm not a human and I don't think like one. I will not treat enemies or threats kindly. They won't get trials. If they hurt my people, they're done. *This* is me." He handed Violet the microphone as she reached him, and to her surprise he stripped off his shirt.

Ooooh, shit. He was going to shift. She grabbed Laurel's arm and tugged her back out of the way.

His pants went next and she totally stared at his sculpted ass, but then he shifted in a bright blast of magic and color. And...he was still the most beautiful thing she'd ever seen. Ever could have imagined on this planet or any other. He'd stepped right out of a fantasy fairy tale but he wasn't the villainous dragon. She wasn't sure he was the hero either. He was just the male she'd completely, utterly fallen for. The one who'd done nothing but protect her, her sisters and the community she cared about.

There were no clouds in the sky today so his blue and purple wings glittered like jewels, shifting under the sunlight as he spread them wide for all to see. Part of her that she was surprised even existed was *rabidly* jealous that others got to see him this way when she thought of him as hers. Which was stupid, of course. He didn't belong to her, but that didn't stop her from wanting to claim him for the world to see. But he was Alpha to his bones; if he wanted her, he'd have made a move. Made it clear. They saw each other every day and lived under the same roof.

Gasps erupted from the crowd, but there were no cries of alarm or outrage. As soon as the gasps died down, there was utter silence.

Violet wasn't sure what it meant, but she held the microphone up to her mouth and started talking, completely disregarding the speech she'd prepared earlier. "I would also like to make it clear that I have Orion's back. And I'm speaking for my entire family because all of us live with him and love him. He's one of us and he's one of you, not some power-hungry jackass who made promises to fix our roads then spent the money on a private jet," she tossed out, referencing one of their former senators. "Or someone who promised our teachers raises, then funneled the money into some bullshit program instead.

"Orion has done nothing but keep us safe this whole time without wanting anything in return, and he didn't even tell us about his protection. He's not doing it for glory or whatever, but because he cares. And I'm not going to try to convince you that he's right as the Alpha of our territory. You either know him and me by now or you don't. And neither of us would ever do anything to harm this place. The threat against us is real, as we all know after last night, and he's the dragon we want by our side as we protect our community."

She let her arm drop, lowering the microphone to her side, and as she did Orion shifted back to human again. Even though she was the queen of the perverts, she didn't stare at him. Okay, she looked a little. Because whew. She was only human. And she really hated that everyone else was getting to see him in all his naked glory. Because the man was beyond stunning.

After he dressed, she grabbed his hand in a show of solidarity—and okay, she just wanted to touch him, claim him in front of the others so anyone looking could just back the hell off—and they headed to the end zone as Laurel started directing everyone to the gymnasium to "cast your votes."

Somehow her sister had set up a voting system similar to what the school had done on prom night for the king and queen, and now they would just have to wait for the results to be counted. Violet didn't let go of his hand as they reached the others, needing Orion to ground her. And okay, she was feeling out of sorts after everyone had just seen him naked. Out of sorts, aka possessive as hell.

When he let go of her hand, disappointment punched through her, but almost immediately he wrapped an arm around her as they reached the end zone and pulled her close. She wondered if he was...publicly claiming her? Or if this was just a friendship thing? And then she wanted to groan at all this internal insecurity.

She leaned into him, wrapping her own arm around his waist and soaking up his strength and presence. And thought that maybe...she could make a move on him as soon as they were alone again. Even if the thought terrified her.

Okay, it was the rejection part that terrified her. Because if he rejected her, it would carve out part of her heart forever.

LAUREL HELD UP ANOTHER PAPER, unfolded it and gave a half smile as she spoke into the microphone. "This voter added a note: 'Orion or Violet, don't care who's in charge as long as it's one of them,'" she said. Then she held up another. "Orion."

And on and on. So far it was a combination of Orion, or Orion and Violet.

She'd kept the voting stations simple, mirroring it after her senior prom, with people writing in their votes, dropping them in boxes, and now she was simply reading them out as a couple other volunteers kept a tally. Crude, but it was working.

So far Orion had like four hundred votes or something. There were a couple drawings with no name listed. And about fifty votes for Orion and Violet, something Laurel was sure would embarrass her sister.

For all Violet did, she didn't like to be in the spotlight. So when she'd grabbed that microphone today, Laurel had been so proud of her sister. Violet always stood up for people, albeit quietly more often than not, but she used her voice when it mattered. Always had.

Once everything was tallied up, Laurel held up the sheet and hid her smile to see five hundred and fifty-six votes for Orion. Almost all the voting adults had been registered. Orion had won by a ridiculous landslide.

The gym was crowded by now, people getting restless in the bleachers and some having already stepped outside to get fresh air. She picked up the microphone. "We have five hundred and fifty-six votes for Orion, and out of those, a hundred and nineteen also have Violet's name. And I'd like to give a special thanks to the jackass who drew multiple pictures of penises instead of actually voting. You're very talented, and if you ever put on an art show make sure to invite me," she said dryly.

Which made everyone laugh, and then a little cheer went up, she assumed because Orion and Violet had just stepped inside, and...were holding hands.

Ooooh, Laurel hoped they'd both decided to stop acting like ostriches and get together already.

She grinned at the two of them and handed the microphone to Orion, who took it with a brief nod. Their new Alpha.

"Thank you for putting your trust in me. Anyone who has military experience, experience with security, or experience with killing vampires, meet me by the end zone. I want to talk about securing our territory from vampires specifically." He handed the microphone to Violet, looked as if he wanted to say more, but then stalked out of the gym with a few men and women trailing after him.

"And if anyone has any medical issues they'd like to talk to me about or need help with anything, I've set up a tent in the parking lot. I'll be here the rest of the afternoon if you don't want to wait for our next check-in." Smiling, she handed the microphone to Laurel, then frowned. "What's that look?"

"What look?" Laurel asked.

"You're being weird."

"Just wondering if you and Orion are like..." She waggled her eyebrows.

But Violet just gave her a wide-eyed look and was saved when Beau strolled up, a grin on his face. "So you like my drawings?"

"Oh my God, I knew it was you!" Laurel cried. They'd gone to high school together, and while he was a little ridiculous, she always found herself smiling around him. Probably because he owned who he was. A hot weirdo. "I see you running away," she called out to Violet, who'd disappeared into the crowd.

"Those were self-portraits." Beau was still grinning, his smile toothpaste commercial white, with only one bottom tooth slightly crooked. And for some reason it made him even more handsome. He'd certainly charmed all the girls back in high school. Well, most of them. Not her.

"What is the matter with you?" she asked.

He shrugged and helped her as she started to fold up the table she'd been using to take the votes. "I ask myself that all the time. So does my mama. Who is thoroughly annoyed about the penis thing. But I knew Orion would win and I knew the drawings would make you smile."

She snickered slightly, ninety-nine percent sure he wasn't flirting with her. He'd always been like this. "You are incorrigible."

"True."

"Why aren't you out with Orion? He asked for anyone who had military experience."

Beau gave her that charming grin that had made far too many women fall for him. "I'm going, but wanted to talk to you first."

"About what?"

"Yeah, about what?" Suddenly Cale was there, large and imposing, though Beau was just about as big as him.

Butterflies launched inside her at the sight of the big male. She hadn't expected to see him today, or maybe anytime soon.

Beau's smile didn't dim a watt, which meant he probably had even less sense than she'd always thought. "About to ask out this beautiful woman."

"If you want to keep that head attached to your body, I suggest you leave now."

Laurel blinked up at Cale.

"I don't think that's up to you," Beau said, still grinning, as if he *wanted* to have his head detached from his body.

Oh. My. God. Before she could respond, however, Daisy—Beau's mother—strode up, and she had the same smile as her not-long-for-this-world son. It was like the woman got more beautiful with age. She had big blonde curls piled on her head and big...assets. Everyone called her Dolly Parton's look-alike more often than not.

"Hey, hon," Daisy said before pulling Laurel into a hug. "I'm sorry for my son. I would say I raised him better, but sometimes I wonder. And who are you?" She grinned up at Cale, who managed to tear his death glare from Beau.

"Name's Cale, ma'am. I'm relocating to this territory."

Wait...*what!* Laurel thought he was only here temporarily. *Oooh. No.* They were only supposed to have a fling!

"Oh, that's great. Are you a wolf like the broody brothers? Or no, I'm guessing you're a dragon because you're as big as that Orion." She patted his arm gently.

Laurel didn't think they were supposed to ask, but Cale just grinned, all politeness for Daisy. Though if he'd been rude to the five-foot-nothing woman, Laurel would have had words with him. "I am a dragon, ma'am."

"Well I hope to see you in your other form soon. Orion sure put on a show earlier." And Daisy seemed absolutely thrilled by it. "I'm going to take my grown-ass son with me now, so if you don't mind, please don't kill him anytime soon. He's the only one I've got."

"I'll try not to." Cale's tone was dry, shooting Beau a warning look.

"That offer for a date still stands," Beau called out as his mom grabbed his arm, then he actually had the balls to wink at Cale.

"Did you two used to date?" Cale asked as he finally turned to Laurel.

She ignored his question. "You're staying here? I thought you were going back to New Orleans?"

He blinked in surprise. "You thought I was leaving?"

"Uh, yeah," she whispered, glancing around the half-full gym. A lot of people had milled outside, but there were still little groups of people talking and catching up. "It's why…" She cleared her throat and tried to ignore the flush of heat that hit her cheeks.

"Why what?" His voice dropped an octave, his expression saying that he could eat her up right here, right now.

"You know exactly what."

His eyes seemed to glow, and she felt herself being mesmerized all over again. This male had a powerful and dangerous effect on her. "You're not getting rid of me that easily."

"But you said you wanted one night," she whispered, mostly sure no one could hear them.

"No, *you* said that. I never said any such thing about one night. So, maybe I stop by your house later tonight? I would like to take you flying."

She blinked. "Like…on your back? As a dragon?"

He nodded, watching her carefully, his green eyes full of heat and something else she couldn't quite define. Possessiveness.

"I…would like to." Talk about the chance of a lifetime. "But that doesn't change anything. We agreed to one night." Yeah, she'd told herself that she was a "new Laurel" but the truth was she was still the control freak she'd always been. Even after a wild night of nonstop sex. And Cale made her feel completely, utterly out of control.

"Again, I never agreed to that." He leaned down close. "Are you saying you don't want more? Just one more night? Maybe two?"

Heat curled through her as images from just that morning flashed in her mind. Of the sensual, visceral memory of the way he'd made her come so easily. "Fine. A couple more nights, but then that's it," she whispered, wondering if she was lying to herself. Nope, not wondering. She was definitely lying.

He leaned close enough that his mouth was only inches from hers. "I won't agree to that, but we can discuss it in a couple days. I like you, Sunshine, and I know you like me too. I know you like my mouth on you, because all you could say last night was 'Cale, harder, faster. Cale, again, again—'"

She slapped a hand over his mouth as her entire body heated up. "Stop it," she whispered.

He gently pulled her hand away. "Why? I can smell how much you want me."

Oh, that was so embarrassing. And also kind of weird. "You can...smell me?"

"Yep. And I can smell that you didn't wash me off either. I want to eat you right now—"

She did the only thing that could possibly shut him up. She grabbed the front of his shirt and kissed him hard.

Of course he took over in an instant, and when he finally pulled back she remembered that they were in a gym with people. *Oops.* Dammit, he made her forget everything but him and what he did to her.

"I'll see you around six tonight," he murmured against her mouth.

She wasn't sure if she responded or just stared at his perfect, tight ass as he walked away. What the hell had just happened? He was supposed to be one night only. Fun. Wild. She'd wanted to break out of her shell, and now... Well, apparently she had a date with a dragon.

A tall, bossy one who looked far better without his clothes on.

Screw it, she wasn't going to get caught up in her head over this. She was going to enjoy whatever was between them until it ended. Because this was the new Laurel, the risk-taker.

Okay, that was a lie. She was never going to be a wild risk-taker. But she could have fun for a while. And if she got her heart broken...she'd deal with it later.

CHAPTER NINETEEN

Today had been a good day. Unexpectedly so, Orion thought as he walked along the well-worn path with Prima and Cale. He'd flown with them to just outside the New Orleans encampment and planned to offer to let Darius and his people move their tents onto his territory tomorrow.

It was strange to acknowledge that he had a new territory to protect, but deep in his bones it felt right. Just as it felt when he'd run another territory far up in a mountainous area when humans had known of his kind. But that time was long past. So long ago that the topography of the earth had been different, and the language he'd once spoken was nonexistent.

"I'm going to let Darius know I won't be returning with them," Prima said. "At least not for a while. I might return to grab some things but...I don't have much anyway."

"I'm glad you're staying," Orion murmured, grateful for his friend's presence. He needed someone he could depend on as he got things running properly. And there was so much to do.

"I'm courting Laurel," Cale cut in as they reached the edge of the encampment.

"No shit, Sherlock," Prima murmured. "I saw the way you threatened that human male today. Not that he seemed the least bit intimidated by you." Her tone held approval.

"Who is this Sherlock?" Orion asked. He'd heard the phrase before from Mari, but hadn't wanted to ask what it meant and give away that he wasn't human.

Prima shrugged. "I do not know. Just a phrase I've heard the humans use."

Cale just snickered, but said, "Once my courting is complete, do you wish for me to find another residence with my future mate? Or shall I live in the same house as you and her sisters?"

Orion shot the ancient dragon a look. "Do not count your chickens before they hatch." Another human phrase he'd heard, one that made more sense than most.

Cale lifted a shoulder, not concerned. "Just let me know later because we will be mated. Actually I'll just ask her what she wants," he said more to himself.

The one thing Orion had forgotten about being an Alpha, *officially*, was all the extra shit he'd have to deal with. Like obsessive dragons. And it was a headache on a good day. "If she rejects your claim, you'll walk away."

Cale's smile faded as he stared at Orion, his expression hard. "I would never force anyone, much less my sunshine human. If she rejects me, I will respect it."

"If you don't, I'll take your head off myself," Prima added jovially.

"I would take my own head off if I hurt her."

"How would you even do that?" Prima asked.

"I would fashion a scythe of sorts out of the strongest material, forged in my dragon fire and..."

Feeling a headache coming on, Orion walked away from their inane conversation when he spotted Darius stepping out of one of the tents.

The wolf smiled at him, waited as Orion approached. "Congratulations are in order. I've heard the good news."

"Thank you. You may tell your Alpha that I officially accept his offer of allyship. And if your people would like, you may move deeper in our territory today. There is a good spot near where we had the gathering the other night. Plenty of flat land and shade."

Darius held his fisted hand over his chest as he said, "You honor us with your trust."

"You've already shown you're honorable. Thank you for your help in tightening our security after the vampire attack."

"Any leads on the killer?"

"No. I tracked her about two hundred miles southwest, then lost the scent completely."

"It's in the direction of the Opelousas territory."

"I know." And he would be covertly infiltrating that vampire territory soon. But he needed to shore up his defenses here first. Now that he had Prima and Cale as well as his wolves, he felt more secure in leaving the territory for a recon mission of this magnitude. He wouldn't tell Darius that, however. "I would like to speak with your Alpha in person when he is available." Because there were certain things only Alphas could talk about with each other. And he wouldn't do it over a phone, the strange human technology he wasn't certain he cared for.

"Of course. He's almost done with his current meetings and I know he wishes to meet with you as well. Especially after Prima has spoken so highly of you."

"Then I look forward to his arrival." Orion liked Darius but wanted to get all this over with so he could return to Violet. He'd been away from her all day, far too long for his liking.

She'd been seeing patients and likely just catching up with friends in the community who'd stopped by the medical tent she'd set up. But he knew she'd be tired and he wanted to feed her, to make sure she was eating properly. Sometimes she forgot to eat or didn't eat enough. Also, he wanted to go down on her, to taste between her legs until she climaxed against his face. Until she was so spent from orgasms that she passed out on top of him.

As Prima approached with Cale, he stepped back as the two of them started talking to Darius. He ducked into the medical tent, was glad to find Baris there.

The male looked up from a notepad, nodded politely. "Orion. How may I help you?"

"I wish to ask if you'd like to join my territory. I'm not poaching from another Alpha; Prima and Darius both made it clear that you might be up for a change. That it was why you came on this trip. So I'm offering you a place in my territory despite my terrible manners before."

Baris gave him a real smile then. "You were practically docile compared to some shifters when it comes to their mates."

Orion didn't correct him about Violet being his mate. She was not his. *Yet*, his dragon purred. "If you need time to think on it—"

"I do not. I wish to stay. I cannot promise forever, but I'm ready for a change and the air here agrees with me. Everything is so open and green."

"We have various accommodations for you, probably not as nice as you're used to."

Baris snorted softly. "I normally sleep in my beast form. Whatever you have is fine, I am certain."

"I look forward to getting to know you better, then." He nodded politely at the healer, and after they said their goodbyes he ducked out of the tent again. Normally he would have taken longer to vet a healer position but Prima had recommended him and that carried a lot of weight. And he needed to set up certain cornerstones of his territory for it to run properly. He'd need more than one healer, that was certain, because Violet could not do everything alone. And neither could Baris. Not to mention, he had a feeling it would take a while for many of the humans to warm up to going to Baris, if they ever did.

By the time Prima and Cale had finished talking to Darius, and Dr. Luna O'Connor had asked him random questions he wasn't sure how to answer, Orion was finally on the way home to Violet. As he crested over the orchard in dragon form and saw her family's house, a steady beacon for him, the tension in his body eased. Even as the anticipation ratcheted up.

As it always did.

But that lived inside him, that compulsion to be close to her at all times. And the longer he was with her, the more his control waned, the more he wanted to let his dragon half take over.

"Do you need a place to sleep tonight?" Orion asked Prima once they'd both landed and shifted. He only pulled his pants on, not bothering with a shirt. The day had been long and he was ready for a shower and to sleep.

Hopefully in Violet's bed, his dragon purred. *And you shall not be sleeping if you do things right, coward.*

"No, but thank you. I'm hoping to find Mari and talk to her."

He narrowed his gaze. "For what purpose?"

"I'd like to talk about training her, among other things. She clearly has skills and will make an excellent spy for you. You'll need a spymaster and she could be it."

He'd thought of that as well. He would also need a second, and while he would prefer Prima, he knew she wouldn't stay forever. And he needed someone who wanted to put down roots. "How long do you think you'll stay with me?"

"In truth, I have no idea. As long as you need me." She patted his cheek gently, the way she'd done when he'd been just a stripling, had just passed from boyhood to manhood. Barely. She hadn't been much older than him at the time, maybe a few decades or so past him. But she'd been more confident, more skilled as a fighter.

Once he'd been old enough and strong enough, he'd escaped his clan in the middle of the night and flown, hard and fast, over a large sea. Then he'd kept going until the weather had changed, until ice had formed on his scales.

And then, exhausted and near death, he'd crashed into the side of a mountain, and might have died if not for Prima and her sister. They'd taken him in, had finally gotten the whole story of his past out of him. He didn't view her as a mother—they were too close in age for that—but she was like a big sister. One he wished he'd had to protect him when he hadn't been able to. Eventually they'd gotten a little brother of their own, many, many years later, and they'd adored and spoiled him. Orion had been able to see the way it should have been for him, but instead of being jealous he'd simply been grateful for their friendship.

"What if I say forever?"

She gave him a ghost of a smile. "Then I'll stay forever. But it won't take you that long to get this place up and running like a proper territory... May I speak freely?"

He glanced around the moonlit orchard, saw no one near the growing pods or by the barn. Didn't scent anyone nearby either. Not close enough to overhear anyway. "When have you not?" he asked, half smiling.

Her expression remained serious. "Why have you not claimed your human doctor? She is so lovely and clearly cares for you. I think that little human would go into battle for you if necessary. I saw the way she marched up in front of that crowd today. She cares deeply for you."

All his muscles went taut. "We are friends and I am happy protecting her and her family. I don't need more." *Lies. And no one believes you,* his dragon roared. *Not even yourself.*

Prima's eyes went pure dragon as she watched him. "Is it that you don't think you deserve her?"

He looked away, something an Alpha never did. But he couldn't stand what he saw in her gaze. "Everyone I've ever loved or cared about is gone." And the ones who should have taken care of him...had been monsters.

"Bullshit, Orion. I'm right here. So are some of the others from long ago. So, next excuse."

"That's not what I meant," he snapped. He'd lost the clan that he'd formed, his found family. The one he'd created after he'd escaped his murderous parents. "My clan, my people—"

"They died from a sickness, one which our kind had never seen. There was nothing you could have done. Nothing *anyone* could have done."

"I should have been able to stop it!"

"Oh, so you're the goddess now?"

"That's not what I meant." He scrubbed a hand over his face, stared up at the moon and stars blanketing the sky, breathed deep. "They depended on me. And I failed them."

"You didn't fail them. You would have saved them if you could. You survived because your blood was able to fight the sickness."

"Or maybe there's something evil inside me, something even that disease couldn't kill," he growled. Because his parents had done their hardest to beat it out of him. "Did you ever think of that?"

Prima blinked, her eyes returning to normal. "Is that what you truly think?" she asked on a laugh. A *laugh*.

"It's not funny."

"No, but it is stupid. And I'm not calling you stupid. But there is nothing wrong with you at all. The monsters who birthed you were the evil ones, not you. And despite everything, you thrived. Don't let them take away your future with a female who you—"

"Stop, Prima. Please, stop." He didn't need to hear the words. Because she didn't know, didn't understand. How could she? Her own parents had been wild, more dragon than human, but they'd never harmed their children. Had treated them with love and affection. Unlike his own parents—and what if some of what they were lived inside him? What if he passed on that evil?

Sighing, she stepped forward, and to his surprise she pulled him into a tight embrace. "Goddess, I wish you'd listen to me. It would make your life so much easier. But you'll just have to do things the hardheaded way, I suppose."

He hugged her back, her touch one of the only ones he would accept. And only platonically. Because he trusted her in a way he couldn't trust most people. It was the rarest kind of trust, born out of a long history together. "Will you tell me why you're really here?" he murmured as he stepped back. Because he knew her heart was hurting and he wanted to destroy whoever had hurt her.

She started to respond, then looked at something over his shoulder, slightly winced. "Oh, no."

He turned, saw Violet hurrying in the other direction.

"Go after her," Prima murmured. "Because I think she might have the wrong idea about us."

Wrong idea? *Oh.* He was shirtless and had been hugging another female. But...this was Prima. "Maybe it's better—"

"What? That you cause her pain? Goddess, don't be stupid." She grabbed his face. "You deserve to be happy!" Growling, she turned and stalked away, ranting in a long-dead language about his idiocy.

And...screw it. He raced after Violet, easily following her sweet scent all the way to house. The moment he stepped inside, Bowie was there, jumping up on him.

Unable to simply ignore the pup, Orion scooped him up, scratching his head and belly and murmuring words of love as he hurried up the stairs and barreled into Violet's room—to find her in just her underwear.

"Orion!" She clapped a hand over her breasts and scrambled to grab a blanket from the end of her bed before she held it up in front of her.

But it was too late. He'd seen everything. Her full breasts, brown little nipples, the soft indent of her waist and full hips, the—

"You couldn't have turned away?" she snapped.

"No."

Wide-eyed, she stared at him. "I don't even know what to say to that. What are you doing here?"

Bowie was squirming in his arms so he set him down and the pup jumped on the end of the bed and watched him, as if he was also waiting on the answer. His little head swiveled back and forth between the two of them.

"I...was just hugging my friend earlier," he blurted.

Violet snorted in disbelief. "Yeah, I hug all my supermodel gorgeous friends while I'm shirtless too."

He stepped forward, all his attention on Violet, on the sharp intake of her breath, the wild scents rolling off her. "Are you jealous?"

She opened her mouth, as if to scoff, then nodded. "Yes. I am. I saw you hugging the most stunning female I've ever seen. A female who is also a dragon like you, who clearly adores you, who you have a past with. And you were shirtless, had your...*body* all up against hers. Yes, I was jealous! *Am* jealous! And I don't like this feeling!" She took a deep breath, rubbed her hand over her face. "Sorry, I'm not sure why I'm shouting."

"One of your breasts is showing again." The blanket had shifted when she covered her face and he could just see one of her nipples peeking out.

She yelped, then awkwardly wrapped the thing around her tight and he regretted telling her. Regretted a lot of things.

"Is there something I can help you with? Because honestly, I'm ready to go die of embarrassment in the shower and I'd like to do it alone." Violet didn't look at him, and the distress rolling off her was potent.

He stepped forward, wanting to comfort her, even if he wasn't sure he could. He needed to make it clear how he felt about her. "Prima is just a friend. Has only ever been a friend. More like an older sister. I've known her since...longer than I can truly say. I'm a shifter, and nudity or this," he motioned to his chest, "is not something I think about. But if you'd been hugging someone without your shirt, I would have likely incinerated them. Or bit them in half."

She blinked. "Wait, what—"

"I'm sorry I caused you distress. I never want to hurt you, Violet. And you have no reason to be jealous." Of all people, never her. She was the only one he wanted. Had ever truly wanted. Her very being sang to the core of him.

Her eyes narrowed slightly. "Why is that?"

His throat froze and he hated himself in that moment. Hated his past, hated his DNA. Hated that he was so weak when it came to her. "Because..."

She stepped closer, eyeing him speculatively. "Did you say you'd incinerate someone if they hugged me?"

He paused, his dragon clawing at the surface, the way she was looking at him turning him inside out. "Yes."

"Would you be jealous if I hugged someone else? *Dated* someone else? *Hugged* them without my clothes on?"

"I'd kill them." The three words came out more dragon than man, a raw growl from the most primal part of him.

She blinked and he braced himself for it, for her disgust, for— She dropped the blanket and he forgot to breathe.

Just forgot how to do anything but stare as she stepped closer, indecision on her face. But she also kicked her chin up, almost in defiance, as if daring him to make a move. And oh how he wanted to. Goddess, he wanted to.

He was vaguely aware of Bowie darting from the room so he kicked out without glancing backward, shut the door with his foot. He didn't want an audience for this. "Violet." He breathed out her name like a prayer.

Wanted to reach for her, to pull her close to him. But that deep-seated fear clawed at his insides that he would somehow hurt her, ruin this, and lose his best friend. The female he'd come to love in so short a time.

Tentatively, she reached out and placed a gentle hand on his bare chest, and he shuddered, closed his eyes. She had so much power over him. One touch from her and his entire body was taut. Aching. Desperate for more.

She placed her other hand on his chest, then slid down to his waist and his eyes snapped open. "Violet," he said again, because apparently that was all he could get out.

"Kiss me," she whispered, a soft demand filled with uncertainty.

And she should never be uncertain where he was concerned, even if it was his fault that she was.

The difference in their physical strengths had never been more apparent in his mind than it was now. He cupped her cheek in his palm, couldn't believe his hand shook slightly. As soon as he made contact she leaned into him, gave the sweetest sigh as he slanted his mouth over hers.

The moment their lips touched, something inside him clicked into place. A certainty. Deep and dark and territorial.

Mine.

She wrapped her arms around him, pressed her bare breasts against his chest, and all he could think about was that this was Violet naked up against him. His sweet Violet was putting all her trust in him now. And the skin to skin of her breasts against him was everything he'd ever dreamed of.

He would *never* betray her trust, but he was aware that there were far too many out there who abused the trust of those they were supposed to take care of, to love.

He banished that from his mind, taking Prima's advice from before. He couldn't let his past ruin this, even if he wasn't certain he deserved happiness.

As she leaned into him, he teased his tongue against hers. That primal part of him took over and he deepened the kiss, wanting to taste all of her. *Now. No more waiting.*

She moaned into his mouth, clutched onto his shoulders as if she wanted to climb him—and at that thought he had to order himself to breathe again. He was barely functioning.

He slid his hands down her waist, hips and back, running his palms down over her ass, that need to touch every part of her pulsing through him. She shuddered under his touch, the sweet scent of her filling the room, consuming his senses. But he needed to touch her everywhere, wished he had more than two hands to do it.

Retracing his path back up, he stopped at her breasts this time and gently cupped them, filling his palms with them. As he did, that sweet scent of arousal nearly made him stumble.

Moving on instinct, he picked her up, needing to get her flat, fast. She wrapped her legs around him as if it was the most natural thing in the world and moments later he had her flat on her back, the bedcovers releasing a puff of air beneath them.

She arched into him as he pinned her in place, her own hands greedily roaming over him as he'd been doing with her. His cock kicked against his pants, desperate for all of her. His entire body ached for his sweet Violet as the reality of what they were doing settled in, overwhelmed him. He'd led dragons into battle against impossible odds, but she completely brought him to his knees, made him want to promise the entire world.

She surprised him by trying to undo the button of his work pants. Leaning back, he looked down at her swollen lips, lust-filled gray eyes.

"You are everything," he murmured in a language from long ago, and one she wouldn't understand. It was why he could say the words so freely, admit what had been in his heart for the last year. *"You're the*

reason I wake up every morning, sweet Violet. When I look at you, you're the only thing I see, the only thing that matters. The darkest part of me wants to shackle you to me, to keep you forever no matter what." He would never take her against her will, never harm her, but there was a compulsion deep inside him that wanted him to keep her no matter what.

She traced her forefinger over his bottom lip, her expression one of awe as she looked up at him.

He nipped her finger, making her smile, her gaze snapping to his. "Take off your pants." Another soft demand from his sweet human.

One he would follow, but… "Not yet. Soon, sweet Violet."

She squirmed impatiently underneath him, her hair splayed all around her, her kiss-swollen lips beckoning to him. "Yes, now," she whispered, but the words were still a demand. "I've waited long enough."

Her bossiness caused a startled laugh from him and he captured her mouth again as he reached between her spread legs, shoved the thin material of her underwear to the side.

Impatient, he sliced one thin strap of the black material, giving him full access to her slick folds.

She groaned into his mouth as he slid a finger inside her, spreading her, teasing her. Then he slid another, wanting to stretch her and ready her for his cock.

But she had to come first, to feel pleasure before that happened. He didn't think she was a virgin, but she was so damn tight and he knew how big he was. And he wanted her completely addicted to him. The darkest, most selfish part of him wanted her obsessed with the pleasure he could give her so that she'd want forever with him.

"Orion," she moaned, nipping his bottom lip between her teeth.

The sound of his name on her lips in that pleading tone was the most beautiful thing he'd ever heard. It made him want to claim her fully, everything be damned. There was no way he could do that to her, to actually shackle her to him, but that innate hunger was there, right under the surface.

She tried to go for his pants again but he pulled his hips back and started kissing a path down her body. The frustrated sound she made was quickly replaced with one of pleasure as he sucked one hard nipple into his mouth.

"You have a magic mouth," she rasped out as he pressed his teeth gently on the tight bud and began flicking it with his tongue.

Her scent was wild now, filling the small room, flooding his senses. He'd scented hints of lust from her before, but nothing like this raw hunger. It was like now that he'd let his own wall down, she was too. She was letting him in.

She slid her fingers through his hair, clutched his head as he switched breasts. "Too much."

He wasn't sure what was too much, but as far as he was concerned it wasn't enough. Wouldn't be enough until she climaxed. Until he was buried fully inside this incredible female who owned him body and soul. "No. It's not enough." Nothing would be.

He sucked hard on one of her nipples, causing her to dig her nails into his head before he continued kissing a path down the rest of her body. As he reached her lower abdomen, she rolled her hips upward, a silent plea.

He slid his fingers inside her again, slowly this time, and she whimpered. He was so gentle, more gentle than he'd thought possible. In the past, sex had always been rough, after battle, and rare. Never with anyone he cared for. It had always been more about release. And, if he was being honest, a way to punish himself. He hadn't thought he deserved anything good or soft.

Until her.

"You're killing me," she whispered.

"Not even close. We're just getting started," he murmured against the top of her mound. Her clit was peeking out, already swollen and ready for his touch.

He'd wanted to drag this out, to hear her beg, but she was soaking his fingers and her scent was making him light-headed. He'd satisfy that dominant urge later; right now, he needed her to come.

Violet arched her hips again, silently begging Orion to kiss her clit, but he just gently blew on it, clearly teasing her. And she had no self-control left—maybe she'd never had any where he was concerned. "Orion!"

He looked up the length of her, his eyes dark as he watched her.

And she forgot how to talk, or at least forgot what she wanted to say. *Make me come, please?* But the words stuck in her throat. Her heart thundered against her ribs, her whole body pulsing with a type of need she'd never known. He was so gorgeous, this powerful dragon, and the hungry, possessive look on his face as he gazed up at her made her tremble. He'd never looked at her like that before. She'd seen peeks of interest, but he'd always been so damn impossible to read.

Right now it was as if he'd just stripped every barrier he'd ever put up between them. Now, there was nothing in the way, just the two of them in this moment.

Thankfully, he was done teasing because he sucked on her clit while he continued thrusting his fingers inside her. And that was enough to send her over the edge. She'd been teetering on the brink since he'd stalked into her room with his shirt off.

Something inside her had broken when she'd seen him hugging that woman. But she believed him when he said the female was a friend and now all she cared about was him putting out the fire he'd started in her. Though if anything, he was simply enflaming it even more. She arched her hips again as he added another finger.

Pleasure pulsed out to all her nerve endings as he curled his fingers inside her and rubbed that oh so sensitive spot over and over. And when he sucked on her clit again she broke apart, too much sensation punching through her at once.

"Orion." She grabbed onto his head as the pleasure bordered on pain, as her orgasm hit hard and fast. In that moment every thought whited out in her mind as she rolled her hips against his face and fingers, taking every moment of pleasure he gave her.

By the time she fell back against the bed, she blinked, saw that... "Whoa," she whispered at the blue and purplish swirl of fog surrounding them and the bed. "What is that?"

Orion sat up, stared in horror at the beauty filling the room.

She jerked upright. "What is it? Is it dangerous?" It didn't feel or look scary. It was almost like a cocoon of magic, and the way it skated over her skin, featherlight, made her feel warm from the inside out. It had to be part of him—the colors were the same as his scales in dragon form.

"It's not dangerous," he ground out, his shoulders tight with tension as he stepped away from the bed and her. "It's…I've got to go. I'm sorry. This was… I'm sorry, Violet." His voice was ragged as he tore the door open.

"Wait…" But he was gone in a flash, the door shutting behind him with a resounding click before she'd even gotten off the bed.

Hurt and confusion punched through her, even as the blue and purple swirl of magic remained, pulling tighter around her, clearly trying to comfort her. As if it was sentient. Which was a weird thought, but—maybe it was. There was so much about magic she didn't know.

Unbidden tears stung her eyes and the swirl lifted something a lot like fingers, wiping the wetness away. And for some reason, that made it worse. The comforting.

Orion had just given her the most intense pleasure of her life and then *left* her, simply run out with no explanation. With her intense orgasm now faded, her chest hollow, she stood and stumbled toward the shower, the weird magic trailing with her even as it started to dissipate.

She tried to stop the tears but that would have been like trying to hold back the ocean. She'd put herself out there with him, had thought things had finally changed for good, that maybe they had a chance at something.

But he'd run off without a word, looking at her as if she horrified him. As if what they'd done horrified him.

As the hot water pounded down around her, she stuck her face under the stream and let the tears come. She loved Orion, but didn't think she could live with him anymore. Not after this. Not after he'd left her alone and bleeding inside.

CHAPTER TWENTY

"That was the coolest thing I've ever done," Laurel breathed out as Cale tugged his clothes back on.

She didn't bother hiding her stare as he covered up all his gorgeous naked skin. He liked when she looked anyway.

For their date, he'd flown them out to one of the waterfalls for an evening picnic. And flying on a dragon was, hands down, the best experience.

"If I was a dragon, I'd fly all the time!" She opened the giant picnic basket he'd brought, pulled out a blanket and started unfolding it. "Seriously. I'd do nothing else."

"I'll take you flying anytime, anywhere," he murmured, grabbing the other ends of the blanket and helping her lay it out. "Was flying cooler than riding me in my human form?"

She blinked, let out an unexpected laugh. "I can't tell if you're joking."

He lifted a big shoulder, a grin curving his luscious mouth. "I was at first, but now I want to know."

"Oh no. I like both sides of you and I'm not playing whatever weird game you and your dragon half have going on." Because he talked about his dragon as if he was separate from his human side. She wasn't quite sure how it worked.

He grinned full-on now. "You're very insightful. But I know the answer is my cock because it's more impressive than anything else."

She snort-laughed, unable to stop herself, then a full-body laugh overtook her. "I don't know if it's confidence or you're just nuts."

"Is my cock not impressive?"

"I'm not feeding your ego," she murmured. He had to know how big he was. He saw the thing every day—and she was still tender from the many, many times they'd had sex. She kept unloading the basket. "Oh my God, all these cheeses. Where did you get these?"

"I stole them from Prima's tent. As well as some of the jams. She is sure to kill me later, but it's worth it." He pulled out a few more containers, including some grainy-type bread that looked amazing.

"Then I better not let them go to waste if this is your last meal." She sat as he pulled out... "Is that champagne?" The green glass bottle had no label, but there was a cork in it that reminded her of champagne.

"Yes, and this I did not steal. I traded for it, especially for this date. For you."

Oooohhh. She didn't know what to think of that. She hadn't even realized people could still get things like champagne and was curious how, but saved those questions for later as he popped the bottle and poured her a glass. "Thank you for this," she murmured, lifting the glass to her mouth. The bubbles tickled her nose and it brought back a rush of memories of a different time. Of parties and deadlines and the manic life she'd once lived. Had thought she wanted. Now she wanted something a little more meaningful... Maybe with the dragon shifter who'd been giving her incredible orgasms.

He sat next to her, stretching out his long legs as he poured a glass for himself. "What's that look?"

"Nothing. Just...this is really nice." And she wasn't sure what this sexy dragon even saw in her. Sure, she was pretty, but she wasn't some out of this world knockout. And most days she felt like she was faking everything. Her three sisters were so accomplished and their parents had been world-renowned scientists. She always felt like she paled next to her whole family. That she was nothing special.

Frowning, he set his glass down next to him, turned more toward her. "What is going through that pretty head? Because I can scent something off." The intensity of his green gaze was a bit unnerving.

"That's not fair that you can smell the change in my mood." And it was something she'd have to get used to. Or maybe not, since she wasn't sure if this thing they'd started was going anywhere. It wasn't a one-night stand anymore since they were now on an official date but...she didn't want to get too ahead of herself. Not when she found that she really liked him, for more than just sex. And he was staying here—the thought of falling for him, getting her heart broken, and then watching him move on to someone better had a tight ball forming in her stomach.

He shrugged. "Tell me what you're thinking, please."

It felt sort of pathetic but... "Honestly, I'm just wondering why you like me. Why we're here at all tonight." She tried to shrug, but the action came out jerky. He'd taken what she'd offered and they'd both had a good time. That should have been it. It unnerved her that he was changing the script so drastically.

He blinked in surprise. "Why wouldn't I like you? You're fascinating, funny, a little OCD and, okay, beautiful. I like being around you. I like your smart mouth."

"You couldn't have known any of that when we first met—and when I propositioned you for a one-night stand."

"True. But I do now. And from the moment I scented you, I knew you were..." He cleared his throat.

"What?"

"Nothing. And you still haven't told me how you made your way back to your hometown after The Fall. I want details." He picked up his glass again, his gaze intent on hers.

They'd talked last night—was it only last night?—about where they'd been during The Fall, and he'd admitted that one of his relatives had been involved with the attempted overthrow of the world. He'd seemed so ashamed, even though he hadn't been involved. And she'd offhandedly told him she'd tell him her story later.

Not actually thinking that later would come.

"Ah, I was in Georgia, which isn't too far away. I lived in Atlanta, or on the outskirts really, as the city had grown so much. When everything went pear-shaped, I got in my car with one bag of essentials and just drove."

It had been eye-opening how little she'd packed that day. How little she'd actually cared about in that condo she'd called home for years. The Fall had crystallized everything, made her see clearly for the first time what was truly important in life. Family. Safety. Friendship.

"I was lucky enough to be able to get gas on the way. I think it was because most people were staying put, waiting to see what happened. I just knew I didn't want to be stuck there for the aftereffects. I wanted to be with my parents..." She trailed off, the pain of losing them a constant that lived inside her. "And my sisters. And I knew how rural this place was. It was a good bet that it wouldn't be targeted by whatever was going on at the time." There had been so many conflicting news reports in the beginning and then the videos had been so wild she hadn't actually been sure if they'd been real or if they'd been deepfakes.

She'd just known to go home. Her instinct had kicked in and she'd listened to it.

"That was brave," he murmured.

She snorted and took a sip of her champagne—which was amazing. She savored the taste on her tongue, the sensation of bubbles.

"It was, and I don't like how you ignore compliments."

Blinking, she looked at him. "What?"

"Whenever I compliment you. Or when someone else does—because I saw you get a lot of them at the gymnasium—you brush them off."

"I do n..." Frowning, she trailed off, then looked away from him. Okay, maaaaybe she did. "So, why are you staying here anyway? I would imagine New Orleans is bigger, with more amenities and stuff."

"Oh no, we're not changing the subject."

"Uh, I most certainly am. Don't you know that's rule number one on a date with me? You let me get my way."

He barked out a laugh. "Is that right?"

"Yep."

"Does your way include…orgasming?"

Heat curled through her at his words, his tone and, oh, that look on his face. One that promised all the pleasure in the world. Her heart rate increasing, she set her glass down. "Definitely."

He grinned wickedly. "Then tell me what I want to know."

She smacked his shoulder. "You can't blackmail me for information with good sex."

"I don't think it's blackmail. I think it's extortion. Sextortion."

She laughed again, surprised by how at ease she was with the big dragon. She felt like she'd known him forever. "Fine…I don't accept compliments well. It's not a big deal. Growing up I always felt like I had to compete with my sisters and their accomplishments."

His grin slid away, a frown taking its place. "They made you feel less than?"

"What? No! My sisters are the best. The absolute best. They're just so, well, talented. One's a doctor, one's a vet, and another—well, I'm not exactly sure what Mari used to do, but she's really impressive on so many levels. And I was what, an event planner?" She rolled her eyes, looked away from him because it was easy to drown in that green gaze and forget everything and anything.

"You organized your entire community in a day and got almost everyone to vote. And when Darius and our people arrived, you're the one who set up the welcome party. I know I wasn't there but I heard about it. You're good with people, they trust you. Rightfully so. So, when I say you're amazing, you can just say thank you." His tone was so damn sincere.

She stared at him, not sure how to respond. Finally, she whispered, "Okay." Because hot damn, it was a whole lot to be under that kind of intense scrutiny. And his belief in her filled her with warmth, soothing the deeply buried insecurity she'd carried forever.

He leaned closer, brushing his lips over hers, just a bare touching of their mouths. But she felt that barely there touch all the way to her core.

"You're amazing," he murmured.

"Thank you." Her cheeks warmed under his praise, but it felt amazing that he saw her. Saw right through her and called her on her internal bullshit.

When his phone buzzed next to them she glanced down and saw the word *Beau* as an incoming text flashed on-screen—asking how their date was.

She looked back up at Cale, her eyes wide. "Wait, is that Beau? My Beau?"

"He's not yours," Cale growled, his dragon in his gaze. "But yes, that's Beau."

"Are you guys, like, friends now? I thought you wanted to chop his head off or whatever."

Cale shrugged, that grin firmly in place. "Keep your friends close and your enemies closer."

"So...he's your enemy?"

Cale paused, then shook his head. "Nah. I wish he was easy to dislike, but he's funny and I like his mom. She made me cookies."

"Oh my God, that's pathetic." She snort-giggled again because it was beyond ridiculous. But also adorable.

"I know." He shook his head, laughing as he reached for a container and opened it to reveal a half-eaten tin of what looked like snickerdoodles. "But for some perspective, they were really, really good cookies. And how can I kill that annoyingly handsome dumbass when his mom is so nice? I think she's the only reason he's still alive."

"That's not the only reason you like him. You're texting with him! Only friends do that."

"Fine, I like the dumb human. He's funny as hell. And he's the one who traded me for the champagne. Said you deserved a proper date with someone who treated you right. And he also threatened my manhood if I hurt you, which I respect." He lifted a cookie, as if in salute.

"Boys are weird."

"I'm not a boy."

Laughing, she laid her head on his shoulder, soaking up all his heat. No, he definitely wasn't a boy. He was all man. Or dragon. Whatever.

And he was under her skin, had just snuck in undercover and now she didn't want to give him up.

Because this male had layers. Lots of them, and she wanted to peel all of them back, get to know every little thing about him. Even if it broke her heart. Because being with Cale at all was definitely worth it.

CHAPTER TWENTY-ONE

Orion was still cursing his cowardice hours later as he flew around the edges of the territory. He'd tightened up security with the help of both humans and supernaturals—including a witch he hadn't realized lived in his territory—but the area was vast enough that there were ways to slip through.

Especially for a murderous vampire.

As he swooped low along the thick forest, the sound of a couple waterfalls below filling the air, all he could think about was how badly he'd screwed up.

The hurt on Violet's face.

The confusion.

The pain.

When he'd run like a goddamn coward.

The biggest coward, his dragon snarled angrily. *She was ready for you, perfect, everything you've ever wanted. Dreamed about. And you screwed things up beyond repair.*

Yeah, he had. And he needed to make things right.

But when his mating manifestation had appeared, he'd panicked. Panicked being an understatement. He'd thought he was dying when he saw the manifestation, hadn't actually understood what it was at first.

Until reality had slammed into him.

His parents had never told him what his clan's manifestation would look like. They'd told him he would never find anyone who would want to mate him because he was garbage, so it didn't matter. But he'd heard enough over the years to know it would be noticeable.

He'd assumed that since it hadn't shown up before, it wouldn't show up at all. That the twisted part of his DNA would remain dormant forever. Because he'd known there would be no one but Violet for him.

There is nothing wrong with you, his dragon growled. *I can still feel her pain through the mating connection. You are hurting our mate. That is the only wrong thing right now.*

He paused in flight, spreading his wings wide as he skimmed the treetops. His dragon had protected him from many of the beatings, the broken bones, the abuse, and sometimes from memories. He only knew because once he was an adult, his dragon allowed him to remember some things.

They were worse than he could have imagined.

Angry at the memories, at the monsters who'd terrorized a little dragon, he dove down through the trees, almost beckoned to the spot he'd first seen Violet.

As he landed, he shifted to his human form and inhaled the freshness of the area. Everything was mostly untouched by humans here. He could scent his wolves had passed through here at one point and...

He paused at the other scent.

The one that did not belong.

And it was fresh.

Something dark hung in the air, dangerous. Hungry for blood.

He casually walked to the edge of the waterfall, keeping his body loose, as if he hadn't scented the evil. He looked down at the spot he'd first seen Violet waving up at him, her smile open and friendly.

He hated that violence was about to mar this place, but there was no way around it now. Whatever evil being had come here tonight would die.

He could hear a whisper of movement behind him as he looked up at the moon, pretended he was unaware. As he felt the air current shift around him, could hear the faint sing of a blade, he stepped off the edge of the waterfall.

Ready, he landed on a giant boulder below, ignored the crack of the stone under his fall, and rolled backward behind the cascading water.

As he jumped to his feet, a female with dark, glowing red eyes stepped through the curtain of water, a blade in her hand and vampire claws extended from her other. "I thought that was too easy," she murmured, eyeing him up and down as if she was thinking of the ways she'd like to dismember him.

The feeling was mutual.

"You killed the human family," he said, wanting a definitive answer. He scented her, knew she was guilty, but he still needed her to admit her crimes.

"I've killed a lot of families." She glanced around the interior of the shallow cave, had to see that there was no way to escape except back through the water.

Not that he was looking for one. He ran from no one, least of all some vampire who killed children.

"But if you're talking about the little human family on the outskirts of your territory, then yes." She smiled, seemingly happy with herself. "The little one's blood was delicious," she hissed, her eyes glowing brighter for a moment.

The scent of truth rolled off the vampire and Orion barely restrained himself from attacking her now, from shifting and biting her in half. Because he wanted answers first.

Then the female would die.

He made a scoffing sound. "Pathetic."

She narrowed her gaze.

"Killing weak humans," he added, in case she needed clarification. "Even the young of my kind don't do that. But I wouldn't expect much else from a lowly vampire." He made another scoffing sound, eyed her with disgust. "Your kind have no honor. It's not your fault, I suppose. You were weak when you were turned and now you're still inadequate. You couldn't even kill the whole family."

"Humans are trash and I'm a bloodborn. Not some weak, human-turned vampire." Pride filled her voice.

Thank the goddess for pride, because now he knew more about her. "Why are you going after humans? If you're truly a bloodborn, and I'm not certain you are, it's beneath you." He played to her pride now.

"It's all about the bigger picture. Humans are food," she snarled, then taking him by surprise she stepped backward through the falling water, disappearing from sight.

He went on instinct, shifted to dragon, his massive wings and body cracking the cave around him as he dove after her.

She was fast, he'd give her that, racing through the forest with the speed of any feline shifter, her feet barely skimming the ground.

But he was faster.

He let his camouflage fall into place as he flew harder, faster, then abruptly changed directions and dove down through the trees, flying straight at her.

She couldn't see him but she must have sensed him, because she jumped up onto a nearby tree, scaled it with feline grace as he breathed fire at her.

The fire incinerated the tree and her—or it should have. Because after it cleared, she was on the ground, her clothes burned away, her fangs out as she hissed at him. "Nice try, motherfucker!"

He dove down, breathing out fire only as a distraction. She might be fireproof, likely from a spell, or perhaps being a bloodborn, but she sure as hell wasn't dragonproof.

As he covered her in fire, killing her ability to see anything, he opened his jaws wide and snapped her in half, the crunch of bones filling the air as he ended her life.

Just as he opened his jaws up, her two halves burst into ash, littering the forest floor below.

He shifted quickly to his human form, stalked through her ashes and bent down, inhaling. She was definitely dead, but he was hoping to get more. A sense of...something. But there was nothing.

Growling to himself, he stood, scanned the area.

No one else was here. She'd been a lone hunter.

And a bloodborn. A very interesting fact, given how rare they were.

He thought about her earlier words. The ominous undertone of them. *It's all about the big picture.*

Since there was nothing of hers to retrieve and deliver to Lucy as proof of her death when he told her that he'd killed the bitch who'd killed her family, he left the ashes and shifted back to dragon form.

He might have screwed up with Violet tonight, but at least he'd done one thing right.

Now he needed to figure out exactly who'd sent the vampire on her killing spree.

Though he was fairly certain he knew who at this point.

The neighboring territory to the west was a problem. One he'd wished would just keep to themselves, but clearly that wasn't going to happen.

So he was going to take care of the problem, one way or another. Though he knew that this problem was going to end with violence. It was the only way.

ORION STEPPED INSIDE THE HOUSE, and despite the early morning hour, heard multiple female voices coming from the kitchen. Anticipation buzzed through him even as he greeted Bowie, who was turning in wild circles at seeing him again.

Even with how heavy his heart was over Violet, he softened as he crouched down and greeted the big-eyed pup who only had love to give. "I missed you too," he murmured before heading into the kitchen.

Disappointment slammed into him to find only Mari and Rose drinking coffee.

"I need to find someone who looks at me like Bowie looks at you," Mari murmured, snickering as she glanced down at Bowie, who was sitting in the doorway next to Orion, his tail wagging and moving his whole body.

Orion frowned at Mari. "What?"

"He might as well have cartoon hearts in his eyes," she said on a laugh. "So what's up? You just getting in?"

He nodded, headed for the coffeepot. "I killed the vampire who murdered Lucy's family. I delivered the news to her at sunrise."

"Oh." Mari patted him awkwardly on the shoulder, but thankfully it was short-lived. "I'll stop by and see her today. I think it's been good for her staying with her best friend."

He nodded, cleared his throat. "Ah, where are Violet and Laurel?" He was really only asking for Violet, and was pretty certain they knew that.

Rose stretched as she stood, picking up her coffee as she did. "I think Laurel is out with that big dragon friend of yours. They had a date last night and I'm pretty sure it went well since she never came home," she said, snickering. "Oh, and I think Violet is with that hot panda shifter. Did you know he's a panda? I have so many questions for him," she murmured more to herself as she headed out the side door.

"Wait."

Rose paused, halfway out the door. "What's up? My chickens aren't gonna feed themselves." She was smiling as she said it, but he couldn't return the smile as that possessive beast inside him reared up. His mate was with another male. Even if he liked the panda healer, his dragon was furious.

"When did Violet leave?"

Rose blinked. "Oh. Last night, I think? Pretty late too." She glanced at Mari, shrugged, then let the door shut behind her.

Last night? So she'd gone to see that panda after they'd... *After you ran away?* his dragon snarked. *Maybe he finished the job you started.*

"Oh shit!"

Orion blinked at Mari's curse, then realized she was staring at him—and the shattered coffee mug in his hand.

Hell. He scooped Bowie up on instinct, not wanting him to get any shards in his paws. "Sorry," he muttered to the room in general.

"Why don't you take Bowie out for a run or something and I'll clean this up? Because you look like you need some air."

No, what he needed was some Violet. But he just grunted a nonre-sponse and hurried back out the way he'd come, taking Bowie with him.

"I'm taking you for a run," he murmured as they stepped out into the chilly morning. "Then I'm going to find Violet, boy." And he wasn't going to be a dumbass this time.

He was claiming his female.

CHAPTER TWENTY-TWO

Violet finished wrapping Holly's ankle, then stepped back and helped the woman stand. "How does it feel?"

"Better, thank you."

"You'll need to stay off it for a few weeks—or I could have Baris come visit you and let him work his healing magic." Violet had already told the younger woman about Baris, but the twenty-year-old shook her head.

"Ah, I'm okay. I mean, maybe in the future I'll be down to visit a healer but I don't think I'm ready. A lot is happening all at once so I'm just going to let my body do its job. Besides," she murmured, glancing around the gymnasium, "if I keep my foot up, my brother's got to do all my chores around the farm," she said on a snicker. "And I'm taking this petty win because he narced me out last month to Nana when I snuck out."

Violet wasn't even going to ask for details. Smiling, she shook her head as Holly's grandmother approached. While she spoke to the other woman, she was very aware of the larger-than-life presence behind her.

Prima. No last name, just Prima, the dragon with killer cheekbones, a body made for war, and deadly eyes.

Violet had been called here to the gym where Prima had been doing some sort of self-defense class with some humans because Holly had hurt herself. "Because of my own clumsiness"—Holly's words.

Violet turned to Prima as Holly and her grandmother headed out, saw that everyone else had either left or were in various stages of picking up duffel bags. She cleared her throat. "It's nice of you to offer a self-defense class."

Prima simply gave a sharp nod. "I think we need to clear the air."

Oh, they really, *really* did not. "Oh, no, I think I'm good?" *Why did it have to come out as a question?* Violet was rarely intimidated. She'd finished medical school at one of the top schools in the country, had gone through a rigorous residency where she'd been one of only two women in the program, dealt with bullshit sexual harassment and misogyny on the daily. But this tall dragon looked at her with alien eyes, and deep inside, in her lizard brain, Violet knew this woman was capable of great violence and could kill her in a second.

Prima's mouth lifted up a fraction. "Orion and I are friends, and since I will be staying here indefinitely, I simply wanted to make sure that was clear."

"Oh, yeah, he told me you guys were friends." And Violet was feeling raw right now. Raw, vulnerable, completely stripped bare. She did not want to talk to this gorgeous stranger. "We're good, I promise."

Prima's eyes narrowed a fraction. "Yes, your body language and tone are very at ease."

"Are you…is that sarcasm?" It was hard to tell when her tone was so neutral, her expression so flat.

"Yes."

"Oh." Violet sighed. "Look, I was feeling weird yesterday, but I believe Orion and you that you're just friends. It's a moot point anyway because, well, whatever." She wasn't opening up to some stranger. Bending down to grab her bag and supplies, she said, "But I appreciate you coming to me to clear the air. Hopefully I can take one of your classes sometime." Uh, lies, because she didn't want to get her ass kicked by this woman. But she was going to be nice to the scary dragon before she ran away.

Prima frowned and plucked the bag from her, hefting it on her shoulder as if it weighed absolutely nothing. "I'll walk you to wherever you're going." And she clearly wasn't asking. "Why is it a moot point? I can smell him on you. I thought you two had finally moved on to more than friends."

Blinking, Violet looked up at her. "What?"

"The two of you have been intimate. So explain why it's a moot point because I do not understand."

Alex, I'll take what's the most embarrassing thing ever, for two hundred. "Um, I don't know that I'm comfortable talking to you about this." And the smell thing was going to take some getting used to.

Prima nodded as they reached the exit doors. "Fair enough. But I worry about Orion. He...has a sensitive soul. Which is strange for an Alpha, but I think it's because of the way he was raised."

Okay, this dragon knew what she was doing because she'd sucked Violet into this conversation with talk of Orion. She was desperate for a glimpse of his past, of knowledge about the male, what made him tick. And Prima had just tapped into that hunger for more knowledge. She wasn't going anywhere until she got answers. "What do you mean?"

Prima paused, looked up at the lightening sky. The sun had risen maybe an hour ago so their class must have started right at daybreak. "His parents were monsters. Or perhaps that is unkind to monsters. They were pure evil. They hurt him, abused him, tore him down every chance they got before he ran away. And that's when we met."

"Wait..." Violet gently touched Prima's forearm as she processed the woman's words, needing to steady herself. Orion had been abused as a child? Hurt?

"They broke his bones on a daily basis, told him it was to make him stronger. That he was weak and no one would ever want him. That they should have killed him when he'd been born."

Throat tight, she looked around wildly, needing to sit. *Oh God. No. No, no, no.* Her sweet, maddening Orion had been abused... Her stomach roiled and she had to fight the rising bile.

"Come." Prima guided her to one of the benches outside the school. "Perhaps I should have eased you into this, but it's too late now. My friend does not have any experience with real relationships. And I am not the queen of them, so perhaps I should keep my mouth shut, but he has only ever had sex in his past. Nothing else. Nothing gentle or loving either. If something happened between the two of you, then I'm going out on a limb and saying that he reacted poorly afterward because of his past. And while I don't think that is always an excuse, he—"

Violet patted Prima's forearm again. "It's fine. I mean, what happened to him is *not* fine." She hoped his parents were dead, that they had suffered. "But..." She eyed the female with the tangled hair and dragon eyes. It was a little startling to look into the beast's eyes, but in that moment she realized that while this woman might be capable of violence, she was also capable of a lot more. Clearly she loved Orion.

"Okay, look, something did happen between us. And I'm questioning if I should even tell you, but whatever. Orion and I were intimate, then there was this blueish purple foggy stuff that sort of looked like the color of his scales. It was sooo beautiful... It surrounded us, then when he saw it, he freaked out. He left and it almost comforted me before it dissipated." And that was the weirdest thing she'd ever said, she was pretty sure.

"Ah, that's the mating manifestation." Prima nodded in approval as she sat back slightly, crossed one of her long legs over the other.

"What's that?"

"With dragons, it's something that appears with our future mate." Her jaw tightened, her expression darkening for a moment before she almost appeared to shake herself. "He might not have known how to handle it. And I do apologize for ambushing you like this with so much information. Orion will perhaps not be happy with me, but I care for him. I remember how malnourished he was the day we found him. How beat down by life. I..." Swallowing hard, she looked into Violet's eyes.

"What happened to his parents?" Violet asked, even though it was none of her business. But this female had just dropped a bombshell on her and some deep part of her wanted to know they'd never come after him again.

"They're dead." Prima said it with such a finality, as if she had no doubt.

"Good." She bit her bottom lip, resisted asking if Orion had killed him. If he had, and he wanted to share that with her, she'd let him.

Prima paused, looked away, her profile striking as she stared off. "He doesn't know this, but I killed them. My twin and I, to keep him safe, in case they ever thought to come after him. I don't know that they would have, but I wouldn't risk it. So we hunted them down and destroyed them with no mercy. I'm telling you this so you understand that I don't want to see him hurt again. So I will cross *any* line for him."

"I don't want to see him hurt either," she whispered.

Prima finally nodded, then took Violet by surprise and patted her cheek gently. "I don't think you do. Just be patient with him. But don't let him retreat from you."

"What do you mean?"

"Be like a dragon female."

Violet blinked.

"Don't take no for an answer." Then she abruptly stood. "He's close, I can scent him."

"Who... Wait, Orion?"

Prima nodded, glanced around the grassy area behind the gym. "Remember what I said. Don't take no for an answer. Whatever you want, go get it. Demand it. But make him chase you. That's the most important advice I will give you. He needs to come for you. If he thinks he'll lose you, it'll kick that dragon obsessiveness into overdrive." Then she took Violet by surprise and—stripped all her clothes off.

Blinking, Violet watched as the woman strode out into the field and turned into a beautiful dragon with glittering jade wings. She breathed out a burst of purple—purple!—fire as she shook her wings out, as if she was showing them off. Well, she should, because they were gorgeous. Then the beast turned to look at her, snapped its jaws once more as if to reiterate her point.

Don't take no for an answer. And make him chase you.

What kind of advice was that? Grabbing her discarded bag, Violet decided that she could enact at least one of those—make him chase her.

Even as she headed back into the gym, planning to use an alternate exit, she wondered if she should be taking advice from Prima. But then decided that if she was going to listen to anyone, it was an immortal badass who'd lived longer than Violet could truly process.

ORION INHALED DEEPLY as he landed in the grassy area outside the gymnasium of the school. There were multiple concrete tables out in an eating area, and he scented that many humans had been here recently. And Prima. Her scent stood out among the humans.

And then there was Violet.

Hers was the only scent that mattered.

Feeling possessed, the mating instinct pushing him forward, he stalked into the gym, looking for her. He needed her, needed to claim her.

As he moved across the gymnasium, her scent grew stronger, pulling him in like the addict he was. He couldn't have ignored it if he'd wanted to.

And he didn't.

He still questioned himself, whether he should be here at all, when he knew he didn't deserve her, but he wasn't walking away from her.

He wasn't sure how he thought he'd have been able to keep his distance forever. That was a fool's thought.

Finally, his dragon side breathed out. *You grow a brain.*

Goddess, his other half was a giant dick. But he wasn't wrong.

He followed her sweet scent out another exit door, his frustration growing. Where the hell was she? He tried radioing her, but either she didn't have her radio on her, or she was ignoring him. It was a fifty-fifty chance at this point.

As he trailed her, he wondered if she was with the panda. Or had been with the panda. If she had been, he'd be rescinding the offer to let the male live here.

And possibly killing the guy.

He locked that thought down because he wasn't sure about his self-control now. Wasn't sure about anything other than claiming Violet.

Fifteen minutes later he followed her scent trail up to an unused house on her property. There were a few scattered around the thousands of acres and they'd all been used for various things, according to her—usually a place for workers to stay during certain seasons.

He opened the front door and quietly stepped inside. There was a slight rustling from the back. One of the bedrooms.

Feeling his dragon shove to the surface, he headed in the direction of the noise and froze to see Violet pulling out what looked like fresh sheets for an unmade bed. "What are you doing?" he demanded, striding into the room, looking around for the dumb panda even though he couldn't scent anyone else.

He knew she was alone, he was simply acting irrationally because of his mating instinct. Knowing that didn't help the adrenaline surging through him.

She lifted an eyebrow. "It's nice to see you too. You're looking lovely today, Violet," she said in a slightly mocking tone. "And it's nice to see you too, Orion. I know you didn't just barge in here and start demanding to know what I'm doing."

He blinked at her hard tone. It was one he'd never heard from her before. Frowning, he realized he'd never scented whatever was coming off her before either—sharp and, okay, amazing. Because she always smelled good enough to eat. Even when she was angry. He peeked into the bathroom, saw it was empty.

When he stepped back out, her head was tilted to the side slightly. "What are you doing? Did you think someone was in there?"

He shrugged, which made her blink.

"So…you followed me here?"

"Yes."

She blinked in surprise, maybe at his honesty. "Why?"

"Because you're mine."

She blinked again, and this time the scents that rolled off her were a mix of fire and anger. Or maybe something else.

"Where were you last night?"

"You mean after you made me climax then ran away?" She laughed but there was no humor.

He didn't like the sound at all. It was harsh and scraped over all his senses. "I…"

She tossed the sheets down onto the unmade bed and stalked toward him, her mouth pulled tight. "Ran. Away." Then she thumped him once lightly on the chest and he savored the feel of her touching him at all.

"Were you with the panda?"

"Wh…what? What panda? What are you talking about?"

Oh, she didn't know Baris was a panda. Her sisters had lied to him. Goddess, she probably hadn't even left last night either. "There is no panda," he growled, not wanting to talk about some other male.

"But apparently there's a confused dragon standing right in front of me, acting all demanding about things that are not his business." She bit out her words, and if it had been possible, she would have breathed fire at him. She had the look of an angry dragon female right now.

"Everything you do is my business," he growled, stepping closer. "Did you leave last night after I left?"

"Uh, after you *ran* away? No, I didn't, I tossed and turned all night wondering what I'd done wrong. What is the matter with you!"

Oh, her sisters had definitely lied. But it didn't matter. He wasn't walking away now. Not ever. Before she could say anything else, he grabbed her wrist and tugged her close to him. Then he leaned down, ran his nose along her jaw, shuddered as he inhaled the sweet jasmine and lavender scent of her.

He definitely couldn't walk away. She was part of him.

"Don't start something you can't finish," she whispered, arching into him.

Nope. Not walking away. But he did back her up against the nearest wall. "I'm not a good male," he whispered, his mouth at her ear, not looking at her as he spoke the words.

"I beg to differ." She ran her hands up his chest, her touch soft and delicate.

"You don't know anything about my clan, what I come from." He nipped her earlobe.

She shuddered, arching into him again. Unfortunately they were both still fully clothed. "I don't care where you come from. I just care about you… Why'd you leave before?" she asked, a soft demand as she slid her hands up, up, up, and around the back of his neck, holding on to him. "Why'd you leave me?"

He stilled at her questions, the answer freezing in his throat.

"Do you not want to claim me because I'm human? Is that why you're fighting the mating instinct?"

He jerked back in surprise, stared down into fierce gray eyes. Her hair was pulled back into a loose bun, but wisps had come out, framing her face.

"Yeah, I know about the mating instinct. So, your dragon wants me, but I'm too weak because I'm human, is that it?"

"No, of course not! Who told you that?"

"Who told me about the mating instinct is none of your business. But I don't need anyone to tell me I'm too weak. I know I am. I'm human, and compared to you I'm—"

"You're *everything*." She wasn't weak. She was walking perfection. She was *his*.

"Just not good enough to mate?" she pushed, that light burning in her eyes.

"I'm not good enough for you," he growled.

She rolled her eyes in response. Actually rolled her eyes. Then she ducked out from under his arm. "You know what? When you figure out what you want, maybe we can talk, but until then—"

Something inside him panicked as she walked away from him, headed for the door. He moved lightning fast, the predator in him refusing to release her. He was at the door, had it shut behind him, his back against it as she approached.

"I'll just go out a window," she growled. "You can't keep me here forever."

Oh, but I can, his dragon purred.

The thin shred of his control, if he'd ever had any at all, snapped in two. "I'll tie you to my bed and never let you go."

Instead of disgust, that distinctive heat rolled off her, punched into him as if she'd physically touched him. "Yeah?" She took a step away from him, moved toward the window, her expression one of pure defiance. "Prove it."

Instinct took over and he had her pinned against the wall by the window in a second, that drive to keep her close to him riding him. "You're playing with fire."

"Yep."

He crushed his mouth to hers, though he was fairly certain she moved at the same time he did. The lust rolling off her mirrored his own, was stronger than last night. Wilder, hungrier. Out of control.

She moaned into his mouth, clawed at his shirt in an attempt to get it off him.

He reached between their bodies, tore his shirt off, then managed to get hers off without shredding it. She had her bra off before he could reach around her body, then she clutched onto him again, rubbing her breasts against his chest as she sought out his mouth.

"I won't let you go," he growled against her, wanting her to understand. "You're mine."

"And you're mine," she whispered, biting his bottom lip.

"Do you understand—"

"I understand you're talking too much when I want to feel you inside me." She worked the button of his pants, shoved them down even as he stared at her.

She completely unraveled him. Somehow eased the self-loathing inside him. He wouldn't claim her fully with the mating bite, not now. But he was sure as hell going to claim her in every other way, to take everything he'd wanted from the moment he'd seen her, scented her.

It didn't take him long to have her pants off and he barely restrained himself from incinerating them—because he could do it without burning her. She was part of him, even if she didn't realize it. He'd protected her and her sisters from the moment they'd met, given them a part of himself so that they were immune to dragon fire.

It was a gift he'd silently given for all the kindness they'd shown him.

Before he could slide a hand between her legs, she'd reached between their bodies and wrapped her fingers around his hard length.

"Violet," he rasped out, desperation consuming him. In that moment he thought about the scars covering his body, wondered what she thought of them. But just as quickly, the thought dissipated as she squeezed his cock.

"Are you going to run away again?" she whispered, stroking him again, her touch light, delicate. Teasing.

"No. Never." Not if he had breath in his body. Even then, he wouldn't leave her. He'd somehow come back from the dead for her.

The visible sign of his mating instinct rose up, the blue and purple swirls of magic surrounding them, embracing both of them. This time he embraced it instead of trying to run from it.

"Good, because I love you."

He froze, stared down at her. *No. She doesn't love you.*

"Oh, I do."

Had he said that out loud? *You are unlovable.* And evil voice from his past rose up, whispered in his ear, stabbing into his heart.

He shoved the voice down, ignored it and focused on the stunning female in front of him. The one he loved right back. Unable to find his voice, to even truly believe what she'd just said, he cupped her breasts as he slanted his mouth over hers.

He could show her how he felt, worship her the way she deserved. He savored the way her tongue teased his, the bold strokes of her hand, but the scent of her need in the air was too strong for him to ignore.

And once he got inside her, he worried he'd lose control so he went down on his knees in front of her.

She let out a gasp, but he grasped one calf, slid it over his shoulder, opening her up to him. Gently, he slid his thumb over her already swollen clit and she jerked her hips forward, a soft sigh escaping.

He ran his thumb over her clit again, massaging it now in soft little circles. As he did, she moaned, began rolling her hips against his teases.

"Orion." His name was a soft prayer on her mouth, a plea and praise at the same time.

And he felt like Alpha of the entire world in that moment.

"Just like that." Another soft whisper, the scent of her desire spiking, making it hard to think about anything other than thrusting inside her.

But she was going to come first. Or he didn't deserve the designation of Alpha.

"You smell like heaven," he murmured, running his nose along her folds as he slid two fingers inside her.

And she definitely liked that; her inner walls tightened around him hard.

Instead of massaging her clit with his thumb, he sucked on it—and she rolled her face against him, dug her heel into his back.

He loved her like this, open for him to please, to devour. And he loved her more than anything, more than he'd imagined he could love another being, but he couldn't say the words. Not in English anyway.

"*I love you,*" he growled in a long-dead language, the words ripping from him before he sucked on her clit again.

She came with a sharp cry, her inner walls convulsing around his fingers as he thrust them into her, as he continued teasing her clit.

Finally she dug her fingers into his head, her breathing erratic as she looked at him. "I want all of you now." A not so gentle demand from his normally gentle female. "Inside me."

"Grab onto my shoulders." The growl tore from him as he took his cock in his hand. And as she did, he grabbed her ass with his other one, palmed her perfect backside and guided himself inside her.

"Oh God," she gasped at the intrusion.

"Orion. My name is…Orion," he gritted out.

She let out a little giggle that quickly evaporated as he pulled back, thrust inside her.

"Orion," she moaned out. "You're so big."

He knew she wasn't trying to feed his ego, and he was beyond words. Was beyond anything other than claiming her at this point.

She wasn't ovulating, and it was so rare for dragons to create life anyway, but in that moment he wasn't sure if he'd have cared if she was. No, he wouldn't have, and that scared him. Because the need to claim her, to mark her, to *keep* her was an all-consuming thing.

As he kept her pinned up against the wall, pistoning in and out of her, she dug her heels into his ass, gasping with each thrust inside her.

She was so damn tight, it was taking all his control not to spill his seed inside her. Not to mention this was Violet. His Violet.

His everything.

But...he gritted his teeth as his balls pulled up tight. She was his fantasy female—better, because she was real and she'd said she loved him. He was afraid to believe the words, but he believed in this moment.

As he reached between their bodies and began teasing her still sensitive clit, he claimed her mouth. He knew she could come again, could feel it in the way her inner walls locked around his cock.

She moaned into his mouth, her hands roaming over his chest and arms as if she wanted to touch all of him. He understood the sentiment because he wanted to touch all of her. Every single inch.

He thrust home hard, remained still, his cock pulsing with the need to climax. But he wanted her to feel every inch of him as he increased the pressure on her clit.

She attempted to roll her hips against him, was grinding against him, and his cock kept hitting that spot deep inside her as she did.

Crying out, she let her head fall back as her second climax slammed into her, this one stronger. "Oh yes, yes, yes," was all she said as her entire body shuddered under the impact of her orgasm.

So he let go, pulled back and thrust into her as his own climax built, built, then released inside her in long, hard strokes, filling her with his scent, with his come. He wasn't sure how long he continued thrusting inside her, but eventually they were just breathing hard as he kept her pinned against the wall.

She stroked her hands up and down his back in a gentle rhythm. "Pretty sure I saw stars with that second orgasm," she murmured, laying her head on his shoulder, burrowing her face into his neck.

Something in his chest ached at the trust she was putting in him. "Is there running water in this place?" Still holding her tight against him, he carried her toward the unmade bed.

"Mmm, yeah." She sounded a little drowsy as he sat her on the bed. "Runs on solar energy and a well."

Nodding, he grabbed a towel from the bathroom, wet it, then stepped back into the bedroom to find she hadn't moved.

She was still on the clean white mattress, her dark hair splayed around her face and shoulders. It had come out of her bun at some point and was now free.

She stared at him, her gray eyes heavy with satisfaction, her legs slightly spread as she stretched out, watching him. Wanting him.

He could see it in the way her gaze tracked his movements, roved over his entire body with raw hunger. He knew she could see his scars clearly in the light, but didn't seem to care at all. His cock swelled even harder as she admired him. Sitting on the edge of the bed, he started gently cleaning between her legs, worried she might be tender.

But then he slid his fingers inside her, felt his come and pushed it back inside her.

"Are you…" She trailed off, her cheeks flushing pink.

"I want my come all over you, *in* you. I'm *obsessed*, Violet." The words came out as a growl but she should understand how he felt. "I don't want any male looking at you, which I know is insane and not possible. But it's how I feel. And I want you to smell like me all the goddamn time so all supernaturals know you're claimed."

"Would you have really tied me to the bed to keep me from escaping?" Her eyes went even more heavy-lidded as she asked the question.

"Probably. *Yes*." No use in lying. She'd said she loved him. He wanted to make sure she understood all of him. The truth of who he was. "And I'm not letting you go." He clasped onto her hip as he tossed the towel aside. Then he stretched out on top of her, was glad when she spread her thighs for him, welcomed him.

"Do I look like I want to go anywhere?" She arched her hips slightly so that his cock was at her slick entrance.

He slid inside her all the way, kept her pinned in place. "Wouldn't matter if you did." His dragon half was taking over now, making sure she understood his possessiveness.

"Good. Because I'm not letting you go either. If you try to run from me again, I'll find you." Her tone was as fierce as her expression.

There was something about the sweet, determined way she said the words—the promise—that pierced him to his very core. She'd told him she loved him. He was never letting her go now. And because he couldn't find the words in English to tell her how he really felt, he buried his face against her neck and told her that he loved her in his mother tongue.

Told her that he'd destroy the world to keep her.

CHAPTER TWENTY-THREE

"At this point I don't care about much other than your beautiful naked body under mine," Orion murmured, nipping Violet's earlobe as he cuddled her from behind, holding her back against his chest. "But why were you at this house anyway?" He nipped her again.

"I can't think when you do that." Her voice was a breathy whisper. She settled her arm over his, linking their fingers together over her bare stomach.

It had been hours and they hadn't put their clothes back on. He liked the idea of her being naked all the time. But just around him.

He stopped nipping at her, just reveled in the fact that he was holding her like this—that she hadn't run screaming when he'd told her that he'd tie her to his bed to keep her. Something he wanted to try later. But with soft ties so he didn't hurt her wrists or ankles. "Okay, I'm not doing anything." Though his cock was heavy between them, pressing against her butt—the most perfect ass in the entire world. Galaxy. Now that he'd gotten a taste of her, his cock was going to be hard all the time apparently.

"Ah...what were you saying? Oh, I got called to see someone about an injury this morning. Then when I left I thought I'd get this cabin ready for whoever might want it. Prima maybe. Or even Cale and Laurel because I think they're going to want some privacy."

"*I'm* going to want some privacy," he growled.

Which made her laugh. "At least we didn't get the sheets dirty," she said, laughing even harder. The sheets she'd originally had when he'd stormed in were in a tangled pile on the hardwood floor.

"We're going to have to air this place out though...or maybe we keep it as a secret getaway for just the two of us." He didn't want to share this place with anyone else, especially since it was the first place he'd made love to her.

She half turned, her eyes darkening with need. "It seems so selfish... but let's do that. This can be our place."

Goddess, he loved the way she said "our."

He cleared his throat, hating to break the intimate spell, but they needed to get back soon and he needed to bring her up to date on some things. He didn't want secrets between them. Not anymore. He wanted to be open with her about everything, though it would take time for him to open up about his past. "I found the vampire, the one who killed Lucy's family."

Her eyes widened slightly, then she turned back around but didn't pull from him. If anything, she burrowed back into him, her head resting against his chest. "Does *found* mean you went all dragon on her?"

"Yes." He paused. "Does it bother you that I killed her?"

"No." Her answer was immediate. "I don't even know what that says about me, but she killed a family. A *child*. People I cared for. So no, it doesn't bother me. I hate that there's that kind of evil in the world, but I'm certainly not going to judge the one who's making our home a safer place."

Goddess, he loved her.

Tell her, idiot!

He ignored his dragon half. He'd *shown* her. He'd tell her later, when he could get the words out. Because he was afraid that if he said them, it would mess everything up. That the world would steal her from him. Then he'd be alone again.

He would only tell her once they were mated. Because once that happened, if one of them died, the other would too. Not that he wanted to think about anything happening to her, ever. But if she died, he didn't want to continue on. When a dragon mated, it was for life. They were the most possessive, obsessive of shifters. So he'd tell her only then. When it was safe.

"Can I ask you...some things about your past?" Her voice was tentative.

He tensed, unsure whether he was ready for this. Even with his beautiful mate. "You can ask anything."

"Well, I sort of know about the mating stuff."

He relaxed. "The mating manifestation, as my kind call it, is what you see now." Because it was all over the room, spread out everywhere, the colorful fog spilling out of the windows, and likely surrounding the entire house. "When a dragon first becomes intimate with their future mate, it shows up. Or that is my understanding. It's different for all dragons. For some it's literal earthquakes. For others, it's light or fire. I never knew what mine would look like because of...circumstances."

"Because of your parents?" Her tone was still hesitant.

He stilled, then forced himself to answer. "Yes. I take it Prima told you some things?" A guess, because that female was nosy as hell. And a good friend. The best.

"She did. And don't be mad at her." She squeezed his hand.

"I don't think I could ever be. She and her twin, they saved me. But I was always closer to Prima."

"I feel like I should be jealous but I really like her. And it's clear she cares for you—and I'm so happy you have her in your corner."

He tightened his grip around Violet, buried his face in her hair, inhaled deeply. Goddess, she grounded him in a way he couldn't fully process. But everything was okay when he was with her. It was as if he'd found a place to belong. She was his home. "I am too. And if she told you about my past, my parents, then she trusts and likes you too. For better or worse, she'll be in your corner for all eternity now."

"I like the idea of having a badass dragon friend."

"And I like the idea of you having a badass dragon *mate*. Me." *Claim her now*, his dragon demanded. *Right. Fucking. Now.*

She stilled as he ran his nose along her shoulder, skimmed his hand over her stomach until he slid lower and cupped her mound. "What exactly does mating mean?" she breathed out, her words shaky as he gently stroked a finger over her clit. "I mean, I think I get it, but I want details."

He couldn't remember how many times he'd made her come so far. *Lies. It has been eight*, his dragon informed him. *Not nearly enough. Keep going.* "When we mate—"

"Don't you mean *if?*"

He pressed his teeth to her shoulder without breaking the skin. "*No.* I told you I was possessive."

She shivered against him, the scent of her lust spiraling around them. "This is taking bossy to a new level," she breathed out.

"This is taking what's mine," he said as he opened her legs from behind, slid a finger inside her. Goddess, she was soaked, and it was all for him.

She clenched around his finger, pushed back into him. "Are you trying to change the subject?"

"No, there's nothing to discuss. When you officially become my mate, the manifestation will disappear. But we'll be bonded for life."

"Explain, please." Her voice was shaky as he replaced his finger with his cock, pushed deep.

"When dragons mate, it's forever. If I die, you will too, and vice versa." Aaaand he realized maybe he should have eased her into that. "But dragons are very difficult to kill." And she felt amazing, her tight walls clenching around his cock.

"But…" She moaned as he pulled out, pushed in again. "I can't think, Orion."

He thrust in hard, loving the sound of his name on her lips. Loved the feel of her taking him so deep. "We'll be linked forever. So *if* you decide to mate with me…" His dragon snorted, as if he was going to give her a choice. But Orion would always give her a choice. He would never actually take it from her, not from his sweet Violet. "Then our lives are intertwined for all time. And you will gain a longer life span to match mine. Eventually you'll grow stronger as well, maybe even gain some magical abilities." There was more to it, but she'd reached back, was clutching onto his hip as he slowly, steadily thrust into her.

Goddess, she was so tight, clenching him so hard.

"I...we'll talk later. Oh, yes, harder, *please.*"

He loved when she begged. Loved when she did anything.

He increased the pressure on her clit as he continued thrusting, having learned what she liked. Which was basically everything. She was so reactive to his touch, and maybe that was more of a mate thing.

It didn't matter that she was human, she was his. Forever.

As he pushed into her again, he gritted his teeth, ordering his cock to behave when all he wanted to do was come inside her, mark her again. Again and again, the pressure was riding him hard. That hunger to sink his canines into her neck as they both came was a live thing inside him.

Suddenly she jerked against him, her inner walls convulsing around him as she started climaxing again. "Orion!"

He let go of his own control, clasping onto her hips as he continued to piston inside her, released himself once again in hard strokes.

Even as they both came down from their orgasm, his cock didn't go fully down. He'd never understood how wild the mating instinct could be until now. Until Violet. But even then, he hadn't understood until he'd gotten his first taste of her.

She turned in his arms, looped a leg over his thigh and her arm over his back as she cuddled into him. "I didn't think it was possible to climax so much." Her gray eyes sparked with hunger and love.

For him.

He still wasn't sure he'd processed it. He brushed his lips over hers, deciding that they didn't need to get back just yet. Maybe not for a while. He wanted to imprint himself on her before they returned, to make sure she knew who she belonged to.

Him.

And once he was certain she was ready, he planned to claim her forever.

CHAPTER TWENTY-FOUR

Violet felt like a new person as she rode on Orion in dragon form toward their house. Just completely different. Probably because of all the orgasms.

So many of them, she was still floating around in a cloud of pleasure.

He was so intense and dominating in bed, and she hadn't expected to like the dominating thing so much, but holy hell. It had been soooooo incredible. And she wanted him again, which seemed ridiculous.

He'd turned her into a sex maniac.

As he landed next to the barn, not bothering to camouflage himself —which she loved, because he felt free to be who he was with her and didn't give a damn what anyone else thought—she hoped that things wouldn't change now that they were back.

They'd been in a sort of sex bubble, and deep down she was worried he might pull away from her again.

After she slid off him, he shifted with such quick fluidity it stunned her. There were sparks of magic, something she wasn't sure she'd ever get used to, and then he was standing there in human form, all naked and gorgeous.

She glanced around, saw Rose heading their way, so she shoved Orion's bag of clothes at him. "I don't want my sister seeing you naked," she murmured. She didn't want *anyone* seeing him naked, and didn't care if nudity wasn't a big deal to shifters. Also something she wasn't sure she'd get used to.

"I don't relish the idea of her seeing me naked either," he said as he pulled his pants on.

"Hey, guys." Rose grinned as she looked between the two of them.

Violet narrowed her gaze. "Why are you smiling like that?"

"Because you two finally did it." And Rose looked ridiculously pleased about it. Then her even more ridiculous sister thrust her hips forward like a total perv and cackled as she did an Austin Powers imitation.

She really did love Rose. "How...what?" She glanced over at Orion, who just shrugged as he tugged his T-shirt on, clearly fighting a smile. "How do you know?"

"Because Mari and I told him you went off with the panda and he looked like he was about to blow up." Rose grinned at Orion. "It worked, right? Come on, it totally worked!"

To her surprise, Orion laughed. "You and Mari certainly knew which buttons to push. Congratulations, it worked."

"What panda?" Violet asked.

"Baris, the hot healer. He's a panda shifter."

Violet's mouth fell open for a moment as she turned to look at Orion. "Baris is a panda?"

"And that's why I didn't tell you." Orion tugged her close, claimed her mouth completely before pulling back. "And I don't think you should be around him. Ever."

Rose fell into a fit of laughter, but Violet ignored her. "You know that's not happening, right? We're going to be working together."

"I know," Orion gritted out, his dragon in his gaze.

It was still a little startling to see, but she liked all of him. "You can't eat him or kill him or whatever you're thinking, *dragon*. Please tell me you know that."

Orion's eyes shifted back to human and he shrugged. "No promises. But if you burn those panda pajama pants, I might consider letting him live."

She knew he was kidding, but pinched his butt anyway. "So where is Mari, anyway?"

"Still on patrol," Orion answered before Rose could. "She's with Bentley," he added as he looked down at Violet. "I've been in contact with them via radio."

"When did you…" She trailed off, looked at Rose, who was staring at them with open curiosity.

Violet wanted to ask when he could have contacted them, but decided to save the questions for later. When they didn't have an audience. She felt as if an eternity had passed since they'd jumped each other this morning, but it was only around two in the afternoon. Holy hell, how had she had so much sex in such a short amount of time? So many orgasms? It felt like a week had passed.

"You look like you're trying to do some complex math," Rose murmured. "And I've got a horse to check on. But congrats, you two," she said, stalking off.

"Oh, thank you." They weren't really mated though. Not technically. Orion had told her all about mating and said she *would* be his mate, but hadn't indicated when that would happen. He hadn't really asked, either, and she simply couldn't be mad about that. She loved this dragon with every part of her.

Turning into Orion's hold, she looked up at him as she slid her arms around him. "I feel like I'm in a post-sex haze right now."

Growling, he tugged her even closer. "I know. I've got to check on the border and do a few other things, but in a couple hours we'll be…" He trailed off, looked over her shoulder.

Glancing in that direction, she saw Darius and Hazel walking toward them. Keeping her arm around Orion, she turned to meet them and smiled.

Darius nodded politely at her, then focused on Orion. "I know you're busy so I'm going to get right to it. King's meetings are over and he'd like to meet now if possible. I know this is last-minute, but he's got a break and he wants to meet you face-to-face. To formally create a tie between our territories."

"It's an Alpha thing," Orion murmured to Violet when he saw the look on her face. "We do need to meet in person and officially solidify this alliance."

"Oh."

"You can also bring a list of things you'd like or need for the territory," Hazel added. "I think Luna or Baris probably already told you, but we've got a lot of medical supplies and machines we're happy to give you. I know Baris has already been in communication with Greer, our 'head healer' so to speak, but you're a human doctor so I'm guessing you'll have different needs."

"I…yes, that would be great."

"Violet comes with me," Orion said. "If this is an Alpha meeting, she's going to be my mate so she needs to be there."

Darius nodded, as if that was a given.

But… "How long will I need to be gone?" she asked.

"King wants to plan a visit here hopefully next week, but this meeting would just be at the edge of our territory. It shouldn't be more than a couple hours. His mate will not be there as she's dealing with some unruly vampires." His tone was dry as he said it. "Not violent ones, just troublemakers. Whether you go or not is up to the two of you," Darius added.

"I don't like the idea of being gone when some of the humans here won't be comfortable with Baris. Once he's been here longer and we're more integrated with supernaturals, I'll be fine leaving with you but… for now I think I should stay," she said.

Orion's expression went dark. "I'm not leaving you."

"Prima's here. She can be my chaperone if you're worried about vampires." Which was a real threat, she understood that.

His jaw tensed and she realized that yep, that was what this was about. And probably he didn't want to be separated for too long because of this wild mating pull. Unless she was the only one feeling it? No, he had to be feeling this too. He was the supernatural one.

Orion looked at the other two. "Give us a moment?"

They both nodded and headed back in the direction of the barn. Their new encampment was set up on the other side, and once they were out of sight Orion focused solely on her.

"The meeting with King can wait."

"Can it?" She wasn't sure of supernatural rules or...any of that stuff. Oh God, she needed a crash course on that.

He paused. "Technically it would be better if I went now and solidified everything. Because I'm going to be infiltrating the territory to the west of us. I believe the vampire in charge has been sending vampires to attack our borders to goad me or us into action. Into doing something stupid. Before I infiltrate them, I'd like to have met King first. I want to see his face, smell his scent, and know that he's honorable and will indeed be our ally if we go to war with those vampires. I believe that he is, or Prima wouldn't have lived in his territory at all, but I still need to meet him."

"Then go today. Get it done and then..." She sighed. "We'll talk about you apparently invading another territory." She hated the thought of him in danger, even if he was a badass dragon.

"We'll also talk about mating." His jaw was tense again, as if he was gearing up for some sort of argument.

And she remembered Prima's words—not that she needed them to know what she wanted, how she felt. Because Violet could be like a demanding dragon female any day of the week where Orion was concerned. "What's to talk about? I thought we were getting mated." She lifted an eyebrow, knew her expression was challenging.

He blinked. "Just like that?"

"You want to chase me? Because that can be arranged," she whispered, stroking her hands down his back all the way to his butt. She squeezed once, making him groan.

"Goddess, Violet. I want you to think about everything I told you. I don't want you to have any regrets, because if we mate, there's no turning back." His voice was tight, as if he was forcing the words out.

"I don't need to think about it. I've been thinking about you every day since the moment you arrived here."

His jaw ticked and the dragon was back. "If you had regrets, it would destroy me."

Oh God, the look in his eyes destroyed her right now. She tightened her grip on him. "You don't have to be afraid of that." But she hadn't been raised the way he had been. She'd had loving parents and sisters and could only imagine the horrors he'd had to live through. She figured the only way she could truly get him to understand that she'd have no regrets was to show him. And that was something only time would do.

"When I get back, you're mine. Forever." His dragon was there in his gaze again, and she could also see the adoration in those eyes as clearly as in his human ones.

"Yes." It wasn't a question for her. He was everything she'd ever wanted, could have even imagined. He was better. And he'd been protecting her, her sisters, their whole community for a year. She'd won the lottery with this dragon.

He hugged her tight as she buried her face against his chest, holding on for dear life. It was only a few hours that he'd be gone. Not a big deal.

At least that was what she was telling herself. She didn't want to be separated from him right now. Something deep inside her was terrified that if he left, things would go haywire.

But she knew that was just this intense mating thing going on between them. Nothing more.

CHAPTER TWENTY-FIVE

"So, you're just stuck to me, huh?" Violet asked Prima as they walked down the steps of the Powell family's house. Months ago the Powell family had moved to a house closer to her family's farm. Prima had come with Violet to this visit and the three homes before.

She'd been quiet, except with the kids. With them, she'd been funny and a chatterbox. It was an interesting change to see. She'd even changed into her dragon and let the kids climb up her tail and slide down her wings. Talk about surreal.

"Yep. My orders were clear."

Violet snorted. "I can't even see you taking 'orders.'"

"Well, when it comes from one of my best friends, it's not hard." Prima gave her a speculative look as they reached the end of the walkway that led to where they'd left their bikes. The bikes seemed to almost offend Prima, but she'd ridden on one without question. "So, when are you two getting mated officially?" Prima demanded.

"Aren't you a nosypants?" Violet asked as she got onto her bright teal Huffy. She set her medical bag in the big basket in front.

"I've been called worse, and yes, I am. So?"

"As soon as Orion gets back. He wanted me to take time to think about it, but I don't need time. I just need him."

Prima gave her a big grin then and only sort of looked terrifying as she started pedaling. "I knew I liked you, Violet. You are a worthy mate."

"That's the first time you've said my name." Usually she called her "pretty human" or "tiny human" or nothing at all.

Prima lifted a shoulder as they headed down the roughly worn concrete path. "Well you're going to be the Alpha's mate soon, which basically means you're soon going to be an Alpha couple."

"But I'm not supernatural. Or physically strong. At all," she added for emphasis as a new thought occurred to her. "I mean, I'm not walking away from him or anything, but will that matter for Orion?"

"Alphas aren't always the strongest physically. The majority of the time they are, but definitely not always. One of my nieces is one half of an Alpha couple, and while she's a dragon she's soft like you. But there is no doubt that she's in charge as much as her mate is. Maybe more so because he'd destroy the world for her. And I don't mean that figuratively."

"I didn't think you did," she murmured as they reached a four-way with the handmade signs Laurel had made giving directions. Not that she needed them. "So why don't you run a territory of your own? Because you're Alpha enough. Right?"

"Look who's nosy now."

"I've always been nosy. I have three sisters, it's like part of my DNA. We're always all up in each other's business. And speaking of sisters, I have another question. Where is your twin? Orion said you had one."

"So many questions," Prima said with a grin, kicking her legs out to either side and coasting along as if she was a child. She looked young in that moment with her shiny, tangled hair flying behind her and her face aglow, but then her expression shifted. "To answer your first question, the reason I don't run a territory is because I don't want to. Not now, anyway. At one time I was worshipped as a goddess. But that was so long ago sometimes I forget about it. In another lifetime I helped lead my family's clan." There was a sort of wistful note in her voice, however. But then she continued. "And my twin is currently in another realm handling something."

It was staggering to think about how old Prima actually was—heck, how old Orion was. She knew they were similar in age, but Orion's eyes weren't as alien as hers. Prima's could turn otherworldly. Violet had heard of other realms, and while it was a lot to think about, she considered it the equivalent of discovering other planets—and she had no doubt there was more life out there. "How many realms are there?" she asked abruptly.

"Who knows?" Prima lifted her shoulder in that casual way of hers. "I like these bikes. I've never tried one before, because, well, why would I? But I can see the novelty of them."

Violet snickered. They weren't a novelty to her, they were a valid method of transportation, but she just smiled. "Do you think maybe we could sit down and go over…supernatural rules? Or things I should be aware of, I guess. Not today or anything, but sometime soon? When I mate Orion, I want to make sure that I understand how to interact with other supernaturals." So she didn't inadvertently insult someone and start a war between territories.

"Of course. I think there are some books floating around somewhere. But I'll have to check with my nieces and nephews. One of my nieces is excellent at research and has probably written a book herself. She is certainly brilliant enough."

Books? Something she could reference if she had questions? Okay that spoke to the book nerd in her. "Thank you."

As they continued riding, a peacefulness descended on them until Prima suddenly jerked to a halt. "Do you smell that?"

She halted her bike and inhaled but only scented the crisp afternoon air. "What am I supposed to be smelling?"

"There's a fire." She turned slightly. "To the west. Come on, you can ride on me. I'll carry the bikes." Without waiting for an answer, she stripped in seconds, barely giving Violet enough time to grab her medical bag and move away from Prima as she shifted.

Prima's wing knocked into a nearby tree, but she ignored it as she scooped up the bikes. Violet knew what to do by now and quickly climbed up one of her outstretched jade-colored wings, simultaneously marveling at the glittering scales while worry clawed at her insides.

A fire was never a good thing. Perhaps it was just someone lighting a bonfire, or burning trash or…it could be anything at all. But if it was enough for Prima to move into action so quickly, it couldn't be good.

As the beautiful dragon swooped low over the trees, Violet held on tight, scanning the horizon for any signs of fire.

And when she spotted a billowing column of black smoke to the west, coming from the direction of abandoned homes, her stomach tightened. A fire could quickly get out of control and they didn't have the manpower to handle anything huge. If they couldn't get it under control, it could be devastating.

The closer Prima flew to their destination, the more Violet's fear rose. They were close to Lili and Aurélie's home. *Oh no. No, no, no.* The young woman and her grandmother had been packing up to leave, to move closer to everyone else in just a few days.

Moments later Violet saw that it wasn't their home on fire, but one a couple doors down. She shoved out a breath, relief punching through her. Hopefully they were unharmed. Prima took a sharp dive toward the street below where Mari, Cale and a few others were working to haul things out of the house.

As soon as Prima landed, Violet slid off her and raced toward Aurélie and Lili. The older woman was sitting in the grass, her breathing shallow.

"She's panicking," Lili said, crouching next to Violet as she checked Aurélie's pulse. "But I think it might be more. The smoke shifted this way and we've both been breathing it in."

"You're right," she murmured, looking into Aurélie's eyes. "Can you talk to me? How do you feel?"

"Okay…" She took another shallow breath, her entire body shaking.

"Lili, grab me a blanket if you can find one." She looked over her shoulder, saw that Prima was attempting to put out the other fire with some sort of dragon magic. But it had jumped to another house. Violet shoved down the panic that wanted to grow and spread inside her. She needed to focus on helping where she could. She turned back to Aurélie. "We're going to transport you to my medical center"—a small setup next to their home's barn—"and get you on oxygen. And I'm going to ask a healer to take a look at you as well. Okay?"

"Yes." Aurélie nodded, her white curls shaking with the movement.

That was when Violet knew this was bad; the older woman wasn't arguing or giving her any lip. "Mari!" she called out to her sister. "How'd you get here?" she asked as her sister dropped a bag of something on the lawn.

"Rode on Bentley. He's a big ass wolf. But we've got a vehicle a couple houses down. Not a motorcycle," she added.

"Help me, then." Violet stood, helping Aurélie to her feet as Lili wrapped a blanket around her.

More supernaturals were arriving then, moving into action to put the fire out and pull out the rest of the contents of Lili and Aurélie's home in case it ended up catching fire. They had this all under control and Violet needed to get the older woman away from the thickening smoke.

"What happened?" Violet asked once Mari was on the road, headed back to their property.

"Not sure yet. I was out on patrol with Bentley when we smelled smoke."

"I don't know either," Lili said, sitting on the other side of her grandmother. "I was in the middle of packing when we heard a sort of boom. Like a small explosion."

Violet frowned at that, but looked at Aurélie. "We're going to get you on oxygen as soon as we stop. Just hang in there a little longer."

The older woman let out a little cough, but nodded.

Luckily the drive back wasn't long and Aurélie was going to be fine, by the looks of things.

By the time she finished getting Aurélie settled, and had convinced her to let Baris do a full-body scan using his healer's magic, she stepped out of her clinic an hour later to find Thomas heading her way.

"Hey, everything okay?" She needed to check in with Prima, to find out about the fire, but Thomas looked panicked.

"No. It's my uncle. He took a bad spill. I tried radioing you but couldn't get through."

She frowned, looking down at her radio. The light was green, but she'd probably been too far away before. "Let me grab my bag and we'll go. Did you drive or bike here?"

"I drove. Used that stuff from Mari to power my truck."

"Okay good, we'll get there faster." And it was getting dark, the sun already setting. "Give me a sec." After telling Baris where she was going, she grabbed her bag and hurried out into the cold night air, thankful that she could depend on someone else right now. They needed more doctors and healers and she was hoping they could convince more of them to move here.

With that thought, she laid her head back against the passenger seat headrest of the dusty pickup and let out a sigh, wondering when Orion would be back. Hopefully soon.

She'd missed him the last few hours, even with all her patient visits. There'd been a low-level ache in her chest, a constant reminder that he was separated from her.

"I'm sorry," Thomas murmured.

Frowning, she opened her eyes, had started to ask what he was talking about when she saw the needle plunging into her thigh.

"I'm really sorry," he repeated as blackness engulfed her.

CHAPTER TWENTY-SIX

Blinking, Violet opened her eyes and sat up. Then wished she
hadn't.

Nausea made her swallow hard, her skull throbbing as she looked
around in total confusion. *What the hell?*

She stared at the bottles of wine lined up neatly in the crisscrossed
storage unit across from her. It covered the entire wall. Next to it were
two long, slim refrigerators that were clearly working. A little blue light
emanated from them, showing off that they too were full of wine.

She looked down at herself, saw that she was still wearing what she'd
had on the last time she remembered anything. Jeans and a thick
sweater. And she smelled like smoke—oh God, Thomas had injected her
with something. And now she was apparently in some fancy wine
cellar?

She shoved a hand out, struggled to her feet, had to prop herself up
on the exposed brick wall next to her. Blinking, she saw there was
simply wine everywhere.

What. The. Hell.

Tentatively, she took a step forward, blinked again and weaved on
her feet. "Nope. Not good, Violet. Not good at all," she muttered to
herself. As she took another step, she patted her pockets for anything

she could use to call for help. No phone, no radio, nothing. Not that her phone had worked half the time since The Fall anyway.

At least she was still dressed. Hopefully that meant she hadn't been kidnapped for some gross trafficking situation.

Ugh. Nausea swelled again, and as it did the sound of a heavy lock clicking filled the air.

Focus, focus. She turned, tried to figure out where it was coming from. The room she was in was long and all she could see were stupid bottles everywhere.

Maybe she could use one of them as a weapon?

Before she could really develop any sort of plan, a male in a cashmere sweater and slacks appeared. And he was definitely, *definitely* not human. Not with those fangs and slightly glowing amber gaze.

His dark hair was perfectly styled; his shoes had to be expensive. They looked like alligator. And why was she even noticing?

She stared at him, her throat dry, a steady drumbeat still thumping in her skull as she tried to focus on his movements. But he was so fast.

One second he was at the little alcove entrance she hadn't seen at first, then he was in front of her, peering down at her curiously. He lifted a hand to touch her cheek but she batted it away.

Or attempted to. Mainly she flopped her hand out like a fish, which made him laugh.

Oh, so she amused him. Screw this guy. "What. Do...you want?" she slurred out.

He tapped her nose once, still laughing to himself. "Your mate. Who, unfortunately, isn't your actual mate yet. I thought you two would have sealed the deal, as the kids say these days. That was my understanding anyway. I'd planned to kill you, which would have killed your mate." He made a tsking sound, turning his back to her as he approached one of the rows of reds. "But that is quite all right, my dear. I can still use you to my advantage. Because that big, dumb dragon will come for you."

"He's not dumb," she snarled, her words still slurring. Good one, she berated herself. Damn it, she needed some kind of weapon. A wooden stake? Something through the heart had to kill anything, right? Or she could slice any one of his arteries if she just had a scalpel or something really sharp. Ooh, maybe she could break a bottle and use the glass.

Considering she could barely lift her hand, let alone stand straight, that was a dumb idea. But she had to get the hell out of...wherever here was. "Where am I?"

"My wine cellar, of course. Isn't it incredible? I'm Vitus, by the way," he said, as if his name should mean something. When she just stared at him, he continued. "I commandeered this mansion once I carved out this territory. It used to belong to some famous tennis player who sadly didn't survive. His blood was delicious, however," the vampire droned on. "And since my former estate was destroyed in The Fall by those blasted dragons, I had to find something new, didn't I?" The question was clearly rhetorical. He picked up another bottle, inspected it, then nodded to himself before tucking it under his arm. "Yes, this will do nicely."

"So...I'm bait for Orion?" She was struggling to process everything, had to throw a hand out on the nearest shelf to steady herself.

"Oh yes. That dragon has been a thorn in my side for months. Your territory is absolutely ripe. But he's been thwarting all my attempts to snatch up a few snacks. So I'm annexing all of your territory into mine. It'll be simpler that way."

Did he just say thwarting? *What the hell.* Oh no, it was a villain speech. She wanted to puke again. Yep, she was definitely going to be sick.

"You're not going to kill him," she growled. Orion was a powerful dragon. He was fireproof and bombproof and whatever-proof. No way was this pretty boy asshole killing him, and Orion *would* come for her.

She wrapped her fingers around the nearest bottle, tried to pull it out of its slot, but couldn't actually do it. *Damn it!*

Suddenly the vampire was in front of her, his fangs on full display, gleaming under the overhead lighting. "I thought you were a doctor. That you were supposed to be intelligent. I swear it's the same with all you humans. That human who handed you to me thought I was going to turn him into a vampire. Fool. He was so easy to convince too. Didn't mind betraying you." He gently swatted her fingers away from the bottle. "The only things humans are good for are food and sex. So I killed that human and of course I'm going to kill your dragon. You're going to watch me do it." His eyes slightly glowed as he stared at her, as if waiting for a response.

She stared right back, mainly because she couldn't think of anything to say. She was barely keeping her bile down as it was.

"Cat got your tongue?" he sneered, flashing his fangs again.

Violet bent forward and puked all over the brick floor.

"Oh, for the goddess's sake," he snarled, moving away from her at rapid speed before she could spray him. "Someone clean this up," he called out, his voice fading as his feet echoed up the stairs once again.

Violet stumbled away from the mess, then collapsed near the opposite wall, the brick cool against her face. She needed to shake the drugs off. To get up, then get the hell out of here.

She wasn't going to let Orion die. Nope. Not happening.

She might not be able to take down the obnoxious and terrifying vampire, but she was going to escape and warn Orion. That was the plan, but another wave of darkness dragged her under in spite of how hard she tried to keep her eyes open.

VIOLET WASN'T sure how much time had passed when she opened her eyes again. But as she sat up, she saw that the puke had been cleaned up, and there were clean clothes set out for her along with a tray of snack foods.

She ignored the food and clothes and stood, relieved to discover she could think clearer this time. Before, she'd been in a deep fog, unable to swim her way through before passing out again.

After taking a few steps, she realized that she wasn't going to be sick this time. Walking deeper into the room, she saw the little opening alcove the vampire had come out of, and as she took another step, saw the winding set of stone stairs he'd come down. If that vampire thought she was going to just sit around and eat his probably drugged snacks while she waited around for Orion to show up, he was the stupid one.

Grabbing onto the metal railing, a chill snaked through her as she quietly ascended them—and saw that there was a huge lock on the heavy wood and metal door blocking her way at the top. She pressed her ear up against the paneling, but didn't hear anything.

They hadn't even tied her up so they clearly didn't think she was a threat. He'd made his disdain of humans clear. That was going to work to her advantage, because she was about to prove them wrong.

She hurried back down the stairs, did a quick walk-through of the long room and couldn't find any other way to leave but that door.

Her stomach growled, but she ignored it. No way was she eating any of the food they'd left. They'd probably drugged it.

Think, think, think. She started opening cabinets, looking under the little double sink and... "Bingo," she whispered, studying the bottles of chemicals and other supplies.

Might not work, but she was going to try to make a poor man's version of sulfuric acid and burn her way through the door's lock. Then she was getting the hell out of here.

CHAPTER TWENTY-SEVEN

Orion turned away from Prima and the others, his dragon right under the surface, ready to destroy everything in his path. He was barely keeping his rage and fear in check. Bowie sat next to him, whining softly, clearly picking up on the tension coming from the small crowd of people. Bowie's presence was one of the only reasons he hadn't completely lost his dragon senses.

"I have no excuse, Orion. I'm sorry," Prima said, her words tight, her expression gutted in a way he'd never seen before. "This is all my fault."

"We're not placing blame," Mari snapped. "We're going to find my sister. And it's not your fault," she added.

"Mari's right." He gave Prima a hard look, too many emotions punching through him right now. He'd returned at the same time Prima had come back from putting out a fire. She'd been looking for Violet, who'd left to take care of someone without telling her.

He'd been able to retrace Violet's steps, track her to somewhere near John's farm, but then he'd lost her. It was as if she'd just vanished. Once Orion had realized that something was wrong, that Violet was gone, they'd reached out to everyone, to see if anyone else was missing and started searching hard.

"We keep up the grid search of our farm and John's. Has anyone seen Thomas?" His uncle said he'd left but hadn't come back.

"No." Cale shook his head, his expression dark. "We need to accept the possibility that they were both taken."

He said the words Orion had been thinking from the moment he hadn't been able to find Violet. He'd already scoured the territory line, had everyone in the community out looking for her. And the shifters from New Orleans had been out on the borders as well, helping patrol and search at the same time. Everyone was pitching in, but hours had passed. Too many. And it was dark and freezing out.

She was missing. He had to face that fact.

If something had happened to her and she was lost or... no. He didn't know how to handle this. "She was taken," he growled in response to Cale. The truth was, he didn't care about Thomas, barely knew the human. As an Alpha, he knew he should be more concerned, but all he cared about was Violet.

She could be anywhere right now. Could be hurt, could be—

"Snap out of it." Prima was next to him in the blink of an eye, her dragon in her eyes. "You'll spiral if you go down that path. If you think she was taken, then you know what to do. And I've got your back."

"Same." Cale nodded.

"We all do," Mari added.

Though he didn't think Mari fully understood what Prima and Cale meant. He was going to infiltrate the vampire territory to the west and burn down everything until he found Violet. Because they were the only ones who could have taken her.

"Mari, you stay here, remain in contact with Bentley. The two of you are in charge while we're gone."

"I want to go with you." Her jaw was set tight.

"No. Not for this. We're going to be flying and...you just can't. I need you here." He wasn't going to explain himself to her or anyone. "I'll bring your sister back." Otherwise he wouldn't be coming back. If something had happened to Violet, he was done with this world.

Mari nodded, and so did Rose and Laurel, their expressions all mirrors of fear and worry.

Suddenly his radio crackled. "Orion, can you hear me?" It was Bentley.

Hope surged through him as he answered. "Go ahead."

"I'm at the west border near the water tower on Delphine Road. There's a message for you. It's about Violet."

Orion didn't remember moving, didn't remember shifting. But he was in the air, flying faster than he ever had toward Bentley's location.

He was vaguely aware of Prima and Cale behind him, their scents trailing in the air, but he could only focus on Bentley's words. There was a message about Violet.

Whoever had taken her was going to die very soon. Every one of them.

He spotted Bentley standing in the middle of the road next to a stranger, his body language tense. The human female next to Bentley shrunk into herself, hiding behind him as Orion let his camouflage fall and landed in the middle of the road.

He roared, all his fear coming out in a burst of uncontrolled rage. Then he shifted, stalked toward the two of them.

Bentley held up his hands. "She's not part of this. She's human and she's scared."

"I know she's human." He could scent that much. "Talk," he snarled.

Bentley took a breath, but held out an arm as if to protect the human. "She can't talk if she's terrified. I told her we would offer her safe haven and I meant it."

"It doesn't matter," the human, who he realized couldn't be more than twenty-five, whispered.

He shoved back the guilt that erupted as she stepped out to face him, her entire body shaking. And he also realized she was likely malnourished and felt like the monster he probably looked like. "Why doesn't it matter?" He softened his voice, hoping he looked less feral than he felt. "And where is Violet?"

She swallowed hard, but then straightened. Her blonde hair was pulled back into a braid, and while she was clean, she was far too thin and her clothes were patched everywhere. "Violet is unharmed, but she's a prisoner of the vampire who runs the town, ah, territory, I live in. He took over after The Fall. He…" She swallowed hard. "He told me to deliver this message and said that if I did not come back, he'd kill my mother. So if you kill me, she's dead. I have to return."

Violet was unharmed. He repeated those words over in his head, the vise around his ribs easing. He could breathe again. "What's your name?" he asked, softening his tone further. The fear rolling off her was potent, choking his senses.

"Sadie," she whispered.

"Okay, Sadie. Can you tell me more? What's this vampire's name? What else did he say? And what does he want?"

"His name is Vitus. He wants to fight you. Tonight."

Orion glanced up at the sky, knew the sun would be up in less than an hour. He didn't know a vampire named Vitus so this couldn't be about an old feud, which was something. This was a territory issue. "Do you know where Violet is being held?"

She nodded jerkily. "In the big house. The mansion. But I don't think I'm supposed to tell you. He told me not to answer anything." Her expression tightened. "Oh God, he'll know. He'll question me and—"

"Stop. I have a way around that. Bentley, get Scarlett." One of the witches who lived in his territory. "Even if he questions you, one of my witches will be able to cast a light spell to ensure that all your answers come across as the truth," he told Sadie.

She blinked once, twice, then tears started rolling down her cheeks. "Okay," she whispered. "He lives in the mansion and I'm pretty sure she's being held there, but I don't know where. I've never been inside it."

"Tell me everything you know."

"He wants you to fight him for the woman. But…" She swallowed hard. "I heard him tell one of his men that if for some reason he loses"— she used a mocking tone, and he saw a bit of spine peeking through— "to kill her anyway. He's mean and petty. And I don't like to use this word, but he's crazy." She stood a little straighter now. "All the humans in our territory are basically blood slaves. The vampires rule everything but there are some wolves too. They're just as bad, maybe worse. They keep us from escaping during the day when the vampires are sleeping. I think they and the vampires are planning on invading your territory when you meet him to fight."

Orion nodded, having expected that once she'd told him the vampire wanted to fight him. Of course the vampire would want to invade while he was gone. "What else do you know about Vitus?"

"Not much," she said, no longer shivering. "But I think he's really old. And powerful. I've seen him do some sort of like, magic-y things. I don't know what else to call it. He's killed people with his mind. Thrown them using telekinetic powers, I guess? But it's not like I've spent a lot of time with him. I've only seen him kill a few people and I've heard a lot of rumors. He sent me because I'm a throwaway. He doesn't care if you kill me. I think he probably expects you to."

"I'm not going to kill you," he said, disgusted and full of rage for this monster. "Has he kidnapped anyone else?"

"From your territory? No. I don't think so. The only message I was given was that he wanted to fight you." She reached into her pocket, pulled out a piece of paper. "Here. It's circled on the map."

He took it. "What time did he say?"

"Sunset."

"Did he say anything else?"

"That he'd kill your human if you tried to attack beforehand."

Orion measured the human female. Her shuttered expression. "What are you leaving out?"

"He was graphic in what he said he'd do to your female. You look very murdery. I don't think you need a description, and honestly, I don't want to say the words anyway."

The human was right.

He turned to find Prima landing with Scarlett on her back. Scarlett slid down quickly and Prima stayed in her dragon form, crouched and ready.

He...couldn't believe she'd let Violet out of her sight. Even if he *understood* how it had happened. He never should have left. Hell, if this was anyone's fault, it was his. He should have protected his female.

Shutting out those thoughts, he quickly told Scarlett what he needed her to do, and the witch, a kind mom of three kids under the age of five, nodded and got to work.

He stood next to Prima's beast as he watched Scarlett work her incantations. "I'm not angry at you. Or...at least I understand what happened." He *was* angry, but that was mainly at the entire goddamn world. Himself included. "And I need to ask you for a favor. I'm going to fight the vampire soon." Because he wasn't waiting any longer. No, he would infiltrate now using his camouflage. He would save his Violet. "And I need you to remain behind and protect the territory. My wolves are capable but we don't have the numbers. And you're one of the strongest dragons I know." She could take on an army by herself if needed. He'd seen her do it.

"I can cast a confusion spell," Scarlett said, turning from the human and walking toward them. "Along our border. I can make it specific, for vampires only. So if you think it's going to be mainly vampires invading, I can cast a fairly wide net along the west edges of our territory. It won't last forever, but it can screw them up enough for our people to take them down."

He believed her. Orion hadn't even realized she was a witch until she'd told him—so she was good at masking herself, even from someone as ancient as him. "Do it. Is the human okay? Did you sense that anyone tinkered with her mind?"

"She's good. The spell will last. And," she lowered her voice, glanced behind her then back at him, "I added a very light tracking spell to her clothes. It's not perfect, but I didn't want to actually spell her because that can be detected, especially since I just cast a truth-blocking spell. So I should be able to track where she goes after this."

"Good work, thank you."

"Of course. I want to get Violet back too." Her voice cracked but she looked away, cleared her throat. "When my husband died, she was there for me. For all of us. I'll do whatever it takes to bring her home."

Thank you. He thought the words, but couldn't force them out past his tight throat. He needed Violet more than his next breath.

And he was going to save his female. Save her, then claim her forever.

CHAPTER TWENTY-EIGHT

Heart pounding, Violet shoved open the heavy door, carefully stepping over the sizzling metal lock on the marble floor. The acid had worked. She stripped her gloves off, tossed them behind her.

Wine bottle raised, she was ready to hit anyone who got in her way, but...the hallway was empty. She might have a real chance to escape without a fight. One she wasn't sure she'd win anyway. The whole objective was to get out of here before being spotted.

Fear pounded in her ears as she raced down the hallway, blindly looking for an exit. She was only getting one shot at this. The gold-framed art on the walls was a blur as she hurried along. As she moved, she realized that there was light streaming into the hallway from an open door.

Faint, natural light.

Oh God. Had the sun already come up? She wasn't sure how much time had passed when she'd been unconscious.

Vampires couldn't stand light, right? She didn't know all the supernatural rules, but she was pretty sure that was one of them. If she could get outside, she should be okay.

Pressed against the wall outside the room, she slowly peered inside. It was a bedroom with a pristinely made, four-poster bed and thick-looking silk curtains covering what had to be windows. But the door to the adjoining en suite was open and that was the source of the natural light.

At the sound of voices coming from somewhere far too close, she ducked into the room and slowly eased the door shut.

Moving quickly, she hurried to the curtains and clawed at them until she found the opening. *Come on, come on. Get the hell out of here!* she ordered herself.

As she got past the second layer of fabric, she allowed herself the smallest breath of relief as she reached the glass panes. An expansive lawn and thick row of hedges sprawled out before her and she realized she was on the side of this mansion.

Easing the locks up on the window, she was glad these were single hung windows; huge windows that she could just open from the bottom and step right out into an azalea bush.

A gust of icy wind hit her in the face as she eased out and she wished she had thicker clothes. But there was nothing to do about it now. For a moment she was still, watching to make sure no one had spotted her. Even though it took time, she shut the window behind her and crawled through the damp bush, adrenaline and fear punching through her as she looked back up at the mansion. From her new position, she saw tennis courts, a pool, and a much larger expanse of grass to the back of the home.

Shoving down the panic that wanted to take root, she sprinted for the hedges. She didn't think they could chase her in the sunlight anyway.

Don't look back, a voice inside her shouted. *Only look forward.*

At this point, it was all she could do. If she'd been seen, she'd been seen. She had to run and take this chance. It was the only way.

Keep looking forward! Get to Orion. She had to shove her way through the hedges, winced as the thick branches tore at her sweater and scratched her skin. Didn't matter, she was burning her clothes to ash anyway once she got free.

She forced herself to be hopeful as she found herself facing a pond and forest. There was a barn-type structure in the distance to the south so she headed east toward the forest. She hoped to hide there. To at least put distance between herself and this pretty prison.

Her thigh muscles strained as she reached the tree line and she was glad for all her hiking and biking. As she moved deeper into the forest, she heard a howl.

Then another.

Oh, no. *No, no, no.*

She'd been attacked by wolf shifters before. What if there were more and they worked for the vampire... Jesus, of course they did.

On a burst of adrenaline, she put on speed, jumping over a log in her way, and this time she didn't bust her ass and sprain her ankle. The cold burned her lungs but it didn't matter.

The sound of running water was faint, but she could hear it. She'd spent a lot of time in the woods as a teen, and even if she wasn't totally sure where she was, she knew she could mute her scent with water.

Even if it was freezing right now.

But that was a worry for another day.

Heart still racing, she didn't stop, just followed the sound of water as the howls came closer.

She figured they were maybe a mile behind her. Maybe less. The eerie cries of the wolves echoed and she'd been running at full speed. And she hadn't been covering her tracks.

Nearing the edge of a stream, she took a deep breath and waded in, biting back a cry of pain as she did.

The cold slapped her senses as she submerged all the way to her neck and let the water guide her downstream. Pure determination was the only thing helping her keep it together right now. She looked around at the slowly brightening sky, realized the howls were getting farther away as the speed of the water picked up.

She raised her legs, avoiding an underwater boulder as the icy waters carried her faster, faster. She needed to get out soon, she knew that. Or she'd eventually go into hypothermic shock. But she needed to get closer to home first. By now she knew where she was. Or had a really good idea, given some of the old, decaying tire swings and ropes she'd just passed.

Clenching her jaw tight, she tried to stop her teeth from chattering but icy fingers wrapped around her, making her movements sluggish. It was time to get out.

Swimming toward the shore was a struggle, but she forced her arms and legs to work as she fought the current, scrambling for purchase on the slick rocks. She clutched onto a fallen tree and rolled herself on top of the thick trunk, breathing hard and shaking. It was so damn cold she felt it to her bones.

Come on, she ordered herself. *Get up!*

After she'd sucked in a few breaths, she pushed up, her palms scraping against the bark, but she had to get home. To Orion. Nothing else mattered.

Ignoring the pricks against her palms, she finally made it across the fallen tree, only to sink into the swampy mud of the shore. *Of course*, she inwardly growled as she managed to yank one foot free, then the other.

Her shoes made loud squishy sounds as she trekked over the thick grass. For a moment she debated losing them completely, then saw a cabin through the trees that looked vaguely familiar. *Oh my God.* She knew exactly where she was, and it was close to the western border of Cassandra's farm.

This place had been a summer camp for boys, but had been abandoned even before The Fall. Sitting on the grass, she managed to get her shoes off then tossed them in the river, hoping that if those wolves were still after her, they'd follow the scent of her shoes and not her. Either way, she couldn't wear them at all now. They were too heavy and slowing her down.

Ignoring the shock of pain to her bare feet, she raced across what had once been a play area for kids. But a sound above made her look up, hope punching through her. Maybe Orion had found her.

Just as quickly, that hope turned to terror when she spotted Vitus, *flying* toward her. "You fly!" And it was daytime! *What the hell?* He was a vampire! "No way, that's not fair!" she screamed, feeling manic as she tried to duck away from him.

Laughing maniacally, he swooped down, still dressed in the clothes she'd seen him in earlier, and snatched her up under her arms.

"You're going to pay for ruining my clothes and making me chase you," he snarled. "But I must admit I admire your ingenuity. Most humans bore me, but you've got spirit. I might keep you after I kill your dragon, change you into a vampire. I need more like you working for me."

A chill that had nothing to do with the bitter cold snaked down her spine. "Over my d-dead b-body!" She struggled in his arms as much as she could, fear taking hold and making her lash out.

"Stop thrashing around!" He tightened his grip on her, wrapping his arms around her in a viselike grip, but she noticed he descended slightly when she struggled.

So she started kicking out, flailing like a lunatic while she screamed at the top of her lungs. If Orion was out there, she wanted him to hear her. "Orion!" She screamed his name three times before she felt fangs sink into the side of her neck.

Suddenly she couldn't move or talk at all, but she could feel the cold invading her as he flew over the treetops.

When the mansion came back into view, defeat like she'd never known took hold and dragged her into the waiting darkness.

CHAPTER TWENTY-NINE

Orion kept his camouflage in place as he flew hard in the direction of Violet's screams, his dragon going faster than he'd ever flown before. He hadn't planned to wait until tonight to fight Vitus. He wasn't playing by some vampire's rules.

No, he'd already been heading in the direction of the mansion using the map the human had given him. But the sound of Violet's terror spurred him into action.

He shoved his fear down, compartmentalized it as he flapped faster, straining all the tendons in his wings. He had to get to her. It couldn't be too late, he told himself, even as he put on another burst of speed.

She'd stopped screaming, abruptly cut off, and— *No.*

The mansion came into view, and he spotted Vitus floating gently down right by a huge pool. So the vampire could fly and come out in the daytime.

A bloodborn, then. Had to be. And bloodborns were inherently powerful, born stronger than those made.

He watched as the vampire dropped Violet carelessly onto the concrete by a big metal grill.

Just. Dropped. Her.

A red haze descended over his vision and he arrowed straight at

Vitus with all the force of his dragon, pulling his wings in tight, his mouth open to blast the male with fire.

The vampire suddenly turned, flew upward in a burst of power. It was too late to stop himself; Orion slammed into the side of the mansion, stone and plaster crumbling under the impact.

His instinct was to stay and fight, but he had to get Violet out of here. That overrode everything.

The vampire landed on Orion's back and something scraped over his scales.

He roared as something burned through his back, his enraged shriek echoing around them. The urge to shift suddenly came over him, but he forced it back. *Almost.*

Arching his back as he fought what had to be poison, his wings remained out, slightly smaller than normal as he turned to face the vampire hovering above him in the air. He wasn't sure what the hell the vamp had injected him with, but it had to be a venom of sorts.

The vampire hissed at him, his fangs longer than a normal vampire's, thick claws protruding from his curled fingers—and that was when Orion saw the orangish liquid dripping from his claws. *Venom.*

He blasted out fire at the male even though he was half human now. A brilliant blue fire he'd never seen before shot out of his mouth, the color quickly fading back to the normal orangey red.

The vampire twisted in midair, but the blue fire clipped his left leg. He screamed as the skin burned away, flew upward, then directly down at Orion at a sharp angle. Attacking from above as he screamed obscenities at him in a language he hadn't heard in ages.

Orion shot straight up into the air, straining all his wing muscles at the in-air takeoff. But he needed to get the vampire farther away from Violet. Was desperate to put distance between them.

Maybe Vitus read his intentions on his face or maybe he was just a clever, evil bastard, but the male turned and dove toward Violet instead of following him.

No!

If one drop of that venom touched her, she was gone, her human body too weak to withstand it. His own body was working overtime to fight the invasion.

He breathed out the blue fire, aiming straight for Vitus. It was a direct hit, slamming into his back, blasting a hole straight through him.

The male screamed, fell as if his strings had been cut, slamming into the concrete below. The vampire was only forty yards from Violet now. Still too close.

The male rolled over, his midsection already starting to heal.

Orion wasn't going to let that happen. He blasted more blue fire at him, even as he fought through the effects of the poison. His dragon was taking over again, stronger than the bloodborn.

The blue fire blasted from him again, incinerating the vampire completely. Instead of ash, a blinding white flash of magic burst in the air, scattering to the wind.

Orion landed next to Violet, crouched next to her far too still body and lifted her into his arms.

Her breathing was shallow, but she didn't open her eyes, and she was far too cold to the touch.

Fear punched through him. "No, you're not allowed to leave me. I order you to live," he snarled, gently opening her mouth with his fingers and breathing some of his essence into her. It wasn't the same as the mating link, and he was taking away her choice by giving her a much longer life.

But it was the only thing he could do to save her.

She was going to live. Otherwise, he was following her into the afterlife.

"Violet, wake up now," he ordered. "Right now! Open your eyes." Goddess, he needed to see her gray eyes looking up at him. What if it hadn't worked?

He'd been too late—

"Orion," Violet whispered, blinking at him.

He swore his heart stopped for a moment, even as he fought to drag in a full breath. "You're okay. And I'm going to get you dry clothes soon, I promise."

She threw her arms around him, burying her face against his neck and holding him tight. "Is the vampire…gone?"

"He's dead, my love," he murmured into her hair. As he held her, he saw one of the curtains moving in one of the upstairs windows. More vampires. "I need to get you home, but…" He turned as Cale landed in the middle of the tennis court in dragon form, completely destroying it before he hopped his way over to them, massacring the lawn and pool as he went.

He shifted before them. "I just neutralized two vampire nests. Is the leader dead?"

Orion nodded toward the pile of whatever the hell that white bundle of magical stuff was. "Yeah, but we're going to make sure he's really gone. There are vampires inside, maybe humans. Stay with Violet while—"

"No." Violet leaned back, gripped his upper arms tight as she clutched onto him. Her eyes were wide, her pupils far too big. "Don't leave me."

Nodding, he brushed his mouth over hers. "I'm not going anywhere. Cale, if there are humans inside, get them out, then raze this place to the ground."

Cale gave a dark smile and strode right through the nearest window, just kicking it in and walking through like an agent of chaos.

"Come on." Orion lifted Violet in his arms and took to the air.

"You look like an angel," she murmured, staring at him in awe and definite shock. "With your wings coming out of your back like that. I didn't know you could half-shift."

He decided not to tell her that he was poisoned and it was the only reason he was still like this. Suddenly the roof exploded as Cale burst through it in his dragon form. Then he turned midair and started burning everything in his path.

Orion knew Cale had this handled, and he had the only thing that mattered. Violet. His precious mate.

As he flew east, he spotted Prima incinerating a pack of wolves trying to flee, and Bentley and his brothers attacking anyone who managed to get free.

His people had things handled for now.

He had to get Violet home, needed Baris to look her over, because her breathing was still shallow and she was freezing cold. Even though he'd given her part of himself, he had to face that in some situations, the dumb panda was useful.

CHAPTER THIRTY

"All you can do at this point is rest." Baris sat in a small chair next to Orion's bed—where Violet was currently curled up next to Orion.

Bowie was literally lying across the two of them like the most wonderful weirdo ever. His paws were on Violet's stomach, his back half on Orion's.

"You're going to be okay," Baris said. "Orion's essence is speeding up the process but you lost a lot of blood from that vampire bite." He cleared his throat. Paused. "I don't think you would have made it if he hadn't intervened. That bastard took far too much from a human."

Orion wanted to go back and kill Vitus all over again.

"Well, how long will I be stuck here?" Violet asked, frowning. "Because I could get out of this bed right now," she said around a yawn.

Baris sighed. "Clearly. Look, I know doctors and healers are supposed to make the worst patients, but we will survive without you for a day. You can't take care of others if you don't take care of yourself."

"But—"

"Nope. There were no casualties and I can easily handle the injuries."

"But some of the humans—"

"Will just have to get used to me since they can't see you right now. They'll be fine."

She held up a hand when he started to cut her off again. "Wait. I just have one non-doctor-related question. How long until Orion and I can officially mate?"

Orion went very still next to her. So did his dragon. She *still* wanted to mate him, even after everything that had happened.

But Baris didn't bat an eye at the question. "After you sleep. Now, if you need me, I'll be in the medical center for the next few hours. I'm not sure how many injuries there are so I don't know how long I'll be. Once I'm done, you can find me upstairs in Rose's room, where I will be spending the night. Now rest, Doctor." He strode out without waiting for a response.

"Wait, is he hooking up with my sister? What the heck?" Violet started to move as if she was actually thinking about getting out of bed but Bowie shifted and laid his head on her chest, looking up at her with big, disapproving eyes. Then he patted her with his paw, as if to say *stay put*.

He really was the best dog. "Good boy," Orion murmured, rubbing his head. "You're not going anywhere, Violet. Maybe ever again."

She snorted and grumbled to herself even as she ran her hand over Bowie's head, scratching behind his ear. "I'm fine." She yawned. Again. "Okay, I'm exhausted. But I feel like I should be doing...something."

"Everything is under control for now. There's going to be a lot to deal with later, mainly housing people, but the vampires from Vitus's territory are mostly dead at this point. Once I killed off the leader, everyone else was easy to take out. He wasn't much of a leader anyway, not a true Alpha." That vampire had been a greedy, sick monster who'd only cared about himself. Orion had known enough supernaturals like that for one existence.

Not that it was just supernaturals. Humans could be just as awful, like Thomas. His body had been found by Prima in the woods, drained of blood. That bastard had gotten off easy with a quick death as far as Orion was concerned. If he'd found him...that human would still be alive and screaming in pain.

"There are humans who will need help," she insisted, laying her head on his chest.

Orion settled back on the bed with her, pulling her close. Goddess, she was really here, and in his arms. "And Baris is bringing in some backup from New Orleans. We just allied with them and they're more than happy to help a bunch of injured humans." It was almost a point of honor.

"You like King, the Alpha?" she murmured, her eyes drooping a little more.

"Yeah. He's got a good core, I can tell. Right down to his marrow, he's an honorable wolf. I understand why Prima said I'd like him."

"Well that's good," she murmured again. "Do we have enough food for the humans? Enough—"

"My mate." He brushed his lips over hers, briefly silencing her. "We have more than enough. There is literally nothing you need to do except sleep. We aren't in danger, the threat is over for now, and hopefully for a long time. That vampire is dead and gone, and I had Scarlett do a scanning spell over his weird remains. He's gone, nothing left of him. He was simply a nasty bloodborn vampire who wanted to expand his territory for the purpose of using more humans. And The Fall gave him the opportunity to exploit a lot of them."

He still had questions about what the bizarre blue fire that had come out of him was, but it had killed the vampire, so Orion wasn't too concerned.

"I hate that," she growled.

"I do too, but you can rest for one day. Please."

"I like it when you say please. Maybe later you can say 'please mate with me, Violet'?" She yawned again, but he recognized that faint trickle of need rolling off her.

"Sweet goddess, Violet, you really are a terrible patient."

To his surprise, she snickered and turned her face into his chest. "I know, I'm the worst. I think… I think if I make myself stay busy, I'll be able to forget about that dungeon, which wasn't a dungeon at all but a very nice wine cellar." She paused. "It's too bad we didn't grab some of those bottles before Cale demolished that place."

He kissed the top of her head. "Do you want to talk about what happened?" She'd told him the bare details, had been clear that she hadn't been seriously injured except when Vitus had drunk so much of her blood.

"Not really. But I do want to hear more about your past. Not from when you were young," she hurried out. "But when you had your own clan. You mentioned it but never really gave details. I want to know everything about you, dragon of mine."

His heart expanded at the endearment. "The story has a sad ending, my love," he whispered, kissing her head again.

"Oh. You don't have to tell me, then."

Sighing, he tightened his grip on her even as he began petting Bowie's head. "I want to. I want you to know all of me."

So he did.

He told her of the dragon clan he'd formed by happenstance. Of all the mercenaries and misfits who'd once lived up on a mountainside with him during a time when humans had known of their existence and, in some cases, worshipped them. He told her of the found family he'd created, then the wild sickness that had gone through their mountain and the lands surrounding it.

Most of his people had died, been killed by an invisible bacteria or drug or...he still wasn't certain what it had been. A disease, to be certain. Their only healer had died and Orion had been helpless to stop the ravage of a disease he hoped didn't still exist.

"You've had so much loss," she whispered, looking up at him, her eyes full of love.

"I have. But so have you. So has everyone, I'm certain. I...was afraid that if I committed to you, that I'd lose you. That if I officially committed to helping our community, I'd lose everyone here just like I lost my people before." Deep down he figured he'd always have a fear of losing her, but that was a mate thing.

Reaching up, she cupped his cheek. "I think today proved that you're not going down without a fight. Neither of us are."

He leaned closer to her, kissed her again, was so tempted to deepen it but he knew she needed rest. His sweet, fierce human who he'd almost lost today. "I love you, Violet."

She smiled up at him, as if she'd been waiting to hear the words. "And I love you right back."

Then she closed her eyes and fell asleep on his chest in seconds.

CHAPTER THIRTY-ONE

Violet stepped out of Orion's bathroom, showered, teeth brushed and wondering where the heck her soon-to-be mate was. Bowie was gone and—

The door opened and Orion was there, a soft smile on his face. The kind he only reserved for her.

"How are you feeling?" he asked as he set a covered tray on the nightstand by the door.

"Good." And so very horny for him. Like, ridiculous amounts.

She loosened the tie on her robe as she walked toward him, took pleasure in the shocked look on his face. Her dominating Alpha actually held up a hand, as if what—to stop her from getting naked? *Oh no, not happening.* "You better lock that door. Unless there's anything we need to deal with right now?"

She wasn't even totally sure how long she'd been asleep but it was now dark outside. And Baris had been right—the community wouldn't fall apart without her for a day or two. That was sort of the point of being part of one. She could depend on others. Like right now when she wanted to mate with her big, sexy dragon. Because she wasn't going another moment without being mated to the male she loved.

"Violet, what—"

"Getting naked." The robe hit the floor as he locked the door.

"Are you sure?" he growled even as his gaze roved all over her like the very hungry dragon that he was.

It made no sense but she almost swore she could smell something spicy and wild in the air. "You smell so good," she groaned, sliding her arms around him, then let out a little yelp when he pinned her flat on the bed.

"Violet," he breathed out, looking worried. "You've been through so much."

"And I know my mind. And you. I love you, Orion. That's enough for me. *You* are enough. All of you. I love you so much it's hard to contain all my feelings. Maybe because I've been fighting them for an entire year. You're mine, Orion. So claim me, make me yours forever."

His eyes flashed pure dragon before the man looked back at her. "You completely unravel me, Violet." Then he kissed her, his mouth crushing hers with a hot claiming she felt all the way to her core.

She wrapped her legs around him, heat surging through her as she felt his thick erection already pressing at the juncture of her thighs. Didn't matter that he still had pants on, she arched into him, rubbing herself over that thick length because, sweet flying dragons, his cock was incredible.

"I love you so much," he growled, nipping her bottom lip.

She hadn't been sure he'd be able to say the words before. He'd been so reserved, even after he'd gone all dominant and told her she'd be mating him. There'd still been something holding him back because she'd *felt* that he loved her, even if he hadn't said the words.

But she'd needed to hear them. Desperately. "I'll never get tired of hearing that," she said on a moan as he sucked one nipple into his mouth.

He growled something around her breast as he shoved at his pants, his entire body vibrating with energy. And the mating manifestation consumed the entire room this time, surrounding them so she couldn't even see the bed.

Just him. Orion was all there was for her anyway.

She helped him kick his pants down his legs while she tore at his shirt, the hunger rising in her like a swelling tidal wave. This need, the hunger, it was like nothing she'd ever experienced.

He eased two fingers into her as he switched to her other breast, teased the hard bud.

"I need your cock in me." The words were a desperate plea.

"Goddess," he growled. "Say it again."

"Your cock. In me." She wrapped her fingers around his thick length, stroked hard, and grinned when his big body shuddered over hers. She loved that he was so gone over her the same way she was over him.

It bordered on obsession, but she didn't care. She'd take this every day of the week for the rest of her life. However long that was. As long as she had Orion.

He teased the head of his erection against her slick folds, groaned again before he thrust inside her in one long push.

"Orion!" She arched against him, belatedly hoped no one was home to overhear them, but oh well. It was hard to care when he pulled back, thrust again. "It's not going to take me long," she gasped out.

"Oh thank the Goddess," he gritted out. "You feel so amazing." Reaching between their bodies, he began teasing her clit while continuing to thrust inside her.

With each stroke, she raced at that ledge, that release, her inner walls clenching tighter and tighter around him. "I'm coming!" She wasn't sure why she announced it but holy hell, pleasure punched out to all her nerve endings. And as she reached her peak, he sank his canines into the soft part of her skin where her neck and shoulder met.

He'd explained it to her before, that this would officially bond them for life, but knowing it and experiencing it were very different. She hadn't even realized something was missing but now that she had Orion in her life, nothing could ever compare.

As she experienced the pleasure-pain of his bite, another round of pure bliss surged through her as he sucked on her neck, removed his canines, then kissed the wounds closed. And suddenly it was as if every single pleasure point in her body sang with the feel of being linked to him. She swore she could feel his hunger and need for her along their mating link, and had never been so overwhelmed in her life. But in the best way possible.

"Violet," he growled out before he came inside her, thrusting over and over as he found his own release.

And when he looked down at her in the aftermath, there was nothing but love in his eyes as he gently cupped her cheek. "You're my mate. My home."

"Always." She would always be his home and vice versa.

She was mated to a tough dragon Alpha with a kind, marshmallow inside, and she was never letting this incredible male go.

CHAPTER THIRTY-TWO

Three weeks later

"I have a mating gift for you," Prima said quietly, handing Orion a small bundle of cloth.

He could feel something hard inside it, glanced around at the ongoing party. It had taken weeks to get the displaced humans housed in their territory, but things were moving much smoother than he'd anticipated. And tonight they'd decided to throw a party and had invited anyone who wanted to come. Many from the dead vampire's territory were here, but many were not, and he understood. They were dealing with their trauma in the way they knew how. Something he could relate to.

"I know we are not officially blood, but you've always been like a brother to me. Even before I had one. And since you mated with the perfect female, I had to think of the perfect gift for both of you. I've been working on it for weeks."

He opened the folded cotton and stared down at two glittering gold rings. One big enough for him and one small enough for Violet. He lifted them up, looked at them under the moon and starlight, his gaze tracking over the intricate etchings of violet flowers on his and a hunting dragon on Violet's. "They're beautiful," he breathed out.

"Some humans have a tradition of marriage, and while I know you two are already mated, I thought your human mate might like a physical symbol of your love for her. And I created both of these with my dragon fire. So…" Trailing off, she lifted a shoulder, not needing to explain further.

But her words stunned him as much as the gift. Metal forged with dragon fire was rare and gifted the wearer with the ability to see a dragon even if they were camouflaged. Orion had no gifts where metal was concerned, but this… "Thank you, Prima. Truly. This is a gift we will both treasure."

Now his mate would be able to see any sort of surprise attack, if it were ever to come. Not that he planned on letting her out of his sight or territory, he thought, his gaze trailing to where she'd been standing with her sisters only moments ago. Wait, where was she?

"She headed for the house," Prima said, clearly reading his expression as she clapped him once on the upper arm then headed back to the party, her hands shoved into her pants as she moved to stand next to Bentley.

He slid the bigger ring on one of his fingers, then hurried after his mate, her sweet scent calling to him right back to their house.

Their house. *A home.*

Inside, he found Violet with her three sisters standing in the living room. And his mate was crying.

"What's happened?" he demanded, looking for a threat as he swept into the room. Bowie was right next to him, whining as he looked at the sisters.

"Oh, nothing." Violet waved away her tears with a watery laugh.

He pulled her to him, kissing the top of her head. "Why are you crying? Why is my mate crying?" he asked, looking at her sisters now.

"These are happy tears," she murmured. "My sisters have given us a mating gift."

Oh. He looked at the big quilt laid out on the couch in front of them as Mari stepped forward. "This is a double wedding ring quilt. It's been a while in the making because we asked Cassandra and some others to start on it months ago," she said on a laugh.

"You guys just took longer than we thought," Rose added, smiling up at him too. "So it's a good thing because these things take forever."

"A double wedding ring quilt symbolizes love and romance, and our grandmother gave one to our mother and..." Laurel cleared her throat. "And we're giving one to you and Violet as a mating gift."

"And a gift welcoming you officially to our family," Mari added. "In case you didn't realize, you're never getting rid of us. You are a Robichaux now, no matter what."

Orion Robichaux. He liked the sound of that. Dragons didn't do last names. They were part of clans—and he'd never claimed his original one. He liked being part of this new clan a whole lot better. "Thank you for the gift. It means the world to me." In a way that he couldn't properly express with words.

Violet and her sisters had given him a family. Goddess, his chest ached with love as he looked at the three sisters, then down at his mate, who was looking up at him with adoration in her gaze.

"I'm proud to be one of you," he rasped out as he held up the ring Prima had given him, and slipped it onto Violet's ring finger. "And this is a gift from Prima to both of us." He showed her his own even as she stared at hers in awe.

"That dragon is trying to outdo us," Mari grumbled, no heat in her voice.

Violet laughed lightly as she stared at it. "It's beautiful. I'll have to thank her later. And thank you guys again. This is so unexpected. I—" She broke off, tears streaming down her face. "You guys are the best," she said, holding out her arms for them.

The three females tackled both Violet and Orion, and even Bowie jumped up on them, barking happily, making sure they knew he was part of this.

"Pretty soon we will have to commission one for Laurel and Rose," Orion said as they stepped back. Because he had no doubt Laurel would be mating Cale soon, and it appeared that Rose would be mating with the panda. He would tell Violet about the gift her ring carried with it, but only once they were alone.

Laurel's face went crimson, but she laughed lightly. "Ah, yeah, probably. Cale is pretty adamant about mating, so…" She shrugged.

"Oh, and you're just soooo chill about it," Mari said, cackling. "Please! I heard you two last night."

"Ew, gross!" Laurel's expression turned to one of horror.

"Not doing that! I heard him tell you how much he loves you, and you are so into this mating thing. So don't even play around. You love that big goofball."

Laurel simply grinned and shrugged. "Fine, whatever. I love him so much it's embarrassing."

"And you and the panda?" Orion said, looking at Rose, eyebrows raised.

Rose grinned too. "I'm just using him for his big dick."

Violet sputtered even as Orion covered his face. Goddess, would he ever get used to these females?

"She's kidding!" Violet said, laughing now, her entire body shaking as she leaned into him.

"I mean, I'm not about the dick thing, but yeah, Baris is pretty insistent about mating too. As in, it's happening by the week's end." And Rose looked pretty smug about it.

"Then I will make sure my sisters have these quilts made too," he said, pulling Violet to him in an embrace, the need to touch her at all times nothing short of overwhelming.

But the other three piled on again and he swore his heart expanded three sizes—a reference he now understood thanks to a movie Violet showed him.

These were his people, and Violet was the love of his life. However long his life was, he would spend it loving her, protecting her and all those they cherished.

—THE END—

ACKNOWLEDGMENTS

For all the wonderful readers who want more of this world, you all are the best! I'm so grateful you want more of these dragons. To Kaylea Cross, thank you for helping me get this book into shape, and for all the other things. Jaycee, thank you for another gorgeous cover (both versions). I'm in love with them. For Julia, thank you for your thorough edits and for helping me keep this world organized. I'd be lost without my trusty style sheet (which is now fifty-eight pages and has a TOC so maybe not a sheet anymore!). I'm also grateful to Tammy for proofreading this beast. To Sarah, I'm grateful all the time for all the things you do! There are too many to list. And of course to Bowie, the inspiration for book Bowie. You are even cuter in real life.

ABOUT THE AUTHOR

Katie Reus® is the *New York Times* and *USA Today* bestselling author of the Endgame trilogy, the Ancients Rising series and the MacArthur Family series. She fell in love with romance at a young age thanks to books she pilfered from her mom's stash. Years later she loves reading romance almost as much as she loves writing it.

However, she didn't always know she wanted to be a writer. After changing majors many times, she finally graduated summa cum laude with a degree in psychology. Not long after that she discovered a new love. Writing. She now spends her days writing paranormal romance and sexy romantic suspense. For more information on her books, check out her website: https://www.katiereus.com

COMPLETE BOOKLIST

Ancients Rising

Ancient Protector

Ancient Enemy

Ancient Enforcer

Ancient Vendetta

Ancient Retribution

Ancient Vengeance

Ancient Sentinel

Ancient Warrior

Ancient Guardian

Darkness Series

Darkness Awakened

Taste of Darkness

Beyond the Darkness

Hunted by Darkness

Into the Darkness

Saved by Darkness

Guardian of Darkness

Sentinel of Darkness

A Very Dragon Christmas

Darkness Rising

Deadly Ops Series

Targeted

Bound to Danger

Mistletoe Me, Baby

Hunting Danger

Covert Games

Chasing Vengeance

Redemption Harbor® Security

Fighting for Hailey

Fighting for Reese

Fighting for Adalyn

Sin City Series (the Serafina)

First Surrender

Sensual Surrender

Sweetest Surrender

Dangerous Surrender

Deadly Surrender

Verona Bay Series

Dark Memento

Deadly Past

Silent Protector

Linked books

Retribution

Tempting Danger

Non-series Romantic Suspense

Running From the Past

Dangerous Secrets

Killer Secrets

Deadly Obsession

Danger in Paradise

His Secret Past

Paranormal Romance

Destined Mate

Protector's Mate

A Jaguar's Kiss

Tempting the Jaguar

Enemy Mine

Heart of the Jaguar

Made in the USA
Monee, IL
05 July 2023

38700753R00152